PENGUIN  CLASSICS

BARLAAM AND JOSAPHAT

GUI DE CAMBRAI was a cleric from northern France. Around 1190, he composed *Le vengement Alixandre*, a continuation of the popular story of Alexander the Great, and around 1220–25 he adapted *Barlaam and Josaphat* from Latin into Old French verse. He is thought to have retired to a monastery at the end of his life.

PEGGY MCCRACKEN is a professor of French, women's studies, and comparative literature at the University of Michigan. Her publications on medieval literature and culture include essays, books, edited collections, and, most recently, two coauthored volumes: *Marie de France: A Critical Companion,* with Sharon Kinoshita, and *In Search of the Christian Buddha,* with Donald S. Lopez Jr.

DONALD S. LOPEZ JR. is the Arthur E. Link Distinguished University Professor of Buddhist and Tibetan Studies at the University of Michigan, in the Department of Asian Languages and Cultures. He edited *Buddhist Scriptures* for Penguin Classics and is the author of a number of books.

GUI DE CAMBRAI

Barlaam and Josaphat

A CHRISTIAN TALE OF THE BUDDHA

Translated with Notes by
PEGGY MCCRACKEN

Introduction by
DONALD S. LOPEZ JR.

PENGUIN BOOKS

PENGUIN BOOKS
Published by the Penguin Group
Penguin Group (USA) LLC
375 Hudson Street
New York, New York 10014

USA | Canada | UK | Ireland | Australia | New Zealand | India | South Africa | China
penguin.com
A Penguin Random House Company

This translation first published in Penguin Books 2014

ISBN 978-0-14-310701-9

Printed in the United States of America

146028962

Contents

Introduction

Barlaam and Josaphat, one of the most popular stories in Europe during the Middle Ages, was translated from Latin into dozens of languages. For this reason at the very least, Peggy McCracken's translation of the famous Old French version by Gui de Cambrai, dating from the thirteenth century, deserves to be included in the Penguin Classics series. Barlaam and Josaphat were not simply literary characters; they were regarded as historical figures, and as saints, and credited with the miraculous, though of course mythical, conversion of the subcontinent of India from the perdition of pagan idolatry to the glory of the Christian faith. In 1571 the doge of Venice presented a bone from Josaphat's spine to King Sebastian of Portugal; the relic is enshrined today in St. Andrieskerk in Antwerp. In 1583, Pope Sixtus V authorized November 27 as Barlaam and Josaphat's saints' day; Josaphat was assigned August 26 by the Eastern Orthodox churches. A chapel with the dedication "Divo Josaphat" inscribed over the entrance was built in Palermo in the sixteenth century.

Yet despite the fame of *Barlaam and Josaphat* and its sainted protagonists, it is unlikely that the tale would have earned a place among today's classics without our knowledge of a single fact, one unknown to Gui de Cambrai and the other learned clerics, poets, and playwrights of the Middle Ages and Renaissance who retold the tale, and also unknown to their audiences, whether they read the story from an illuminated manuscript in a monastery, heard it from the pulpit in a church, or saw it performed on a stage: *Barlaam and Josaphat* is based on the life of the Buddha. The extent to which this is so—that is, whether this fact should be emblazoned on the cover of a book or buried in a footnote—is a question worthy of further consideration. However, there is no question that since this fact was discovered in Paris in the middle of the nineteenth century, it has captivated the academic imagination, inspiring generations of scholars to go in quest of *Barlaam and Josaphat*'s origins.

The evidence of influence is found in the tale's echoes of three famous episodes from the life of the Buddha as traditionally told in Asia. In the first, after the birth of Prince Siddhārtha, the future Buddha, the king summons the court astrologers to foretell his son's destiny. All but one predict that the child will become either a great monarch or a great saint; the remaining astrologer is certain that the boy will become a great saint. Alarmed that his son will not succeed him on the throne, the king builds a special palace where the prince will be shielded from all that is unpleasant and unattractive, in order to prevent him from becoming discouraged with life in the world. A very similar scene occurs in *Barlaam and Josaphat*: the king, a devotee of idols and a persecutor of Christians, hears the astrologers' predictions and fears that his son will some day become a Christian. He builds a special palace to prevent such a fate (see "King Avenir's son is born").

The second episode takes place when, after living in the palace for twenty-nine years, Prince Siddhārtha becomes curious about the world beyond the walls and asks his father to allow him to take an excursion with his charioteer. After initially refusing, the king relents, but has anything unpleasant removed from the royal route, musicians stationed in the trees, and the road lined with flowers and incense. However, the plan fails, and during four successive chariot rides the prince encounters, for the first time in his life, an old man, a sick man, a dead man, and finally a meditating monk, and in doing so learns of the realities of aging, sickness, and death, as well as the existence of those who seek to escape them. In *Barlaam and Josaphat*, Prince Josaphat takes two rides outside the city, encountering a blind man and a leper the first time and an old man the second (see "Josaphat leaves his palace"). He does not encounter a corpse or a meditating monk, but shortly after his second excursion the Christian monk Barlaam arrives at the palace, in disguise, to provide instruction in the Gospel to the son of the idolatrous king (see "Barlaam comes to Josaphat").

In the third scene, after returning from his four chariot rides, Prince Siddhārtha, now married and with a newborn son, requests his father's permission to leave his family and royal destiny behind, to go in search of a state beyond birth and death. The king refuses and attempts to distract the prince by having a group of courtesans beguile him with their beauty. But the prince is unmoved. Exhausted from singing and dancing for him, the courtesans fall asleep on the floor at the foot his throne. As he gazes on their sleeping forms, they remind him only of corpses. In *Barlaam and Josaphat*, King Avenir instructs a group of beautiful women to seduce the virgin Prince Josaphat. In one of the most powerful scenes in the story, a slave princess almost succeeds. The chastity of the prince is preserved when he has a vision of the hell that awaits him should he succumb to passion (see "A beautiful princess tempts Josaphat").

This is the extent of the literary connection between the life of the Buddha and the story of *Barlaam and Josaphat*. Prince Siddhārtha leaves the palace that same night and, after six years of ascetic practice, achieves enlightenment and becomes the Buddha (which means "awakened one"). He then teaches the path to liberation from suffering, over the course of a long life, passing into nirvana at the age of eighty. Prince Josaphat follows a very different path, as you will read in the pages that follow.

Although these three central elements of the plot of *Barlaam and Josaphat* clearly derive from the life of the Buddha, precisely how they passed from ancient India to medieval France is still not understood with complete historical accuracy. The connection between East and West was first discovered in 1853, when the German Indologist Theodor Benfey (1809–81) noted that one of the parables in *Barlaam and Josaphat*, the parable of the man in the well (see "King Avenir neglects his gods"), was also found in the *Pañcatantra*, a famous collection of Indian fables in Sanskrit. By this time there was among European philologists great interest in classical Sanskrit and, increasingly, in Buddhism. In 1844 the French scholar Eugène Burnouf (1801–52) had published his massive *Introduction à l'histoire du Buddhisme indien*, a work that was read with great interest by Schopenhauer, Schelling, Nietzsche, and Wagner in Germany and by Emerson and Thoreau in America. Three years later, a student of Burnouf, Philippe Édouard Foucaux (1811–94) published his translation from Tibetan of one of the most famous Indian biographies of the Buddha, the *Lalitavistara* (*Vast Game*), a work that likely dates from the third century CE.

In 1859 the French savant Édouard Laboulaye (1811–83) saw a direct parallel between *Barlaam and Josaphat* and the life of the Buddha, noting the clear similarity between the stories of the chariot rides. However, he did not identify a specific Buddhist text as the source of the story. This link would be provided in 1860 by the German folklorist and translator of *Barlaam and Josaphat*, Felix Liebrecht (1812–90), who argued that the *Lalitavistara* (which he had likely read in Foucaux's 1847 translation into French) was the source. Liebrecht turned out to be wrong about the *Lalitavistara*, but from that point until the present day, great scholarly labor has been invested in the task of tracing *Barlaam and Josaphat* back to its original source. Despite these efforts, the direct route has yet to be precisely mapped. Still, there has been much progress, ranging over continents and languages.

Gui de Cambrai's *Barlaam and Josaphat* (as well as the many other European vernacular versions) can be traced back to Latin sources, the earliest of which dates from 1048. This Latin text is a translation of the Greek version, long associated with Saint John of Damascus (d. 749), an attribution that was accepted long into the nineteenth century. The famous German philologist Friedrich Max Müller (1823–1900) imagined that a delegation from India had brought the *Lalita-*

vistara to John of Damascus, who then translated it into Greek (without explaining how the learned Christian saint could have known Sanskrit). However, it is now assumed that the Greek story was translated, not from Sanskrit, but from Georgian, and not in Damascus, but in Greece, more than two centuries later, by a different Christian monk: perhaps Euthymius the Georgian (d. 1028), abbot of a monastery on Mount Athos. The Georgian tale he translated, and to which he added all manner of Christian sermonizing, is called *The Balavariani* and was likely composed by Georgian monks living in Jerusalem during the ninth or tenth century.

To this point, the line tracing *Barlaam and Josaphat* back in time is clear and straight. From here, however, it begins to become more obscure. Two Arabic works survive with the title *Kitāb Bilawhar wa Būdhāsaf* (*The Book of Bilawhar and Būdhāsaf*), with the earlier of the two dating from sometime between 750 and 900. It is clear from the considerable overlap in the parables they recount that the Georgian version of *Barlaam and Josaphat* derives from this Arabic source, although scholars now assume that the exact Arabic version used by the Georgian monks has been lost. The Georgian monks took the basic story of a royal father who extols the virtues of life in the world and a royal son who extols the virtues of asceticism (a story with little overtly Muslim content) and then Christianized it, turning it into the story of an idolatrous king, a persecutor of Christians, and his virtuous son, who is converted to Christianity by the pious monk Barlaam. The prince then converts his father, and eventually all India, to the true faith. The many parables in the story were also easily Christianized, and references to the rather mysterious figure of the Buddha (al-Budd in the Arabic tale) were simply excised.

Here the trail goes cold. The Buddha lived and taught in northern India during the fifth century BCE. His teachings eventually spread throughout Asia, establishing a strong presence in what is today Pakistan and Afghanistan (we recall the colossal Bamiyan Buddhas that were destroyed by the Taliban in 2001), regions that had recently come under Muslim control at the time that *Kitāb Bilawhar wa Būdhāsaf* was composed. But Buddhism had also been known in Persia during pre-Islamic times, and scholars speculate that *The Book of Bilawhar and Būdhāsaf* derives from a Persian source, now lost.

There is also no conclusive evidence that would identify the original Buddhist source of the story. There are many versions of the life of the Buddha, versions that evolved over many centuries, and most of them contain the three scenes—in one form or another—that also occur in *Barlaam and Josaphat*: the prophecy of the astrologers, the chariot rides, and the attempted seduction by courtesans. The path from language to language, however, marks the path of influence clearly: Josaphat in Latin is Ioasaph in Greek, Iodasaph in Georgian, Būdhāsaf in Arabic, and *bodhisattva* in Sanskrit. Bodhisattva, "one who aspires to enlightenment," is the primary epithet of Prince Siddhārtha prior to the time that he achieves enlightenment and becomes the Buddha.

I noted above that the story of the Buddha's influence on the composition of *Barlaam and Josaphat* was first discerned in the nineteenth century. This is accurate, but the similarities between the two stories were noted centuries before. In his famous work, *Description of the World*, Marco Polo describes the island of Sri Lanka, where his ship made port on his return voyage to Venice, perhaps in 1291. In the chapter that he devotes to Sri Lanka (which he calls Seilan), he provides a detailed account of the life of the Buddha (whom he calls Sagamoni Borcan, the Mongolian name for the Buddha, which he likely learned at the court of Kublai Khan in China). Indeed, Marco Polo's is the most detailed account of the life of the Buddha to appear in a European language to that point. It is also remarkably sympathetic, especially compared to the disparaging European descriptions of the Buddha found in the works of Christian missionaries to Asia in subsequent centuries. Polo says that if Sagamoni Borcan had been a Christian, "he would have been a great saint of Our Lord Jesus Christ, so good and pure was the life he led."

In 1446 an unnamed editor of Polo's book inserted this

sentence into the description of the Buddha's encounters with death and old age: "This is like the life of Saint Josaphat who was son of the King Avenir of those parts of India, and was converted to the Christian faith by Barlaam, as is read in the life and legend of the holy fathers." In fifteenth-century Europe, Barlaam and Josaphat were far more famous than the Buddha. A century and half later, in 1612, the Portuguese soldier and chronicler Diogo de Couto (1542–1616) argued that the Buddha, whom he calls Budão, was in fact Josaphat, and that over the centuries the people of India had forgotten the true identity of the Christian saint. In his travels in India, de Couto even claimed to have found the palace that King Avenir built for his son.

But these brief references would go unnoticed for centuries, during which time *Barlaam and Josaphat*, once so famous, came to be forgotten, together with so many other saints' tales from the Middle Ages. The story would lose its audience in Europe, although it found a new one in Asia. In 1591, Jesuit missionaries published the story in Japanese, as part of their efforts to convert Buddhist Japan to Christianity.

In the sixteenth and seventeenth centuries, European travelers—whether they were explorers, traders, soldiers, diplomats, or missionaries—encountered the Buddha in many Asian lands. But because the Buddha has a different name in each of the languages of Asia, and because he is depicted in many different artistic styles, they did not recognize his images as representations of a single historical figure. Instead he was so many Asian idols, known by different names: Xaca in Japan, Fo in China, Buddu in Ceylon, Sommonacodom in Siam, Sciacchiá-Thubbá in Tibet. Only at the end of the seventeenth century was it discovered that the idol worshipped in Siam represented the same god worshipped in Japan. Over the course of the eighteenth century, it would be concluded that this god had been a historical figure, although where he came from remained a topic of debate. Some thought he had come from Egypt. Others said he was originally the Norse god Odin. Only in the nineteenth century, with the rise of the science of philology, did scholars in Europe develop the ability to read Buddhist texts with a high degree of accuracy—texts in Mongolian, Tibetan, Chinese, Pali, and Sanskrit. It was then that European attitudes toward the Buddha began to change.

Long condemned as an idol known by many names, the Buddha would, through the work of scholars like Eugène Burnouf, be transformed into a philosopher—a teacher of ethics who revealed the path to enlightenment to all who would follow it, regardless of their social class. In a Europe where the authority of the church was under attack, he was an Asian sage who had founded a religion that had no God, a religion that had no priests, a religion that was not a religion.

And so the head-spinning ironies abound. Islam, long (although wrongly) condemned for bringing about the demise of Buddhism in India, becomes the conduit for the story of the Buddha to travel incognito from Asia to Europe. The story of the Buddha, whom European missionaries would excoriate for centuries as an idol and as a purveyor of idolatry, is transformed by Christian monks into the story of a prince, called Prince Josaphat rather than Prince Siddhārtha, who converts the pagans of India from idolatry to Christianity. The Buddhist prince who is a bodhisattva becomes a prince named Būdhāsaf then Iodasaph then Ioasaph then Josaphat, and as Josaphat he becomes a Christian saint. Yet as that saint fell into obscurity, the original bodhisattva—once but one of many Asian idols known by many names—coalesced into the figure of the Buddha and came to be respected as the founder of a great world religion.

And perhaps here we have the ultimate irony. A story about a heathen, the Buddha, is turned into a tale about the conversion of heathens, a story that would become a forgotten fantasy. Forgotten, that is, until the heathen reached into the darkness and pulled his Christian brother into the light, restoring *Barlaam and Josaphat* to the fame, surely a most complicated fame, that it justly deserves.

DONALD S. LOPEZ JR.

Translator's Preface

Gui de Cambrai's *Barlaam and Josaphat* is one of many medieval versions of the life of Saint Josaphat and his teacher, Saint Barlaam. The story appeared in Latin in the eleventh century and was subsequently translated into virtually every European vernacular language—ten versions appeared in French alone between the twelfth and fifteenth centuries, and three of those are verse translations.[1] We will never know with certainty what made the story so popular among medieval audiences. They may have appreciated the relatively simple lessons in Christian doctrine and belief, or they may have enjoyed the many parables that Barlaam uses to teach Prince Josaphat about Christianity. The setting of the story in India may have had some appeal, or audiences may have been drawn to the story of conflict between a pagan father and his Christian son.

The early part of the story has long been recognized as a retelling of the life of the Buddha: a young prince is raised in isolation from the world because his father fears he will renounce the secular world to become an ascetic, as foretold by astrologers; the prince subsequently discovers illness, old age, and death, and chooses to renounce the world in order to seek a spiritual reward. The Buddha's story traveled through many cultures and languages as it was transformed into the story of a Christian saint. Scholars believe that a version of the life of the Buddha was translated into Middle Persian (this translation does not survive), and then into the Arabic *Book of Bilawhar and Būdhāsaf.*[2] The Buddha appears in the Arabic version of the story as the prophet al-Budd, but the main protagonist is Prince Būdhāsaf, whose name is likely derived from the Sanskrit word *bodhisattva*. Although the Arabic text retains elements of the Buddha's life story, the ascetic religion promoted in the text is not clearly associated with Buddhism or Islam. *The Book of Bilawhar and Būdhāsaf* uses parables to illustrate and emphasize the evils of the world and the dangers of worldly values. It preaches the renunciation of the world and its pleasures and promotes ascetic values. Those values were firmly grounded in Christian belief when the text was translated into Georgian, probably in the eleventh century. The Georgian translation is preserved in two versions. In both the long version, translated under the title *The Balavariani*, and the shorter version, *The Wisdom of Balahvar*, a pagan Indian prince receives the teachings of a Christian hermit and embraces Christianity, refusing the worldly values of his idolatrous father.³ The Georgian version of the story was next translated into Greek, also probably in the eleventh century. From Greek, the story was translated into Latin, the lingua franca of clerics in western Europe, and *Barlaam and Josaphat* was subsequently translated from Latin into the many vernacular versions that circulated in medieval Europe.

The Greek translation of the story was long thought to be the original version of the story, and the eighth-century theologian John of Damascus was thought to be its author. This attribution has been discredited by modern scholars, but many medieval translators—including Gui de Cambrai—identified John as the author of *Barlaam and Josaphat*, and the story's attachment to a well-known theologian could have been another reason for its popularity. Gui de Cambrai even makes John of Damascus a character in the story.

Gui de Cambrai translates his *Barlaam and Josaphat* from a Latin source, he tells us twice, at the request of his patron, Gilles de Marquais. Gui's name indicates that he was from Cambrai, in northern France, but we know little about him. He has also been identified as the author of *Le vengement Alixandre* (*The Revenge of Alexander*), a continuation of the popular *Romance of Alexander*, which recounts the vengeance taken by the vassals of Alexander the Great on the servants who poisoned their lord.[4] We assume that Gui was a cleric, since he knew Latin. He had literary skills, or at least literary pretensions, because he translated Latin prose into Old French verse, and his *Barlaam and Josaphat* is clearly written for a courtly audience: Gui addresses noblemen directly in many of his narratorial interventions in the text.

Several times Gui de Cambrai is also named in the third person as the author of the text. Such references may suggest that the text was read out loud to an audience by a minstrel or a professional performer, and in fact the text includes many asides to the audience that could suggest that it was read to, or performed for, an audience. Some scholars have claimed that Gui de Cambrai left his translation unfinished, and that it was completed by an unnamed compiler who may have emphasized Gui's authorship as he added the extensive social commentary to the text. It is also possible that Gui names himself in the narrative, since it was not unusual for medieval authors to refer to themselves in the third person in order to claim authorship of a text and even to vaunt their rhetorical skills. And indeed other scholars insist that the entire narrative was written by Gui, including the narratorial interjections that explain the story, condemn the vices of the nobility, lament the corruption of the church, and excoriate those who have failed to go on Crusades to win Jerusalem from the Muslims.[5]

Gui's perspective is resolutely Christian: he speaks of "our Lord" and "our religion," and he vilifies Jews and Muslims as pagans. As in other medieval texts, Jews come in for special blame for their failure to recognize Christ when their prophets foretold his coming. Muslims are described as idolaters, like the Chaldeans, Greeks, and Egyptians whose religions are also refuted in *Barlaam and Josaphat*. "Idolater" is a fairly common term of abuse for Muslims in medieval narratives, despite the fact that Islam forbids the representation of living beings and especially of God and his prophets. The characterization of Muslims as idolaters reveals the limited knowledge about Islam among medieval Christians, and indeed accusations of idol worship were used to condemn almost anyone who was not a Christian. "Saracen," the name commonly used for Muslims in medieval French texts, also comes to have the fairly general sense of "pagan," and in *Barlaam and Josaphat* it appears frequently as an alternative name for Indians.

Gui de Cambrai's *Barlaam and Josaphat* includes two unique additions to the story of Prince Josaphat. First, Gui includes a holy war in his story. In most versions, after King Avenir divides his kingdom and gives half to his son, he sees the prosperity of his son's domain, realizes his error, and converts to Christianity. In Gui de Cambrai's *Barlaam and Josaphat*, the king sees the prosperity of his son's kingdom, understands that Josaphat has converted all his people and many of King Avenir's own, and resolves to take back the part of his land that he gave to his son. Avenir calls his vassals to war, and they march on Josaphat's kingdom. The king's son defends his land with the approval and participation of his archbishop, John of Damascus; the Christians defeat the so-called Saracens; and King Avenir converts to Christianity. The narrative of the war between the Saracen father and the Christian son resembles an Old French epic, or *chanson de geste*, in its opposition of the Christians' just cause to the error of the nonbelievers, and in its recital of blows exchanged between knights and its detailed accounts of heroic deeds in battle. The resemblance of the war between Josaphat's Christians and King Avenir's pagan Saracens to Crusade warfare is unmistakable—Gui even calls King Avenir's men Turks, and in one of the final sections of the story the narrator inserts a lament about the Christian noblemen who have failed to regain Jerusalem, and he condemns those who took up the cross and promised to go on Crusade but then failed ever to leave their homes.

The second innovation of Gui de Cambrai's *Barlaam and Josaphat* is its debate between personifications of Josaphat's body and soul. After Josaphat secures his Christian realm and witnesses his father's conversion, he leaves his kingdom to seek his master, Barlaam, in his wilderness hermitage. He wanders for two years in search of Barlaam and lives a life of harsh deprivation. His body starves as he cares for his soul, and at this point in the narrative Gui inserts a dialogue in which Josaphat's body complains vociferously about its treatment by Josaphat's soul. Again here Gui imitates another popular medieval literary genre that pits the appetites of the body against the spiritual desires of the soul.⁶ Gui's version is a lively exchange between a whining, complaining body and a strict and unforgiving soul. It allows the narrator to reiterate in a sometimes humorous key the dangers that worldly pleasures pose to spiritual rewards, and to emphasize the values of renunciation that are promoted throughout the story.

Gui de Cambrai's *Barlaam and Josaphat* is not significantly different from other versions of the story, apart from these additions of the war episode and the body-and-soul debate. However, its feudal vocabulary and the social commentary addressed to a noble audience give the poem a grounding in contemporary culture despite the story's location in a faraway, rather vaguely located India. Gui's version is longer than many others, and not only because of its added episodes and narratorial interventions. He also extends the characters' speeches, giving them more emotional depth and offering more details about their motivations. Gui adds wordplay and puns, and uses elaborate metaphors to describe emotional states.

I have not attempted to translate all the wordplay and punning into modern English. What follows is an accurate, though not word-for-word, translation of Gui de Cambrai's Old French. Gui is fond of repetition, not only of words, but also of nearly identical verses or phrases. I have eliminated many of these, and I have often varied the vocabulary in order to strive for a more fluent and economical English translation. Verb tenses fluctuate between past and present in Gui's text, and I have used a consistent past tense. I have also removed many of the brief formulas of oral performance

("Know this . . . ," "I believe") that seem intended to extend the line of verse rather than to offer a significant narratorial intervention. Gui de Cambrai's *Barlaam and Josaphat* may have been read aloud to an audience, but it is most certainly a translation from a written source, as the narrator claims, and not transcribed from an oral performance. However, it does, as mentioned, preserve many interventions from the narrator that directly address an audience. I have placed the narrator's shorter interruptions in parentheses. Longer interventions, sometimes in the third person, are signaled in the notes. Unless specifically addressing women (usually to chastise them), the text uses masculine pronouns to describe Christian subjects, and I have preserved the use of masculine pronouns instead of gender-neutral identifications, to reflect both the Old French usage and the text's perspective. Apart from a few mentions of women devoted to God in the parables Barlaam recounts, women in *Barlaam and Josaphat* represent seductions of the world that lead to the loss of the soul, and the lessons of the story are explicitly addressed to men.

The translation follows Carl Appel's 1907 edition based on two manuscripts.[7] Appel identifies some short lacunae in his edition, but I have not marked these in the translation; I have filled in the lines where the meaning seemed obvious, and I have simply skipped over several missing lines and inserted a transition. I have also added chapter divisions to the Old French text. Gui's *Barlaam and Josaphat*, like the Greek and all subsequent versions, is full of Biblical allusions, citations, and paraphrases, which I have not attempted to document.

PEGGY MCCRACKEN

Acknowledgments

Matthias Meyer and Constanza Cordoni first drew my attention to *Barlaam and Josaphat*. Inspired by an international conference they organized, my colleague Donald Lopez and I cowrote a book, *In Search of the Christian Buddha*, while I was translating Gui's narrative. That collaboration made the translation all the more interesting and rewarding, and I am very grateful for our many conversations about the text and for Don's encouragement to take on the translation in the first place. Doug Anderson now knows more about *Barlaam* than he ever imagined he could bear, I am sure, and I could never have completed this project without his good humor, unfailing support, and willingness to help me translate chess metaphors.

Barlaam and Josaphat

The narrator's introduction

Whoever begins a task well and then finishes it well deserves a double reward. Suffering will be turned to joy for anyone who undertakes a good work and toils to ensure that it is well done. Blessed is a dolorous life when it leads to glory. (As this story will show, human glory is deceptive and of little worth.)[1] Those who serve the devil do not understand what it means to serve God. They believe their sins will earn them more than the good man's works. They are deceived. However, I do not wish to write a long prologue because I would rather begin the story of Josaphat and Avenir.

This Avenir was king of India, and he did not tolerate any religion that challenged his authority. Because he was a sovereign king, he did not believe he should bow before any religion. That is how his story began, and he would never have turned to the good religion if God had revealed this reasoning to be false. (I began this story for Gilles of Marquais and his wife, Marie, so they could live better lives and be ready for their deaths.) Listen and you will hear how King Avenir chose heaven in the end.[2]

In ancient times the good flourished, even though there was much evil in the world, but now evil has taken over and destroys all that is good. The things that used to be valued are neglected now. The logic of evil is compelling, and no one can avoid it. The people who used to thrive here and cultivate good deeds have all gone to other lands to seek better rewards, and they have left no goodness behind. Faith is corrupted. Sin has lit its forge, and the hammers and anvils are ready to shape all manner of transgressions. Sinners will suffer for it later, and yet no one will humble his heart to the good. Now I must turn to my story.

King Avenir and his kingdom

In early times, the holy church taught about God, and as the pagans learned more about him, they understood that they were lost. They saw that living without belief would destroy them, because after they died they would have nothing. The thing that most drew them to God was the Christians' expectation of a good life after death.

At the time when people first believed, there was a foolish king in India. He did not care about God or his power, since he believed that his knowledge and wealth came from other gods, and not from God the Creator. This king, called Avenir, took great pleasure in his reign and he was confident in his rule, for he believed that nothing could destroy or diminish him. He was greatly renowned, and his subjects served him willingly, but in serving their king they opposed the holy church.

King Avenir vanquished all his foes, and he was wealthy, with many friends and fiefs, but his discernment was poor. He spent his time pursuing pleasure and did not realize that his great power impoverished him. He was most rich and handsome, but as you know, gold is less prized when laid over tin; when enamel shows beneath the gold, the vessel has less value. Similarly, the king was fulfilled outside but empty inside. His body was full, but his soul was empty. The body enjoyed its pleasures, but the soul slept in a cruel bed. There was peril in these pleasures, and the body's pleasure was tainted because it put the soul in sin. (At that time, as I understand it, the first growth of Christian belief flowered, and those who believed in God were strong in their faith. More learning, enlightenment, and veneration of the holy church was found in just one man than can be seen today in one hundred.)

King Avenir took great delight in his reign, but his soul did not profit from the pleasures he pursued. And indeed, because he did not yet have a child, the king's enjoyment of his privileges was lessened. (A child is a beloved thing! If children could remain with us always, there would be less to regret in the world.) This is what King Avenir and his thoughts were like.

The Christians in Avenir's lands did not fear the king's laws or his prisons. The more the king persecuted them, the stronger their faith became. Their martyrdom was doubled since they willingly received death when the king demanded it, and they found victory in vanquishing the one who would vanquish them. King Avenir tested his earthly power against the Christians' resolve, and his laws proved ineffective. The Christians did not fear pain or death, and all the king's efforts were in vain. King Avenir was angered by his inability to overcome the Christians. He prepared new tortures and punishments for them. He threatened them with dolorous days and painful weeks, but they held their loyalty to God like a shield before the king's attacks. The Holy Spirit who comforted them would destroy the king's power.

And so things remained there, as between a text and its gloss, and a great gap requires great caution. But the holy church would take her share even from among the king's councilors who despised her and sacrificed to ancient idols. One of these men was noble, wealthy, and very handsome. He denounced the king's sins and left his service, abandoning his land, his household, his domain, and his wealth. He exchanged all the king's marks of favor for the life of a hermit. The king loved this councilor above all men, but his vassal did not care for the world and left it behind, to purify himself of his sins and worship the Lord who dwells on high.

When the king heard about the man's departure, he was sorely tried. He lamented the loss of his good friend, and his heart was filled with hatred for the Christians and the life they led. King Avenir wished to avenge his anger, so he sent messengers to the Christians' hermitage, instructing them to search everywhere until they found the vassal who had abandoned the king. The messengers found the man and brought him back to court. He came without a wealthy entourage: he appeared impoverished, but he was rich inside. The king said to him, "What a state you are in! What happened to your wealth and wisdom? Where are your honor and prowess? You were a lord, and now you are a serf. See what kind of master you serve! The man who would keep his servant in such misery is a bad overlord. What are you thinking? Your pride and your honor have turned to shame! Nature has been denied! You have forgotten what is right and you fight against nature, for it is a sin to have no pity for your children! You have forgotten the name of your father, and you do not remember your children or their mother. They are your flesh! They are your limbs! Why have you done this? Explain it to me! Alas, what an evil time this is. Your thoughts are secret and your intentions harsh—why would you exchange wealth for poverty?"

When the man of God understood what the pagan king wanted from him, he responded willingly and joyfully. He said to him carefully, "If you wish to listen to reason, you must banish two enemies at your court."

The king responded, "Ha, foolish man! You who were once my dear friend, speak to me and show me my enemies."

"King, listen and understand," the man responded humbly. "The enemies I describe are anger and greed. Whoever seeks to understand with his heart must renounce these two things, for anger overcomes and destroys a man, and greed shames him. Sire, these two are your enemies. But if you will listen to a friend's advice, replace anger and greed with wisdom and justice. Then you will be able to devote yourself to learning what is good. Reason uses the understanding of wisdom and justice to bring those who have strayed into the right path."

"I will listen to you, do not fear," the king answered. "Teach me where you first learned this foolishness."

The hermit was quick to reply. "Reason and rectitude have taught me that it is futile to love this dying world," he said. "Happiness that will quickly end offers poor pleasure. This world is inconstant, and the man who devotes himself most fervently to it suffers the greatest loss and destruction. The more he attains, the more he desires; he lives in pain and he will dwell in loss. When I was young, I heard it said that everyone should despise the world, and that is wise advice. The man who seeks God must renounce the world and should not spend his time seeking wealth or possessions. He must place his hope in the sovereign good that is God on high, he who descended to this world for our sakes. He lived and died for us and saved us with his death. He was willing to come down here for us (and his divinity was not lessened because he came to earth to seek and redeem us). Our Lord became our servant when he accepted martyrdom on the cross for our sakes. Because of the sin of the apple bite, our Lord took the form of a man to save us, and all those made in his form are redeemed by his death. Your lord, the devil, sought to martyr our Lord, but he was vanquished by the cross. God in his glory defeated him, and God's victory revealed that his human form covered a divine nature.

"King, now listen and understand, for I do not fear your threats. God is against you, for whoever hates God will never have a share in his inheritance, in which all good things will be given and received. You are not good, and for this reason you are separated from God, who made you in his image. Do you think you are equal to your Creator? You are a creature, and you do not recognize who created you! Serve your Creator. He may well reward you, for he is a merciful Lord, but you must submit yourself to his service. King, become both a king and a servant. You will earn a great realm and uphold a just kingdom. Neither pride nor evil should hinder anyone who seeks such a realm. This world is but darkness and shadows. False belief blinds the pagans, and their pleasures cover them in shadow. It is a serious wager to give up everything and receive nothing in return.

"King, I left you and your love because of your false belief. God is my Lord and my Father, my companion and my brother. He is my Lord because I am his servant and will serve him all my days. He is my Father because he created me and formed me in his image. He is my companion because he was tempted, but his power and his divinity protected him from sin, for to sin is contrary to him. He is my brother because he became a man. If he will help me in my present plight, I will fear no threat. I care nothing for you, your empire, your vassals, your prowess, your sovereignty, or your crown, for you should know that it all comes from him."

The king was furious. He would have threatened his vassal harshly but for the promise he had made him. "Oh wretched man," said the king, "my oath protects you. I would take revenge for your slander if my faith did not restrain me. I will suffer your insults in order to keep my promise. You have poisoned me with your base and foolish words. Rise and leave this place, for I am no longer your friend! If I find you again, you will pay dearly for your foolish claims!" The man departed sad and full of regret that he had not been martyred. The king remained in his court and angrily commanded his people to kill the Christians. Never before had the Christians been so cruelly persecuted by King Avenir.

King Avenir's son is born

While King Avenir was foolishly following a path he thought would lead to honor, a son of great beauty was born to him, and the king held him most dear. Nature took great pains in forming the child, and a more beautiful boy could not be found in any land. His countenance foretold his destiny and prefigured the flower that would grow from the seed. King Avenir named his son Josaphat and wished to demonstrate his happiness at the boy's birth. He prayed with thanks to all his gods, but he was foolish and deluded. He did not acknowledge the Creator to whom he should have offered his gratitude, for the devil caused him not to believe.

The king organized great festivities to celebrate the birth of his son, and he sacrificed many bulls, cows, and other animals to appease his gods. All the people of India came to the celebration, because they feared the king, and all who came made sacrifices. The king received his people with great honor, thanking them for the sacrifices they offered and giving them many gifts.

Astronomers well versed in the arts of magic and deception attended the celebration—there were fifty-five of them, I believe. By the king's order, each foretold the future of the newborn Josaphat. Many said that he would be brave and wise, and that he would surpass all other kings in wealth, power, rank, and valor. One astronomer knew more than the others and saw Josaphat's future more clearly. "Sire, I will not lie," he said to the king. "I will tell you truthfully what I saw: the son you have from your wife will never care about your kingdom. He will seek a higher realm, and he will be the lord of a better land. If the stars do not lie, he will become one of the people we call Christians." The king was sad and worried by this prophecy, but the joy of his son's birth made him forget his sorrow.

Later, when the king had thought further about the astronomer's prediction, he had a palace built a short distance outside the city. It was constructed with great skill, and the king had all its rooms richly decorated. He spared no expense, and the palace he built was most beautiful. He was concerned about his son and believed he could change the boy's destiny. The child grew and became handsome—soon he was a young man. When he reached an age of understanding, his father had him taken to the rooms prepared for him in the palace. The king's plan was evil. He sent the boy's household with him, and he locked young men of his son's age inside, giving them firm instructions. "Hide all of life's ills from him, and do not let him know that all things in the world must die," the king commanded. "Do not let him see any sadness, infirmity, death, old age, or poverty. He should believe that there is nothing but pleasure in the world. Let him see only joy and happiness. Do not wound his sensibility with anything that causes anger, and keep him from hearing any-

thing at all about this Lord of the Christians. If one of his
guards becomes ill, be sure that he is immediately taken from
the palace so the prince does not see him. Replace the guard
with a handsome, healthy, and valiant man, so the child does
not see or understand that there are such things as wounds or
infirmities in the world."

The king arranged the pleasures of the palace to convince
his son that there was nothing in the world beyond what he
could see. He thought he could deceive the child in this way.
To protect his son, the king issued a decree commanding that
there should no longer be any Christians in his lands. The
king swore that any who remained would die a painful death.

The story recounts that there was a rich and noble count in
Avenir's court who believed in the Christian God, but he
concealed his belief because he feared the king. Envious men
spoke against him constantly, because of his faith and valor,
for evil and pride cannot tolerate wisdom and rectitude.
These slanderers often spoke to the king, accusing men and
denouncing those who would defend them. (No one should
attack a man who seeks to defend the true faith.)

One day the king went to hunt in the forest, and I believe
he took with him more than two thousand men to share his
pleasure, including the count who believed in God. The king
enjoyed the pursuit of pleasure, but he began to think about
the count and the accusations against him, and he did not
know what to believe.

While the king hunted in the forest with his great company
of men, the count who had cast his lot with God went in a
different direction. He knew the woods well and he rode
alone, far from the others, because he sought solitude. As he
rode, he looked ahead and saw a gravely wounded man. A
wild animal had eaten one of his feet. The wounded man saw
the count, who did not stop, and called loudly to ask him to
take mercy and to carry him home since he could not walk
there. "My noble lord," he called, "carry me away from here
and you will earn a great reward." The wounded man's plea
touched the count's heart and lightened his sadness. Because

he pitied the man, and because it was right, he agreed to carry him to his house. It was fortunate for the wounded man that his home was nearby and his pain would soon be relieved.

"Tell me," the count said, "and do not lie, what profit can come to me from this service?"

The wounded man replied, "I am a learned man, a doctor of words. No man was ever as accomplished as I am, nor as well trained to counsel others on how to avoid evil." When the count heard what the wounded man said, he did not give it much weight. He took the man to his house and gave him provisions.

The men who were eager to betray the count told the king that he was a Christian. (No good man ever lived without causing envy.) They accused him repeatedly and warned the king that the Christians took courage from the fact that this man who shared their religion was close to the king.

"They try to bring down your religion with their cunning. Noble king, mete out justice on them! If you will trust us, we can tell you how to test him. Say to him, 'Friend, I know that I have done wrong. I sinned against the Christians when I had them driven out of my country. Now I will be baptized. If you will counsel me, I will leave this religion.' Then you will know for certain whether we are right."

The king did not see the treachery in this advice, nor did he understand the intention hidden behind its logic. He called the count aside and repeated the words scripted by those who had no desire for the good. "My friend," said the king, "I have loved you greatly, and so it is right that I tell you all my thoughts and plans. I have done evil things to the Christians, and yet their faith seems righteous to me. I believe I was foolish to persecute and destroy them. Now I repent, for our gods are worthless compared to the God of the Christians. This world is full of vanity and evil: the Christians' lives are more peaceful than ours. By converting I will prove that whoever would abandon worldly pleasures can rejoice, for renown is worth nothing, as is my kingdom and its glory. I can gain no greater glory than baptism. Now counsel me with your wisdom!"

The count did not perceive the deception, and he responded simply as a man of good faith. "King, one thing surprises me: where have you found such resolve? It is laudable to do good deeds, and everyone should learn to recognize what is good. The things that seem good in this life are filled with evil and folly. This world will soon pass away, and everything begun here will come to an end. The world began from nothing, and it will return to nothing. God made all things in the beginning, and everything was made as he commanded. Beginning without beginning, end without end! Whoever has discernment should understand the precept that God has neither end nor beginning. All things began in him and all will finish in him. Without him nothing we see has any value. Leave your gods and believe in the Creator of the world and everything it holds! This life is filled with sadness, and any happiness found here soon fades and comes to an end. All the world and its pleasures are fleeting.

"The faith of Christians is certain and firm. They put all their hope in God, and they know with certainty that God prepares a reward for them according to their acts. This temporal life promises a man something he cannot have, for in the end he must die. That death is not honorable and its sorrow is eternal. King, be wise. Direct your will and deepen your desire to receive such a great reward."

The king was angry when he heard the count's response, but he said nothing. The count was perceptive and wise, and he recognized the king's disappointment. He saw that his lord's heart was troubled, and he left the court pondering how he could make peace with the king, for he greatly feared his anger. He spent the whole night in thought, and then he remembered the man who had said he was a doctor of words. He sent for him and asked for his advice—he had great need of counsel.

The count told the word doctor everything: how the king had tested him and how he had replied. He said the king had avoided answering, but he recognized the king's anger and perceived his own peril. The word doctor understood that the count was in danger from the king. The count asked for his help and offered him a generous reward in exchange for good counsel. "Sire," the man replied, "listen to me. Tonsure your head and exchange your clothes for a hair shirt, then go to the king. When he asks why you have come, tell him, 'I have renounced the world out of love for you. I will leave this world, as you suggested yesterday, for your sake. I will do all you ask. I have come here prepared to follow you.'"

The count was pleased by this advice, and he did exactly as the word doctor suggested. When he arrived at court, the king was taken aback by his appearance, and when he heard his friend's words, he perceived his honesty and true love, and his earlier doubts were removed. He saw the count's sincerity and judged that the accusations of his disloyalty were false. The king absolved his friend of suspicion and honored him, to show his favor. But his anger toward the Christians in his land grew, and his war against them became more violent.

One day King Avenir went hunting and saw two Christian monks. He had them seized and asked why they had come into his land. "You deceivers of men," said the king, "what brings you into my realm? Do you not fear the proclamations that were cried, warning that if you were found in my lands, you would be killed? Do you wish to remain here?"

"Sire, no, we do not wish to stay. We were only going to buy food. We left your lands in accordance with your ban, but we came back here to seek provisions."

The king replied, "You made a bad choice. Do you fear hunger more than death? Anyone who fears death seeks only to escape it."

"King, you do not know how strongly one should fear death," they replied. "Only those who are saved can escape the death that takes us all. We have left the pleasures of the world because they kill the soul along with the body. We do not believe there is any escape from death, and good men who live as we do are glorified when they die. We do not fear death, for we know that whoever lives in goodness does not truly die but passes to a great reward."

The king replied, "Listen to me. You lie! If you do not fear death, why did you flee from my threats? Unless I take mercy on you, death has now found you, since you did not stay away."

"King, we do not fear your threats of death, nor do we recognize your laws, but out of pity for you we will leave your lands so your sins will not multiply. However, we are not afraid to die."

The king was very angry and had them burned immediately. He commanded that any Christian man or woman remaining in his lands should be executed.

Josaphat leaves his palace

While the king was persecuting Christians, his son was locked away in his palace. He spent his days more wisely than his father did, strengthening his heart with knowledge. All who saw him marveled at his learning. He cultivated his body and his soul, but he cared more for his soul than for his body. The king marveled at his son's beauty and wisdom, and he forbade his men to tell Josaphat anything about sadness or death. But human nature cannot be hidden, especially from a child so gifted with wisdom and discernment. Josaphat understood that his father did not want anyone to speak to him about the things of this life. He wondered about the reason for the interdiction and often asked himself, "Why has my father, the king, done this? He does not want anyone to teach me, and I do not know why." The youth often sought to understand his father's decision to isolate him in his retreat, and he always concluded that his father would do nothing that was not for his good. Then he began to consider whether he should ask his father why he had him guarded so closely in his palace and why he lived with so few people. He resolved to do it, then he reconsidered. "My father would not have hidden it from me if he wanted me to know," he thought. Instead, he chose one of his servants and opened his heart to him, asking why and to what end his father had isolated him in the palace. "Good friend," said Josaphat, "if you wish to keep my friendship, tell me why I am locked in this prison."

Josaphat's servant looked at him kindly and understood that his lord was full of knowledge and discernment, and he thought, "If I tell him a lie, he will no longer love me." And so the servant answered Josaphat truthfully. He told him everything: that the Christians had been banished; that the astronomers foretold at his birth that he would embrace their belief; and that, according to the king's commandment, not a single Christian remained in the region. "Your father has isolated us here because he fears what could happen. He hides all the sadness of the world because he wants to keep you from faith, wisdom, and what is right, and to repel sorrow with joy."[1] When the young man heard his servant's response, the Holy Spirit lodged in his heart where he had not been known before.

Josaphat's father loved him above all things and came often to visit him. One day his son tested him. He revealed the sorrow that lay beneath his apparent happiness. "Good father and king, please explain this to me: a sadness has taken hold of me and torments my heart, and I don't know where it comes from."

His father could see from Josaphat's pallor that he was in pain. "Good son," he said, "what sadness has come over you? Tell me so I can relieve it and restore your happiness."

"I wonder why you have imprisoned me here. Tell me, if you will, good father, why you did it and if I have displeased you in some way."

"Sweet son, you have not displeased me. I chose this palace for you so that you might live a life full of joy and the greatest pleasures. I would not wish for all the world that the sight of some sadness should trouble your well-being."

"Father," Josaphat said, "it pains me that I cannot see what lies beyond these walls. Your heart is hard if you will not allow me to go outside and see what the world is like. I desire it so badly that my own heart is in pain. If you wish to make me happy, let me go outside and see the world."

The king considered whether he should agree. By right and by reason, he wished to allow it so his son's sadness might be relieved. "Good son," he said, "I will permit it." Josaphat thanked the king gratefully.

The following morning King Avenir ordered that all the young men and women of the city should be assembled. He commanded them to put on such a display of happiness that no sadness would be seen anywhere, nor should any old or infirm people be visible. The king was foolish and at odds with himself since he tried to seem joyful in appearance though he was filled with anger. The king deluded himself. He wanted to combine joy with anger, but anger does not care for joy.

King Avenir had handsome horses brought for his son and the great train of people and guards that accompanied him. Josaphat was richly mounted, as is fitting for a king's son, and his father commanded that he be allowed to ride about the city as he wished. The young man went out and encountered pleasures of all kinds. He looked intently at everything he saw, for he was not used to seeing such a world or so much happiness. Then he saw two men in his path. The sight was not pleasant, for one of them was a leper and the other was blind. He understood then that happiness had deserted the world. He asked his companions, "Who are these two men?"

"These men are not worthy of your attention."

"Tell me, I want to know what happened to them."

"Sire, we cannot hide it from you. This is human suffering," his companions answered truthfully. "When the matter from which the human body is made becomes corrupted, then bad blood is produced and causes illness."

"Does this happen to all people?" Josaphat asked.

"No, only to some. But many people become infirm, and infirmity brings suffering."

"Can we know who will suffer, or does everyone fear that suffering will come to him without warning?"

"No one knows whether he will suffer," they replied truthfully. "No man of flesh can know if good or ill will come to him. But God knows all things and has prepared all that was, all that is, and all that will be." The king's son did not speak further, but he sighed deeply and his thoughts were troubled, for he had never thought of such a thing.

Two weeks later Josaphat rode out again into the city with his companions, where they encountered a very old man. His skin was wrinkled, his back was bent, and his hair was white. He had a wretched look: he had only a few teeth, his lips were blue, his legs failed him, and his arms were weak. His chest was high and his belly low; his eyes were sunken and his nose sharp, for he had been born many years before. The king's son noticed him and looked at him with wonder.

"Who is this man?" Josaphat asked.

"By your leave, Sire, we will tell you," his companions answered. "This man has lived for a long time. He is old and frail, and his hair is white because he is so aged. His limbs have become weak and he lives in misery."

"What will be the end of this old man?" the king's son asked.

"The only thing that can happen now is for him to die, and he cannot escape it."

"Does this happen to everyone?"

"Yes, by faith, old age comes to everyone, unless death comes first. All people grow old, unless death cuts their lives short."

The young man thought about this and then asked, "Is there any way to avoid death or old age? And do you know if there is some force that can prevent death? It is regrettable that men must grow old and die."

"My good lord, if we speak truthfully, we have to tell you

that the young and old will all die. So it was for our ancestors, and it cannot be any other way. Death is the debt we
owe to nature. No one can escape death—like it or not, we
all must die."

The wise young man's heart and happiness were troubled.
"Now I do not know what to say," he responded. "This life is
most bitter, and this world harsh and evil. No one is safe
within it. Death is cruel since it destroys a man by taking his
life. Two things are to be feared: the first is that although a
man is strong today, he may become infirm tomorrow. The
other thing that causes fear is that no one can escape death."

The king's son was sad and fearful. Death confused and
frightened him, and he pondered it often. "Alas, after my
death there will be nothing left of me," he lamented. "I will
die when death comes, and afterwards no one will remember
me. My life is in danger, and death will cause it to be forgotten. If there is no world after this one, then this one is vain
and full of suffering. This life is cruel if we die without the
hope of living again. Since men must leave the world, if they
can have no other life, then this one is poor and stingy. No
man should think he is wealthy, because no man is so beautiful, young, rich, or valiant, or so wise and powerful, or gov-
erns such a strong city that he will not have to die. For this
reason, wealth is like poverty and flesh is a base matter."
These were Josaphat's thoughts. It weighed upon him that
the whole world would come to ruin, and he feared death
greatly.

When his father came to him, Josaphat hid his suffering
behind happiness. His heart was sorrowful, but his face was
joyful, and he deceived the king because he did not wish for
his father to see what saddened his heart. The thoughts that
gnawed at Josaphat's heart constrained his body. He tossed
and turned, he cried out, he lamented and sighed, and did
not know what he should say. He could not sleep, and he
kept asking himself how he could bear the sorrow of death.
He thought about it constantly. His entire body suffered because he did not know how to escape death, but his heart

bore the greatest grief. He was filled with sadness and despair, and he experienced little joy. He asked his confidant frequently if he knew of anyone who could counsel him. "Sire," his servant replied, "I do not know anyone, for as I told you, the king banished all the Christians from his country long ago, and those who remained were taken and killed. I do not know how to advise you, for there is no one left to instruct you."

The young man did not know what to do. As time went by, his understanding was more and more troubled, and the more he thought about death, the more troubled he became. But God, who sees and knows all things, provided what Josaphat so strongly desired. He sent good counsel to the youth who was so close to the right path.

Barlaam comes to Josaphat

The story tells us that at that time a most wise and holy monk named Barlaam lived in the wilderness. He was a learned priest and spent his days in harsh penitence. Barlaam learned of Josaphat's distress through a divine revelation. He changed his dress, putting on a merchant's attire, and left the wilderness. The Holy Spirit revealed that he would succeed in his mission, and he journeyed through the wilds without tiring. He came to the sea, crossed over it, and went to the city where the king's son lived. Upon his arrival, Barlaam inquired about the king's son and his servants, and people told him all about them. He learned that one of the servants loved his lord above all things, and Barlaam found this man and told him what he wanted.

"Friend," he said, "heed what I say. You are close to the king's son. I am a merchant from another land and I have come here to sell goods, but trade is dangerous. I have a precious stone I wish to offer your lord, to win his love. I have never seen a better stone. I wish to give the precious gem to

your lord—only you and I will know about it. I have spoken
about it to no one, but I describe it to you with confidence because I see that you are a wise man and of good faith. This
stone has great power: it makes the blind see, the mute speak,
and the deaf hear. It cures children, it frees prisoners from
their dungeons, and it makes the foolish wise and the poor
rich. It is most precious and dear: there is no more valuable
gem in the world."

"Here is what I think," Josaphat's man responded. "You
appear to be a wise man, and I see that you are reasonable
and intelligent. But it is hard to believe your words, and hard
to trust them, for I have seen precious stones of all kinds—
emeralds, pearls, and other extraordinary gems—and I have
never seen or heard of one that possessed the virtues you describe. Show it to me, then, for I would not wish to be judged
a liar in the king's court. If I describe the virtues of this stone
and my words are not true, my tongue will be cut out, and I
will never be allowed in my lord's presence again."

"Wait," said Barlaam, "that is not all. A man who forgets
what he should say is most foolish, and I forgot something I
must tell you. The noble stone cannot be shown to any man
who has not lived a chaste life or who has witnessed any evil,
because he would be killed by it. But your lord can see it, for
he is wise and has kept his eyes clear and pure, and he is
chaste. You may tell him about the stone with confidence,
and your lord will be most happy because of it."

"For God's sake, do not show me the stone, for my vision is not pure and I have sullied my body, more on the
inside than the outside. I do not believe that you are a liar.
I will speak to my lord and return quickly." The servant
went to the king's son and told him what Barlaam had described. When Josaphat heard it, the Holy Spirit caused
him to rejoice. He forgot his sorrow and had Barlaam
brought before him.

The wise man came quickly and greeted the king's son
kindly. An attentive man could see by his greeting that he
was a good man. Josaphat thanked him for coming and of-

fered Barlaam his hospitality. The prince invited the visitor to sit before him and then asked his servant to leave.

"Where is the precious stone whose virtues and powers my man told me so much about?" Josaphat asked Barlaam. "Good friend, is it true? Show it to me, if you please!"

Barlaam responded carefully. "You will see the truth about everything you have heard. I spoke truthfully to your servant, I promise you, but you cannot see the stone until I know that you are worthy to receive it. One of my lords recounts a parable that fits this situation, and I want to tell it to you.

"A sower went out to sow, and he dropped his seed along the road. The birds then ate it. The sower prepared other seed and sowed it, but it fell on stone, and when the seeds sent out roots, they lacked water and soil. The plants dried up because of the hot sun, and they could not grow because they needed soil for their roots. The sower sowed other seed among thorns, and these grains were lost as well—the thorns overwhelmed them and they yielded nothing. He sowed other seed in good earth. Then his harvest increased one hundred-fold.

"If I can find in you soil that will bear good fruit, I will sow God and his seed in your heart. I want you to know who the sower represents and what the seed is, and if your heart is ready to learn, I will teach you important lessons. But if your understanding is rocky and full of thorns, I cannot show you my precious stone nor prove its efficacy. It would be perilous for you if you do not know how to receive it. If a man spreads pearls before swine, he will regret it, for he expects too much. You have lived a good life, and I do not doubt that you will be able to see the precious stone and that you will receive such good counsel from the purity of its light that the fruit in you will be increased a hundred times. I left my land for your sake, and I have come from afar to teach you the things you need to know."

Josaphat said, "Dear friend, I have long sought for a wise man to enlighten me. An idea troubles and disturbs me. It burns me inside and out, and my body suffers from it, yet I hide the turmoil in my heart behind a happy face. I could find no one who could relieve me of the burden my heart carries, and this is why I am so afflicted. If I could find a wise man, I would willingly hear any counsel he could offer, for I have long wished for good seed to be sown in me. It will not be burned, nor suffer from stones or thorns. I will water its roots with the rain of my heart. I am most bitter, Master, when I do not find any man who can draw water from the well of my heart. If you know things that will relieve my unhappiness, do not conceal them from me. When I heard you say that you came from far away to help me, my fear was lifted and you gave me hope, for I believe that you can relieve my pain, good master."

"I have tested you," Barlaam said, "and I believe that you are not distracted by outside appearances but see clearly into your heart.

"There was once an exalted king who dressed in beautifully made robes," Barlaam recounted to Josaphat. "He rode about richly adorned with royal ornaments, accompanied by many companions, and filled with great happiness. He saw two poor men in his path. They were thin, barefoot, and dressed in rags. The king saw them and dismounted. He greeted them happily, and he bowed before them and kissed them when he rose. The noblemen who accompanied him—knights, counts, and princes—scorned the king for it, and they spoke among themselves about how the king had abased himself when he knelt before the poor men. They did not dare reproach the king directly, but they scorned him for humbling himself and thought it a great dishonor. One of the king's brothers spoke to him and told him that he had acted most dishonorably, for his honor was sullied when he set it aside to bow to such poor men. The king tried to explain his actions, but his brother did not understand.

"The king had instituted the practice of sounding a trumpet at the house of any man condemned to death—the horn was the signal he would die. The king sent for his herald and gave him the horn that announced deaths. 'Trumpeter, go to my brother's door and sound his death,' said the king. 'When he hears the sound of the horn, he will know that he must die.'

"The herald did not delay. He went to the house, stopped before the door, put the horn to his lips, and sounded it. The king's brother was dismayed when he heard his death announced. He spent the whole night in worried agitation. He was frightened and did not know what to do. He feared the king would put him to death and he did not know why, for he had committed no crime. He was terrified.

"The next day at sunrise, the king's brother rose, made himself ready with his wife and children, and went to the court. He was worried and filled with sorrow, for he feared death. The king saw that he was present and commanded him to come forward. 'Brother,' he said, 'listen to me. Do you weep because of death? You would be right to do so, for death is greatly to be feared. Are you frightened of death because you heard my horn? Do you fear me so much that you have come to put your life at my mercy because of the man I sent to sound your death? But yesterday when I saw the heralds of my Lord and revered them, you scorned me for it! Now you see that you were wrong (for no one should scorn a man if he cannot show reason for it). I was right to bow before the men I encountered yesterday, for they were messengers of the King who created all things, including you and me. We should fear him, for we are his creatures. By this experience you should learn not to reproach a man or judge him wrong if you cannot show why. Those who used you to reproach me are even worse. I will show you how they erred.'

"The king had four caskets of the same size. Two were covered in gold from his treasury, and the story tells us that he had them filled with rotting filth. The other two were filled with the finest gold, but he had them covered in mud and dirt, and put old rags on top of them. He sent for the noblemen who blamed him for kneeling before the paupers, and they came quickly. Then he asked them whether they knew which caskets were the best and most valuable. The men judged by what they saw and chose the caskets covered in gold. 'It is obvious that these are the best,' they said. 'The other two are so filthy that they should be taken away and burned, for they do not belong in a king's court.'

" 'You have judged well according to what you see,' the king responded. 'But you see with your bodily eyes, and the eyes of your heart are blind. Similarly, a man may be judged to be poor and lowly when indeed he has more wealth than can be found in all of Rome.' To show them their mistake, the king had the golden caskets opened. 'Now you can see that what is beautiful and noble on the outside is rotten on the inside,' he said. 'Likewise, the man dressed in rich clothes and adorned with gold is full of filth inside. His body is covered in fine things, but his soul lies in great sin.'

"The king had the other two caskets opened to show them their mistake. 'My lords,' he said, 'look inside. You disdained these two caskets because they were wretched outside, but there was great wealth inside them. Look at this treasure— these caskets are full of gold. They are like people who do not care about this world and its vanities. Poor outside and rich inside, they are not afraid to be beggars, and they abandon the body to save the soul from danger. You who accuse me, consider this and judge whether I should honor and bow to the men of my Lord, the Son of God, and my Creator.'

"Friend," Barlaam continued, "the king whose story I tell you led his lords to faith with his wisdom and admonitions and through this good demonstration. You have done likewise. I have told this story for you, because when I came before you, you honored me, in your mercy, not for any value you saw in me, but because you understood that it was right. You have some understanding of what is good, and so you are not lost."

Josaphat seeks knowledge of God

Josaphat perceived that Barlaam spoke wisely and used stories to teach him a good lesson. "Master," the young man said, "instruct me. Who is the man who went to sow the seed?"

"He is a Lord of great power, Lord of all lords," the hermit responded. "He is God, who holds everything in his hands. He is immortal, but he took human form for our sake. He is divided into three persons, but he does not lose his unity because of this division. The persons do not share a single substance but remain One.

"It is he who created all the world out of nothing. We must worship this God who made the heavens, the earth, and the seas. He made all creatures and designed all nature. Genesis tells us that God made man in his likeness and in his image, and he gave him understanding. He also gave him nobility of character so he might experience both joy and sorrow. Man can sin if he wishes. And when he chooses, he can avoid sin. God made him from the earth. Then he formed woman. He put them both in a paradise full of joy and pleasures, and he gave them happiness and knowledge. He commanded them to be obedient and forbade them to taste but a single fruit (this fruit contained the knowledge of good and evil). He told them that if they ate it, they would die. He showed them the tree and the fruit, when he put them in the garden of delights, and told them, 'If you do not touch this tree, you will never die. You may take what you like from the other trees, but you must leave this one alone.' However, the devil tricked the man and made him bite the apple, and man was condemned because he transgressed God's law. We are wretched and destitute because of our father Adam's sin. We are all descended from the first father, who changed our day into night.

"Some believe that it was his Creator's fault that Adam sinned. They say, 'If God had made him to be good, he would not have done wrong, but since he made him evil, it is no wonder that he sinned.' For this reason they say that God was wrong to condemn men to death. But these claims will not save them: God is perfect goodness and nothing ever came from him that was not good. Moreover, if man were not able to sin, he would have rewards that he did not earn. Why should he have a reward if he does not earn it? The scriptures tell us that God made man in his own image so he would know his Creator and serve him as his Lord, and so he could earn the reward promised him.

"God made only the first man in this way, and not others, it is true. But those who were born to the first man betrayed God when they turned their faith to other gods. Some worshipped the elements, and others made gods out of wood and stone, and sacrificed to those gods in opulent temples they built for them. They no longer believed in a single God, for they made the sun and the moon their gods, and believed in them. Good faith was corrupted, and anger and envy were born, along with murder, felony, theft, deception, and many other sins. Men lost the knowledge of God because they served idols. There was hardly a single wise man who knew God or his name. But there were prophets, and God spoke to them about the evils that were so abundantly present then in all men and about the evil their sins spread throughout the world.

"At that time, when people died they went to hell, to dwell with devils, whether they were good or evil, and this is a fate that no wise man should seek. The world was like that until God was born to a virgin, Saint Mary, and saved us from death. We learn from the scriptures that he was born on earth from a virgin, without a man's seed. He received baptism to show that all should be baptized, for good works cannot earn salvation without baptism. He lived and preached among the people for thirty years. Then he was betrayed, sold, arrested and beaten, and hung on a cross, where he was taken by death. Then he went to break hell open, and he freed those who deserved it. They had waited for forgiveness and the One who had allowed himself to be hung on the cross wished to give it to them.

"The Jews judged him wrongly, for he never did any wrong. Indeed, he could never do wrong, because his divinity prevented him from sinning as a man. Those who crucified him found nothing but good in him. On the third day, he was resurrected and appeared to his apostles. Then he went up into heaven, from where he had descended. He bestowed the Holy Spirit on his apostles, just as he had promised.

"Now I have told you who my Lord is, but I cannot adequately describe his nobility and his lordship or the extent of his power and his dominion. If you receive his favor, you will understand. You will never be disappointed if you fill yourself with his mercy, and you can receive his mercy if you become his servant."

The king's son marveled at what he heard, and Barlaam's gentle words penetrated his soul and his understanding. He embraced Barlaam. "Dear friend," he said, "you have shown me your precious stone, and I now understand that only those who seek to know God may see it. Your words have illuminated my thoughts. They have thrown off the hard and bitter darkness and brought me clarity. Sadness no longer dwells in my thoughts, good master. A new day dawns inside me, and it will light my darkened heart. If you know more, show it to me, for I have great confidence in you."

"Listen, then, my lord, to what I wish to tell you: you will fail in all your good intentions if you are not baptized. Whoever believes in baptism may be saved if he receives it, but he cannot be saved any other way. Our Sovereign Lord sent us a Savior to show us that whoever believes with all his heart, if he is baptized, will surely be saved. Our ancestors saw their salvation from afar, and they desired greatly his coming. We know no other salvation."

"Dear friend, I have understood you," said Josaphat. "You have given me good hope and my doubt has disappeared. But what is baptism? Explain it to me—I want to learn. And then

show me why those who love God should be baptized and
why they cannot be saved otherwise."

"I will teach you," Barlaam replied. "Baptism is the root of
our faith and the firm foundation of Christian belief. Baptism removes the stain of sin. This holy cleansing returns men
to their former state of honor. The scriptures say truly that
baptism is the solder and the joint that join and solder us to
our Creator. Through baptism we are recognized as heirs to
our Father in heaven, who sent his Son to us. He does not
mislead us, for he himself received baptism. Without baptism
a man possesses nothing, and nothing he does can save him
without baptism. If a man is not baptized in good faith, the
devil destroys everything he builds. For this reason, I counsel
you not to wait another moment—seek to be baptized with
all your heart, in understanding and good faith. Make haste
and allow no delay. To tarry would be unwise. Indeed, it
would be dangerous, because no one can know when death
will come, and you will die."

"Good master, tell me, how can this be?" Josaphat asked.
"What hope is lost without baptism? Where does what you
call a heavenly kingdom come from? What will happen at
that unknown time when death arrives to kill me and eat my
flesh and bones? I fear it, but I cannot say how my flesh will
come to nothing. Master, I know well that I will die. I am
sure of death, but I do not know if I can live again after my
death, nor do I know how I should live."

"Good friend," said Barlaam, "in life there are a multitude of torments, and whoever can die and then come back
to life after death is most fortunate. Whoever leaves his
flesh behind for God's sake does not die. He will live beyond death, and the reward prepared for him is better than
any eye can see, any heart can understand, and any ear can
hear. Those who receive this reward will rejoice. The scriptures tell us truly that the gifts of divine glory are valuable
beyond description, and God's gifts would not be so hard to
understand if we could know them according to his understanding.

"Although the body is corrupted through death and loses the flesh that continuously burned and tormented it, the soul looks to eternal life and thinks of nothing else. It waits only for the sovereign day when our Lord will come to judge all the world, and on that day even the apostles will tremble from fear. There will be no long debate or false promises of rewards, and the support of friends will be of no value. Each man will have his reward according to discernment and reason. Whoever deserves a crown will receive it, and his reward will be good.

"God the Creator tells us in the Gospels that there will be no appeal after death—none will escape judgment. Let all people know that they will die and on the sovereign day they will be raised up and judged according to their works. There will be no appeals on that day. Everything hidden will be seen, and pleas for mercy will not be heard. Bad deeds will be revealed and counted, and neither tithes nor sins will be hidden. Everything will be seen and all will be judged. Do not imagine that day according to what you know of this life, and do not doubt that God can resuscitate you after death. He made man from nothing and he will return him to nothing. And since he can forge man from nothing, you should not marvel that he can bring him back to life—no one should question it. He made every creature and he will come in his own person to judge the right and wrong that each one has done in the world.

"The judgment will be just. No count or king will be spared because of his high position. All men will be judged, high and low. God's friends will be in glory and their exaltation will endure, for their crown will be everlasting. They will be seated on his right, but those on his left will suffer as our Lord and Father promised. They will have great distress, many ills, and infernal pains without relief. He will not take pity on them, and none will be able to make amends for crimes committed against God. No ransom will be accepted, and justice will be done. Sinners will be removed from before the face of our Lord, and they will suffer pain and sorrow forever. Such is hell, and such are its captives. But those who dwell on high will have joy and pleasure forever."

"I understand that all men should be afraid," said Josaphat. "It is no wonder if they are frightened, for they should fear the great sorrows and pains of hell that I have heard you describe. But, good master, how do you know that after a man dies the soul will retake its body and be delivered either to joy or to sorrow after it is judged? Tell me how you can know with such certainty what is to come. Explain it to me—I wish to learn."

"Friend, we can know with certainty that which is still to come because of what has already happened," the holy man replied. "God suffered death on the cross for us, and he was resurrected—this is true. His resurrection teaches us that all who die will be resurrected in the end, and they will be judged. And I can truly say that they will be rewarded on that day according to what they deserve. Each one will have his recompense, either for gain or for loss. Death will lose its strength, and its victory will be vanquished. None will ever die after that day, and the fear of death will diminish, for death will no longer hold its power. The resurrected ones will be cloaked in immortality and will never change, nor will their bodies decay. This day will surely come, and it will be filled with anguish and sorrow. Those who do not receive mercy will suffer forever."

Barlaam teaches Josaphat about Judgment Day

"The Gospels use a parable to teach us about Judgment Day. There was once a wealthy man who dressed in silken clothes and lived a luxurious life full of pleasure and joy. A poor man lived outside his gate. This man was dying of hunger, but he took courage in his poverty. The rich man was most wealthy, but he never gave anything to the poor man. He despised him because of his poverty, and would not give him even the scraps from his table. Then it happened that they both died at the same time. The rich man's soul was lost. It went straight to hell, where it joined the company of the devils it had always served. The poor man's soul was saved and carried up into heaven, where holy angels received it with joy. The rich man's soul saw that the poor man's enjoyed every happiness. It cried loudly for forgiveness and Abraham responded, 'You had many advantages in the world. Your body was richly fed, and you were lord of a great house, but this man had only misery, and you never took pity on him. The great difference between your life and his explains why he is happy while you sorrow, and why he has joy and you have pain. Any man who is not charitable wastes his life and loses both body and soul.' With this parable, I have shown you that whoever does evil is damned and whoever does good receives the rich reward of forgiveness.

"Elsewhere the Gospels recount that a rich king organized a lavish celebration for his beloved son's wedding. He invited many noblemen to come to the feast, for he wanted to honor his son on the day he would take a wife. He had a banquet prepared and sent messengers to summon his guests. None of them wished to come to the wedding. They claimed they had other things to do, but their excuses revealed that they chose not to attend the feast.

"When the king understood that none of them would come, he invited others and filled his well-provisioned house with guests. According to the scriptures, the king looked at all those who had come to the wedding banquet and noticed one man who was not dressed in wedding clothes. 'Wait there, friend!' the king said to him. 'How did you enter without wedding attire?' The guest had no response, and the king immediately had him thrown out of the palace, into a dark and sorrowful place.

"The king represents God, who will make a wedding party for his Son, represented by the holy church, but it will be at

the Day of Judgment. Those summoned first were called by
God's messengers, the prophets. They are the Jews and the
pagans who despise the true faith because they are blinded
by their beliefs and do not care about good deeds.[1] The next
to be called were those who proved their good faith by their
remembrance of God, and he shared his glory with them.
One was present who had sinned against God by polluting
his body, and this is the one who was sent away from the celebration. Why, then, was he called 'friend' when he had
demonstrated enmity by abandoning God? God loves everyone—he claims both the good and the bad as his friends. He
even called Judas his friend. Even though God knew Judas
would betray him, he did not fail to call him 'friend.'

"The parable describes a heavenly celebration. I draw it
from my memory and offer it to you according to my own
understanding so I can show you that our Lord prepares a
wondrous paradise for all his friends. One of the Gospels
gives us another parable that demonstrates the same truth.
There were once ten virgins. Five recognized the true faith,
and they had good oil in their lamps. The other five did not
believe, and they did not purchase oil to fill their lamps. Since
they did not have the light of their lamps, they illuminated
their way with the light of the world that kills the soul and
corrupts the body. (The wounded soul and the sullied body
lament and long for the holy church.)

"The virgins were called to a great wedding celebration,
and they went, taking their lamps. Five carried full lamps,
and five carried empty ones. Five were full of wisdom, and
five were filled with evil and had no good in them. The five
virgins who had enough oil to illuminate their hearts came
without hesitation before the spouse and his bride. They arrived at midnight (the invitation was made for this hour, I believe), but they were distressed that the other five were left
behind because they had no light. The bridegroom's gates
were closed, and the five virgins who had no oil were shut
out. 'My lord, my lord, open for us, open the gate!" they
cried out at the bridegroom's door. He responded, 'The law

requires that you remain outside the door because of the works you have done. You may not enter this door where the good are received, for you have misused the intelligence that I gave to enlighten you.'

"Listen and understand and then you will know without doubt what virginity is," Barlaam continued. (Those who do not value loyalty should listen well so they might learn.) "There are three kinds of virginity. The first and best is pure chastity, as when one says, 'This maiden is a virgin.' The second is the virginity of the married couple that keeps its own domain so well that a foreign lord cannot claim that any adultery inhabits it. The third kind of virgins are widows who give themselves to God and do not consent to another marriage. They are beautiful and good, and they will receive a crown in heaven.

"Through the parable about the virgins, you can understand that the day of justice will come, when God will judge us. Those who keep their thoughts pure and their lamps lit will be well received at the wedding banquet of our Creator. Those who come without oil will find the gate closed, for they have polluted their lives so much that God does not know them. I have shown you this parable so you will know the truth and so you will understand the sovereign Day of Judgment.

"On that day all you see will be lost, and all creatures will perish according to their natures. For this reason, those who have done evil rather than good will be lost, as will those who have used their swords against Christians, those who amass gold and silver and have power over the poor, those who drink wine and become drunk, and those who use their authority to steal from orphans. They do not care about divine law and they are far from Jesus Christ. The scriptures say to them: You who have done great evil, where will you flee? And who will help you when God comes to judge the world? What will become of your vainglory? Who will remember it? What will become of your great happiness, which will be changed to sadness? God will judge without appeal

on that day of anger. Judgment will be declared and no excuse will be heeded. The prophets showed the truth through
the parables they included in the Gospels."

"I understand this," Josaphat responded. "According to
the story you have told me, sinners will lament and dwell in
sorrow and should all be afraid. But tell me what I should do
to escape the cruel pains, torments, and sorrowful travails
that await sinners. Teach me the right path, so I can rejoice in
the reward and the crown that God bestows on all his
friends."

"You must first receive baptism," Barlaam instructed, "for
it will be a great benefit to you. Then you must be watchful
and wise. You must guard your heart and refrain from sin so
the devil's temptations do not damn you to death. And if you
sin, use reason to recognize your transgression and seek with
all your understanding to repent. Belief should be born in the
heart. The man who dwells in repentance and who loves and
believes in God will discipline his heart. Through repentance, he can come to true confession and use his belief to
defend his soul against the body's desires.

"Turn your heart to God who formed you in his image.
Trust in him and put yourself in his care. God has called you,
and he gave you intelligence so you could use it to gain understanding. If you do not seek to turn to the good faith, you
will lose your sovereign inheritance, and your soul will be in
great peril."

Barlaam warns Josaphat about idolatry and teaches him about salvation

"You must reject idols, for our Lord hates idolatry above all
things," Barlaam said to Josaphat. "The man who abandons
his Creator is like a servant who leaves his lord. He turns
from wisdom to folly, and his life is ruined.

"I will tell you a parable I heard a long time ago. It is about those who worship and venerate idols and sacrifice to them. They are like the archer who captured a nightingale. The archer drew his knife to kill the bird, and the nightingale spoke to him. 'You will gain little from my death, and it would be wrong for you to kill me when you could never be satisfied by eating me,' said the bird. 'Good friend, consider this: You wish to kill me, but I will not fill your belly. Yet if you free me, I will give you three secrets, and you will profit greatly if you follow their lessons.' The man was astonished and freed the bird immediately. He asked it to tell him the three secrets. 'Listen well,' said the bird. 'Do not seek to take anything you cannot have. Do not regret a loss that cannot be recovered. And do not believe anything that is not believable. Learn these three lessons and keep them in your heart. Good things will come to you if you hold to them, for there is great wisdom in them, I assure you.'

"The archer marveled to hear the bird speak so well. He untied it and let it go, and the nightingale flew away. The bird was happy to escape and rejoiced in its freedom. Nonetheless, it tested the archer to see whether he had learned the three lessons. 'Archer,' it said, 'you took bad advice and made a foolish mistake. You lost a great treasure today, for I have a precious pearl larger than an ostrich's egg in my body. I gained my life through your loss.'

"The archer did not understand that the bird was testing him, and he was filled with regret. He spoke sweetly to the bird and asked it to come back to him. He promised to treat it well and welcome it with honor into his home. The nightingale understood the reason for the man's persuasive words, and it took him for a fool. 'For God's sake, friend,' said the bird, 'you have made a great error. You did not understand my lessons and now you have been deceived by my test. I told you never to regret losing something you could not recover. I see you follow this advice badly. I taught you another thing. I instructed you not to cast your net after something that cannot be taken. I see you err in this as well, for if you cannot fly after me in the air, then your skill, your nets, and your words will not help you catch me again. I told you a third rule (but you did not understand me), that you should not believe anything unbelievable. My archer friend, you tried to seize me because you thought I had a precious stone in my stomach. But I lied to you, and what I said could not be true because such a stone would be bigger than my entire body. Only a fool listens and does not use his intelligence to understand what reason makes clear.'

"A man is foolish to worship and serve gods he has made with his own hands," Barlaam continued. "The more he gives them, the more he loses. Do not believe that these are gods. They cannot hear or see, nor can they help anyone in need. There is nothing in them but the gold that foolish men take out of their vaults and shape into whatever gods they wish to serve. They make their gods according to their own will, and then they destroy them whenever they wish. They create their own lords and then take the creation for a creator. They invent their own religion and they despise the holy faith. They persecute and kill those who would teach them that God made them and can unmake them. The devil incites them to make idols, and he rules their vain thoughts. Take care that you are not led into this path. Believe in our Lord who suffered on the cross to redeem us. He is the God we should love and fear, and he is the God we should worship and serve with pleasure. He is God the Father, and he is our Lord and Creator. He is three persons joined in One, one God in a Holy Trinity. This God sent me to you. Worship him and believe in him. Be baptized, and you will surely be saved. If you are not baptized, you will be damned.

"Consider what you will do. The pleasures of the world are fleeting and quickly lost. They kill the soul and destroy the body. And when men are condemned at the final judgment, pleasure will be a poor adornment. No flesh is so sweetly nourished or so richly dressed that it will not rot from the filth of its corruption. No matter how noble or distinguished its lineage or how great its wealth, none will wish

to look upon it. And there is worse: the soul will find its body
again at the Day of Judgment, but if the body has sinned, the
soul will be betrayed and will remain in hell. If the soul has
acted wisely, it will be saved and have joy forever. For this
reason, I urge you to serve God faithfully in your heart. Do
not be afraid to confirm your belief. If you believe what is
good, good will come to you, and God will remain with you
and help you in everything you undertake. If you serve him
wholeheartedly and undertake your works with a good heart,
he will help you succeed, for everything begins and ends in
him."

"Master," said the king's son, "I believe what you say, with
all my heart. Before you came here I hated my father's gods,
and now I know that there is nothing but deceit in them.
Now I hate them more than ever, and I know that nothing
will ever persuade me to love them again.

"I will say more, good master: I will be the servant of our
Lord God, my Father and Creator. I am ready to be baptized
and serve God with all my power. But I wish to know if I
need more than belief and baptism to be saved. Master, if
you know of something else I need, do not hide it from me!"

"I am pleased to instruct you," said the hermit. "After baptism, you must strive not to sin. Act according to your faith
and you will do well, for faith is nothing without works. Ensure that your life is pure and protect your faith so it is not
lost through your actions. Do you know what could destroy
you and wound your soul? Adultery, along with fornication
and lust, impiety, anger, discord, hopelessness, homicide, avarice, evil intentions, pleasure, and dissent. All these things
destroy the soul. Here are the fruits of the soul, according to
what I know: peace, patience, love, joy, faith and humility,
goodness, charity, repentance, wisdom, gentleness, pity, and
knowledge. These are the fruits that bring the soul to glory.

"Whoever gives his heart to God and does good works
will surely be saved. Be generous and kind. Be ready to do all
good things. Devote your soul and your body to God. God is
merciful and asks only that your whole heart be devoted to

him. This life is fleeting—do not think about tomorrow, but put everything into good belief in God and his providence. If he provides for you, you will not be discouraged. Love God and serve him. Believe in him and love your neighbor as you love yourself. These are the two commandments that the prophets preach and that faith requires. If you follow these two laws, you will come to God."

"Now I understand," Josaphat responded, "but tell me again about one thing. If my unworthiness causes me to err and I sin, must I lose all hope? Can I lose the good because of a bad act?"

"Friend, because of our weakness the Savior of the world took human form in the Virgin and suffered and died for us. We are weak creatures joined to a base flesh. Everything fails, everything falls, and everything declines. But God gave us a remedy to counter our base nature, for repentance cleanses all the sins of the world. No one can ever do so much evil that he cannot come to God, for God is full of mercy. Never will anyone so corrupt his body that God, who is merciful, will not immediately pardon him if he prays sincerely for forgiveness. No one should ever fall into despair because of a sin. Despair itself is a sin that God does not love, and he laments when we do not trust in his pity and believe that he will forgive our sins.

"The Gospels do not lie, and they give us a brief but clear parable to demonstrate this. A shepherd had taken one hundred sheep to graze in the wilderness, and one became lost from the others. The shepherd left the rest of the sheep and went to seek the lost one. He searched until he found it and carried it back on his shoulders to put it with the others. The Gospels tell us that he rejoiced in the recovery of the lost sheep and he sent for his neighbors and his friends to celebrate its return.

"The shepherd is God, who descended to earth to seek us. The sheep is the sinner who comes to God through repentance. When he is found, God will carry him to dwell among the righteous. The story of Saint Peter also teaches us this lesson, and I will recount it to you. He renounced our Lord Jesus Christ on the night of his passion, but through confession and tears of contrition, Saint Peter's sin was washed away, and God pardoned him at the very hour he cried and repented of his sin. This is why I tell you that tears of repentance will make your conscience pure."

Josaphat said, "If I am able to reconcile with my Lord for my earlier life, I do not wish to anger him further by sinning again."

"I must correct you," Barlaam interrupted, "for I see you taking on a difficult task. No one can douse a fire without leaving some smoke. What are you saying? That you will continue to enjoy a life of ease and the pleasures of the world while still avoiding sin? I do not think this is possible (our ancestors could not do it). God tells us in his scriptures that no man can serve two masters. If he loves one, he will hate the other, and no good will come of it. If a man has two lords, he will hold one dear and he will have to abandon the other. Whoever wishes to serve God must hate the world or he will be unable to devote himself to him."

Barlaam shows Josaphat that he must abandon the world

"Whoever seeks to love God with all his heart must abandon the world and choose pleasures greater than the pleasures of this world. Some become martyrs to serve God. They suffer torments in their flesh and stanch the flow of their sins with their blood. Others go into the wilderness to suffer and steward the gold their Lord has entrusted to them. These men leave people behind. They exchange lead for silver, and silver for gold, and they amass a treasure. They leave worldly pleasures and dwell deep in the wilderness. They live on herbs and roots and suffer the cold and the heat, but they do not heed these things, for they seek to heal their souls, and the harsh life they lead delivers them from mortal sins. Their lives show that it is foolish to have hope in the world. Do not doubt it. Whoever listens to the judgments of this world should live in fear, for his love of the world and its delights will destroy him. Whoever makes his belly his god and seeks only its welfare leaves his soul to die of hunger. He has exchanged gold for lead, and he is like the man who fled the unicorn.

"The man ran, crying out in fear—he did not dare turn to face the unicorn. Then he fell into a deep pit. A beautiful tree grew beside it, and its branches were strong and laden with the most tempting fruit that had ever existed. The man grasped the tree as he fell into the pit and its large branches supported him. He looked down into the pit and saw a terrifying sight. A huge hungry dragon loomed below him with its mouth open—it would be most perilous to fall. The man was trapped between the two dangers. If he fell, the dragon would swallow him, but if he left the shelter of the tree, he would find the unicorn waiting for him, and he could lose his life. Then he saw two small animals come to the foot of the tree to forage and eat. He noted their appearance: one was black and the other white. He despaired then, because dangers threatened him from three directions.

"Then he looked up in the tree and saw its sweet fruit, and the sweetness tempted his lips. He could see by its color that the fruit must be very ripe, and the sweetness of fruit pleases and nourishes men. The man wanted the fruit badly, and he picked it to taste its sweetness. His fear changed to pleasure as he gathered the fruit. The sweet fruit made him forget his fear, and he did not want to leave the tree. He bit into the fruit, and the more he ate, the longer he wanted to stay there. The flavor was pleasing to him, but he died of hunger while eating it. The closer he was to the fruit, the more he desired it. The fruit was so sweet that the more he ate, the less he tasted its sweetness, and the less sweetness he tasted, the more fruit he ate. The place was dangerous. Yet the man was so hungry for the fruit that he lost his fear, and the sweetness of the fruit made him forget the danger. The little animals gnawed at the tree until they chewed through its roots. Then the tree fell because it could not stand once it lost its roots. The man fell and the dragon ate him.

"I have recounted this parable to you, but I have not yet explained it," Barlaam continued. "The unicorn represents death, which constantly pursues the body. Do you know what the deep pit is? Good friend, it is the world, where we would live in fear if we recognized the danger of the dragon that lay below and wanted to grasp the man in the tree. The dragon represents hell, which takes sinners. The tree is our life. It is continuously gnawed by the two animals in the pit—one is the day, the other is the night. The fruit hanging from the tree represents the delights of the world, and the sweetness that comes from the fruit represents the devil, who entices men with sweetness and makes them sin. Learn this well: there is nothing in the world as sweet as sin to those who grow accustomed to it. Once desire is ignited, it is difficult to refrain from sin, and it takes great effort to resist gathering and eating the fruit when it appears so sweet and desirable. While man forgets himself eating the sweet fruit, the beasts gnaw away at his life, and he is dead before he even notices the threat. When his soul leaves his body and the dragon's maw takes him, he understands that his gluttony for the sweetness of the fruit has led to great suffering. I tell you that this fruit is filled with poison. The sweetness represents the sin that poisons the fruit. Whoever takes such fruit eats his own death."

Josaphat was pleased to learn the meaning of the story. He asked Barlaam to tell him other parables, for he was eager to hear stories that would teach him how to shun the world and its pleasures. "Master," he said, "tell me more!"

Barlaam said, "I will tell you a story about a king and his steward. The king loved the steward and gave him authority over a large part of his country. The steward accepted the land and managed it for his lord. He had three friends, two of whom he loved and cherished. He shared his wealth with them and made them great lords in his land. He did whatever he could for them. He was less generous with the third friend, who was an intimate of the king. The steward feared him more than he loved him. However, if he had known that one day this friend would intercede with the king on his behalf, he would have loved him better.

"The steward did not wish to lose the affection of the first two friends, and he compromised himself to show his love for them. He broke many vows for their sakes and lied for them frequently. He did not keep faith with his neighbors or his lord, and he wronged many people and had many put to death. He loved and cherished the two men so much that they should have returned his love—they should have been his friends.

"One day the king summoned the steward for a reckoning. The steward had managed the king's land for a long time, and the king wished him to account for how and where he had used the country's wealth. The steward was surprised and troubled, for he feared he had been betrayed. Then he thought of a way he could defend himself. He would ask his three friends for help.

"He went to the first friend and humbly asked for his aid. He needed his friend's support urgently, he explained, for he had to render an accounting before the king. 'Good friend, tell me how I can explain my actions so that I do not incur blame. I have wronged my lord greatly, for I do not know what I have done with his land and its wealth, and now he wants them back. I will lose my lord's love because I sold his land for you. I have given you everything I owned, to make you wealthy. I have put all my silver and all my gold into your treasury, and everything I own is under your control. Now I need your help—do not withhold your support from me, for you know that one should respond to a friend in need. Help me now, I beg you!'

" 'I do not know why I should help you,' his friend responded. 'It is true that I used to love you, but I do not love you any longer. I am weary of your friendship. I have made many other friends and their company is more honest than yours. I am happy with them now and must go to join them. Because I used to love you, I will give you some old clothing, but I will not give you anything else or help you in any other way. I can be of little service to you.'

"The steward was saddened by this response. He went to his other friend and humbly asked for his help. He asked his friend to take pity on him in return for all he had done for him. 'I must defend myself to the king, because of the crimes I committed for your sake,' the steward explained. 'I have put myself at risk for you many times! Now help me, I beg you, so I may remain in the king's good graces.'

"His friend responded, 'I cannot listen now. I am busy with other business. Go away and return later, for I have other things to attend to here.'

"When the steward heard his friend's excuse, he thought he had lost everything. He left, sad and filled with sorrow, and did not know where to turn since his two friends had failed him. He could not expect his third friend to help him when the first two would not. The steward was afraid. He sought counsel everywhere, and when he found none, he despaired. Finally he went to the third friend, to see whether he could hope for any help from him. He went with his head bowed in sorrow and his face turned away. Sad and anxious, the steward approached his friend. He asked him humbly for forgiveness and bowed before him without pride. His friend welcomed him and received him graciously. He put his arms around his neck and promised that he would use whatever influence he had to help him. 'Friend,' he said, 'you have shown me little love. However, I will do what I can to reconcile you with the king, if he will receive me. I will go before you, and the king will have to arrest me before he can seize you. If the king does not arrest me, I will not allow any harm to come to you. Do not lose hope, for you can trust me. I will go before the court for you. Have confidence in me. I will protect you. I will act as a fortress to keep out your enemies and defend you against them.'

"The steward marveled that his friend had received him so well and promised to do as much for him. He remembered his own actions and regretted that he had done so little for this friend. 'I did so much for the others,' he thought, 'and they did not care about me at all. I received no help from them. They would not give me anything, and they left me to suffer. I am surprised that this man for whom I did nothing is willing to sacrifice himself and everything he possesses for my sake. He gave me more than I asked for, and he has proven himself a true friend.' "

The king's son marveled at the wise man's story and asked Barlaam to tell him its meaning.

Barlaam said, "I will explain. Do you know who the first friend is? He represents wealth. Man spends his entire life trying to accumulate wealth, even though it is fatal to him. He runs many risks in order to gain wealth and power, but no matter how hard he works or how rich and powerful he becomes, when his soul leaves his body, his prestige and influence die with him. His heirs will quickly claim his possessions and all he has earned will be of little worth to him. His heirs will not care about his reputation—they will barely remember him. Of all the things he has acquired, he will keep only a shroud, and when he rots in his sepulchre, neither his wealth nor his power will matter.

"I will tell you about the other friend. A man may be proud when he is rich and powerful in this world and has a wife and children and many friends. But when death takes him, those who shared his company will go with him to his gravesite, and their only act of love will be to bury him. Afterward they will return to their own affairs, and they will not want anything more to do with him.

"The third friend represents the good deeds of the Christian. The steward did little for this friend, but he willingly offered to help the steward. He risked himself to save him, and he was a good friend when the steward was in danger from his enemies. The other friends failed the steward in his time of need, but the third friend helped him and saved him from the punishment promised by the King who made the world and will judge it.

"These are the three friends a man finds in the world," Barlaam continued. "Two of them kill and condemn him, but the goodness of the third redeems him. Two lead him to sorrow. The third earns him the love of the King he betrayed. The third friend remains with him and reconciles him with the Lord, who is full of mercy. Shun the first two friends, and take good care of the third, for whoever neglects the first two and serves the third will save his soul."

"Master, I wish to put all the pleasures of the world behind me," Josaphat responded. "Give me more examples of how to resist them. Show me all you know so that through your teaching I can know the sovereign King who made the whole world and rules it."

Barlaam teaches Josaphat to store his treasure in heaven

"Listen, then," Barlaam said, "and I will tell you another story that should offer a warning to all. There once was a city, the most beautiful and richest in the land. It was the custom of the nobles there to name a foreigner as king, and they always chose a man who did not know their laws. Each year they chose a king only to replace him the next one. This man served as their ruler for a year, and during that year he could make whatever declarations and laws he wished. The citizens did whatever he asked, until the end of the year. Just when he was most confident in his reign and thought himself safe inside the city walls, the citizens came to him, stripped him naked, and took the kingdom away from him. They dragged him through the city in great shame, then exiled him to an isolated island in the sea. He lived on the island ever after, poor and without succor. He suffered hunger, exposure, poverty, and sorrow without hope of relief, and he paid dearly for the crown he had enjoyed.

"During this time they elected a wise man to be king, and he tricked them. He accepted the crown and agreed to govern the city. He was not happy about his election and sought to understand the city's customs. He was troubled and wondered what had become of the kings who had reigned before him. He made inquiries, and a wise man told him of the kingdom's custom. He learned that the city's nobles exiled their king every year and chose another, and that when the king had reigned for one year, they shamed and tortured him, and then sent him into exile. This king understood that he would be lost if he did not find some way to avoid the shame and pain he would suffer at the end of his reign. He cared little for the kingdom, and he regretted that he had become its king. He found the honor dishonorable, because it would bring him shame. 'It is a cursed power that leads to such a shameful end,' the king thought.

"He pondered his situation and came to a decision. He had the doors of his treasury opened secretly, and he removed quantities of silver and gold, rich cloth, and all manner of precious stones and sent them to the island where he would be exiled when he lost his throne. He consigned them to faithful men who swore an oath of loyalty to him, and he provisioned the island well. When his reign ended, the citizens seized his crown and sent him to the island. They treated him just as they had treated all the others. But this man had prepared ahead of time. He arrived on the island and found the wealth and the treasure—the precious stones and the silver and the gold—that had been sent there on his orders. He would have great abundance forever.

"The foolish kings who had come before him were imprudent. They did not see that the agreement begun so well would end so badly, and they finished their reigns helpless and impoverished. They were sent to the island of the lost and dwelled forever in need. They never had joy or pleasure again, and they lived in great sorrow. But this last king acted prudently. His wise thoughts and his good heart led him to prepare a rich retreat where he enjoyed happiness and honor forever.

"The city in this story can help you understand this world," Barlaam said. "The citizens are like the devils. They are the constables of this world and elevate us like kings with wealth and worldly power. But later we are dishonored, for while the body pursues and takes pleasure in the riches and abundance of this life, death cuts short its reign. When a man loses his life, the citizens come and find him empty, vain, naked, and impoverished, and then they give him his just reward. They exile him to an isolated island, and the place they send him is hell. They send him into danger and exile his soul. The good king wished to learn the truth and came to understand the customs of the world. Through good instruction, he found the path of good faith and became its lord and king.

"The councilors who taught him are like the preachers who exhort us to leave behind this world where serfs would be lords. They are like me. I have shown you both joy and sorrow. You will have joy if you know how to win it, and you will have sorrow, even in the little time you remain in the world. Your thoughts are your treasure and you can draw the fine gold of your salvation from them. Friend, put your riches in the place where you will have most need of them.

"When I lived in the world, I loved it very much, but then I understood that my happiness was a dangerous illusion. I understood that whoever lives fully in this life receives a poor reward. I saw that the man who had the most still remained poor and sorrowful: he was impoverished in his wealth and powerless in his might. He found no happiness in his possessions, and he was beggared in his wealth, lost in his own path, sorrowful and sad in his joy. I saw that his good health was in fact infirmity, his truth a lie, and his great estate impoverished. He was dead while he lived. Such is the world and its fruits, which always end in death.

"I was in the world for a long time, as I have told you," Barlaam continued. "I saw its privileges and its glory, its power and its fame, its cruelty and its splendor, its sovereignty and its valor. I rejected it all, for it will all perish. I saw that everyone dies and that they are nothing once they are dead. I also saw that the devil makes new friends frequently. He makes one man a king and the other a count, but to the third he brings great shame. He makes one man poor and the other rich, the third generous and the fourth miserly. Worldly wealth is acquired through hard work, and when a man is rich he has more cares because he fears the loss of his wealth, and if he loses it, he sorrows. The devil works against those who use reason to understand the world. He takes many forms and provokes us in many ways. He makes the foolish man appear wise and the wise man appear foolish.

"If your desire is to love the world, you should ignore my sermon and wait to receive the crown from your father, who is deranged by his power and ever more lost. Friend, consider the end of this world—all men will die, both highborn and low. That is their certain fate. Whoever loves the world remains loyal to its pleasures. Evil misleads him and he acts against what is right. For this reason, I beg and beseech you to reject the pleasures of the world and its vanities—they will deceive you. Nothing lasts and everything returns to nothing. Purify your wisdom and your knowledge. Take your treasure and your wealth and send them where you will be forever in joy. If you wish to be with God on high in heavenly glory, you must seek him with your whole heart."

Josaphat said, "Tell me again how I can send my treasure there. Show me and make me wise."

"I will tell you," said Barlaam. "Open your treasury and give generously to the poor. You can find happiness in relieving their poverty. Be merciful and charitable, and give to whoever asks. Be noble and kind. Be a good father to orphans and help them as though they were your brothers. The poor are the messengers through whom you may send your wealth to the island if you would seek heavenly joy."

Josaphat learns about reason and will

"Is this religion you teach newly established, or did the apostles preach it before through signs?"

"Good friend," Barlaam replied, "It would be wrong to teach a false belief. What I tell you is not new. I repeat and renew what God preached and showed us through parables.

"I will tell you about a rich man who came to ask God what he could do to earn divine glory through his faith. God told him, 'Give your wealth to the poor, for you must become poor if you wish to enter my kingdom.' The rich man did not do what God instructed. He kept his wealth and his sin was multiplied. I tell you this directly: a camel can no more pass through the eye of a needle than a rich man can enter paradise. This is the commandment that Jesus Christ taught to all, and whoever will not heed it condemns himself. The saints understood it and had it proclaimed to all. Some follow this commandment by suffering martyrdom. Others flee the world to live as hermits and repent, each according to his own conscience. This is the sovereign commandment that God announces to all people: to withdraw from this vain world in order to seek understanding and do good deeds. Only through great effort is anyone saved while living in the world, and whoever will deprive himself of this world will be a king and lord in the other. This is the true philosophy. Those who understand this other life leave evil and do good. This commandment is most ancient, and it has been followed from the first generation."

"Good master, tell me how this can be," said Josaphat. "If

the commandment was truly made so long ago, then everyone should follow it in good faith, or so I believe."

The holy man replied, "Many men have followed this commandment, but many rejected it when they saw that the rewards were so long deferred. The first faith has been lost by
many, for they will not look to the future. All are called by the
same voice. Some say, 'Lord, I am coming,' and others pull
back. Some do good, others do evil, and those who are the
most disloyal believe that they have found a better faith and
that their religion is better. All men are free to act according to
reason. They can do wrong when they wish, and when they
wish, they can leave what is wrong behind. They have the
power to embrace the world or to leave it, according to their
own will. They can do good or abandon it. They can repent or
they can sin."

"Show me more clearly where such freedom comes from
and why man has it," said Josaphat.

"I will show you through logic," Barlaam responded. "The
freedom to judge is given to all men, for man has reason
through his soul, and he deliberates using reason. First he
uses his reason to identify choices, and then, through deliber-
ation, he chooses. He has a scale in his thoughts, and he
weighs his thoughts in order to choose among them. His will
is free and it is in his power to choose what he desires, no
matter how much his thoughts distract him. Whatever is in
his thoughts directs his desires, for good or for evil. His desires advise him, and he is ready to do whatever they counsel.
But in fact one desire is always more urgent than another.
Desires are diverse, and so are their strengths, and their
strength affects how badly a man wants something.

"If you want to understand this better, consider the veins
of the earth. A spring that issues from high in the mountains
gives pleasing sweet water. Water also comes from below the
earth. One water is sweet and the other bitter. One is clear
and the other cloudy. Similarly, thoughts are sorted by reason. One is clear and the other cloudy. One is good and the
other bad. One is from above, another is from below, and

others from deeper still. But thoughts come and go among the desires. From the many thoughts a man may have, a thousand desires are born. Desires are not equal, but a man uses reason to weigh his choices and choose which he will pursue."

"Master," said the king's son, "please tell me: are you all alone or are there others who preach as you do?"

"Friend, I do not know of any in your country," Barlaam answered. "Your father drove them out, and he martyred many of them, for he does not care about God. What I tell you is taken from the holy scriptures—the prophets foretold these things, the apostles taught them, the Gospels showed them to me, and I have recounted them to you. Throughout the world there are many Christians who follow this life, and there are many good preachers, priests, and pastors who know what I have taught you. I came to you—I do not hide it—with the intention of teaching you what I know, for you were in great need."

"Now tell me, brother, why have I never heard my father speak of these commandments, if they were told to other people?"

"He has heard them, but he did not understand them, because hatred and fear fill his heart and blind him. He gives himself over completely to evil."

"Good friend, I wish he had learned and understood enough that good might come to him."

Barlaam said, "I will tell you what you should do. You must look to God's mercy, for he can save him. If you put everything into his hands, good friend, in your faith you can become a father to your father. You will cause your father to be reborn if you can convince him to believe.

"I will tell you a story I once heard about a king. He was noble, from a great lineage, and he was very brave. He was a good man, generous to his people, and very wise, but he did not believe in God. He had a councilor whom he loved and cherished. This man was wise and valiant, and he believed in God. It weighed on him that his lord was so misguided, and he would have corrected him, but his fear held him back. He was afraid that if he spoke about God, his lord would be angry and condemn him. He did not wish to lose the king's love because of his faith. He was wise and waited for the time and the place to reason with him and show him the truth. If he had not feared the king's anger, he would have already debated with him in good faith.

"One day the king sent for his councilor. He took him on a tour of the city (I believe he did this often), and they rode about together to see if they might see anything new. They wandered through the city until they saw a candle shining brightly in a poor hovel. They stopped and saw a man inside. He was poor and hungry and dressed in rags—he had nothing. Then they saw his wife approaching him, bringing him a glass of wine and singing happily. The goblet was made of clear glass, the red wine was richly colored. Its deep hue could have revived even a man who had languished in illness for ten or fifteen years. The woman seemed more noble than her poverty would admit. Singing joyfully, she offered the wine to the man whom the king considered a pauper. The king watched him for a while, and he and his retinue wondered how there could be such wealth in poverty.

"The man did not complain of his poverty—in fact he rejoiced when he should have mourned. The man and his wife covered their poverty in joy, and the sound of their festive singing showed the king and his men that the couple was rich in happiness. The king and his wealthy princes tried to understand, and the king called his councilor to him. 'Friend,' he said, 'I wonder how these people can believe that there is delight in poverty and pleasure in drinking wine. They are paupers, but they are happy in their misery. They sing when they should weep, and they live when they are close to death. They are free in their prison, and in death they hold to life. They find laughter in their tears and life in death. I cannot help but marvel at it. We are noble and richly dressed, and we take pleasure in whatever our hearts desire, but we do not live as happily as this pauper. He lives joyfully in his misery, and he makes something base into a treasure. He is rich despite his need and turns the truth of his poverty into a lie. He is generous though penniless, and his pleasure belies his misery. He laughs despite his tears, and his household is rich without being wealthy. He is well advised though he has no councilor, he is well supported without receiving help, and he is rich with no belongings, and strong with no power. He is wise yet knows nothing. He has enough yet possesses nothing. He lives while dying. He is impoverished and does not see it. We have never loved our lives as much as this man does.'

"The councilor asked the king, 'Sire, what do you think their life is like?' The king answered, 'It seems to me that it must be very poor and bitter, and full of resentment and misery.' 'Sire,' the councilor explained, 'whoever leaves this world without doing good has, according to those who reject this world, a worse life than theirs and indeed lives in peril. Rich clothing and adornments are worth nothing compared to the glory they anticipate. Just as you suggest that these people seem deluded when they find joy in their sorrow, so these men tell us that the time we spend rejoicing in our good fortune would be better spent in lamentation. Worldly pleasures are deceptive and full of suffering when compared to the sweet rewards that await those who keep their minds on the heavenly glory that will crown them and who seek that glory by doing good deeds.'

"The king was very surprised and responded, 'Friend, tell me, then, who are these people who have a better life than we do? Tell me how they live.'

"His councilor answered, 'I will tell you as much as I know. Without doubt, those who despise this vile world and care only for the heavenly kingdom live a much better life than we do.'

"The king asked, 'Good friend, what is the kingdom you describe?' 'My friend,' the councilor answered, 'the kingdom on high is worth more than anything here below. It is filled with wealth—no poverty is found there—and it holds reward, not punishment. There is happiness without sorrow, wealth without fear, love without blame, and honor without challenge. There is sovereignty without oppression, wealth without inheritance, life without fear of death, freedom without imprisonment, wisdom without foolishness, and possession without loss. He who can win this place will have joy and honor forever, and he will have the eternity that is promised to those who know and love God. Those who call on him will lose only this bitter world, and they will be with God above forever in the enduring glory of his court.'

"The king responded, 'Tell me truly, who is worthy of this life?' 'By faith,' said the councilor, 'this life is easy to enter for those who desire it sincerely.' 'Now tell me,' the king said, 'what must a man do and what path leads him to such great joy?' 'He must find true belief,' said the councilor. 'Whoever believes wholeheartedly in God and his birth and in the Holy Trinity will be saved. This is what Christians believe.'

"The king understood and answered, 'You have hidden this from me for too long. You are my man and I am your lord. You should tell me everything that will benefit me and keep me from danger. If what you have told me is true, why did you hide it from me for so long?' 'I did not neglect to instruct you because I was indifferent or because of ill will,' his companion explained, 'but for fear of losing your friendship. I did not want to tell you anything you did not wish to learn. The things I tell you are true, and anyone who cares for his own well-being should believe them.'

"The king responded, 'I command you not to hide these things from me any longer. You will teach me about them every day, and I will hear you out of love.' The councilor advised the king willingly, and he converted his lord through his teaching. From that time forward, the king was a wise man, greatly esteemed and of great renown, and he lived a very holy life."

Barlaam then explained the lesson of his story. "I tell you, then, that if anyone can show your father the truth and bring him into the right path, he will be baptized. He will leave the false belief that holds his soul in the balance."

Josaphat responded, "Good brother, may God's pleasure and his will be done with my father. But now that I know the things of this world are vain, I wish to leave it. I will go with you to live, for according to what I have heard you say here, anyone who seeks to serve God with a good heart should flee this world."

Josaphat learns the value of earthly possessions

The hermit answered Josaphat with another parable. "By faith, you want to do what a rich and handsome young man once did. He was from a noble lineage, the son of a wise and wealthy man. Another nobleman from an important family also lived in the city. He was wise and brave and had earned many honors, and he lived in great luxury. He had a daughter who was richer and more beautiful than any other young woman in the city. The father of the handsome young man asked for this young woman as a bride for his son, and her father agreed to the marriage, but when the young man learned of the arrangement, he was sorrowful. He did not love the girl, because she did not believe in God, and so he fled. He did not want to live with a woman who did not put her faith in God.

"The young man left his home and went away. He suffered from the heat of the day, and as he passed through a city, he stopped to rest. The heat prevented him from going any farther. He went into a nearby house where an old man lived in poverty with his daughter, who sat alone, sewing a ragged dress. This young woman worshipped God in her heart and prayed for his grace. She gave thanks to him for the salvation he had bought for her with his life. The young man marveled when he heard this. 'Maiden,' he said, 'may it not offend you, but is this a jest? What sweetness have you found and what rich gift have you received that you should offer thanks in this way? Show it to me, I want to see it. Do not hide it from me. Whom do you praise so wholeheartedly?' 'Friend,' said the young lady, 'I am God's servant and handmaiden. My father is poor and aged, but up to now God has been pleased to provide for him and for me too. God has given me everything I have, and I serve him with my whole heart. I am certain that if he wished, he could give me more than I could ever ask for. But God knows that I do not care about possessions in this life, for all the wealth of this world will soon pass away. There is nothing here below that compares to the glory on high. Since I am able to understand reason, I offer thanks to God, who made me and who will take me when he wishes. He will judge my soul and my body. What justification will I have to offer when the judgment comes if I do not thank him now and worship him with a good heart? I do not know what more I can tell you, I am his handmaid. He is my Lord.'

"The young man marveled at her wisdom and her words. He went to her father and identified himself. He described his father's nobility and wealth, and the old man recognized him. The young man asked for his daughter—he loved her and wanted to take her as his wife, for she knew how to understand reason and she was noble, generous, and wise. 'She is so wise that I would have her as my wife,' the young man said. The old man replied: 'Listen to me: it is not fitting for you or for your lineage that you take such a wife, nor would I be happy to have such a rich son-in-law. I am a poor man. I cannot trust a young man who acts so rashly.'

" 'Sire,' he said, 'you misunderstand me. I do not ask for her lightly. I desire her with all my heart. A rich wife was promised to me, one of the most noble in the land, and I fled because I did not wish to marry her. With your permission, I would take your daughter as my wife because she believes in God and because she is so brave and valiant. I would rather have her than any other.'

"The old man responded, 'You cannot have her, if you will

not stay to live with me. She is my only companion and I would suffer if you took her away from me. I am alone and have no friends. If another joins us, he cannot take her as a companion if he would separate us. She will never be parted from me to take another companion. She is my constant company, and I have a share in her. I do not wish to lose my share to another, and if she were taken away, I would lose her. You must become my companion as well if you would take her as yours.'

" 'I willingly agree to do as you wish,' the young man responded wisely.

"The old man tested him. He spoke kindly to the young man, then harshly. He sifted his conscience and his heart through the winnow of his good intentions and separated the chaff from the grain. He questioned him until he was certain the young man was not caught up in some kind of rash love. He saw that his request for his daughter was not impetuous and that he sought the marriage in good faith and prized it more than his own nobility and lineage. The wise old man tested the noble youth until he was certain that he did not wish to marry his daughter to gain wealth but because of her tenderness and moderation. The young man was enriched by poverty, for the father understood his honesty. He led the young man into his chamber and showed him a great abundance of riches. He gave him his daughter and his treasure and everything he had, and the young man received the wealth as an inheritance. He became a lord and the equal of his neighbors, and with time he became even richer and surpassed them in wealth."

"By God," said the king's son, "you told this parable for me. But did you mean that I am like the young man? You have searched my thoughts and I have allowed it. You have wandered through them as if in a wood or along a river. You have gone through my forest, I believe, and you and I have sought to learn whether any wild animal remains there that has not yet been tamed. You waded into my river, and there were no birds that did not belong there. All the strange animals have been driven away by your presence, I believe. Now show me with a true heart whether you know how my river runs. You have searched all my country—my body, my heart, and my thoughts. Do not have pity on me. Pull out the brush and prune the hedge."

Barlaam said, "I see that you have a true heart and I have found firm resolve there, for you are a wise young man. You have made a good start, but you must ensure that a good beginning has a good end. Pray to God, who knows us both, as will I, that he will be a merciful guardian of your soul and your body, and that in answer to my prayer he will send you the true light of the Holy Spirit so your heart will be illuminated and seek to receive the Christian truth and faith. Let his divinity and his strength and his goodness be a shield for you, and let him give you understanding so you can truly believe."

"Master, you must tell me about the glory of God and his strength."

"I pray to God that he will pardon your sins and grant you wisdom," Barlaam responded. "I pray that he will show his power over you and give you the wisdom to understand all that I teach you. The Gospels tell us that the power of God has no limit, for his majesty is infinite.

"Know truly that no one can see God, nor will any man see him before Judgment Day. Then we will see the Creator in his substance and glory, and in his majesty and power. I will show you that God is greater than I can say, for there are not enough tongues in the world to describe his strength.

"Consider the grandeur of his creation. Look at the sky, it never loses its beauty, nor does the earth ever grow old or lose its strength, and they were created long ago. See the springs and the sea whose boundary you cannot perceive. The sea gives and receives each day, and it never loses any part of itself. The sun follows its course each day, and it helps the moon, for it shares its light and illuminates it. You can perceive God's power in the things he has made."

"Good master, you give me answers to difficult questions,

and I see that reason can lead to an understanding of God's power."

"This is true," the old man responded, "but his divinity is so great that human intelligence cannot fully understand or measure the extent of God's power."

"I believe this," said Josaphat. "But now tell me in truth: How many years have passed since you were born? Where is your home? Do you have companions in your faith?"

"I am sixty years old, I believe. I live in the wilderness, and I spend every day and every night in repentance. I have companions who share my belief, and they too dwell in the wilderness and wander through its woods. They have no lodging or home, for they put their minds on higher things."

The king's son replied, "Explain this to me: you tell me that you are sixty years old, but when I look at you, this does not seem right. I do not think that anyone would take you to be younger than one hundred."

"By faith, friend, you are right. I was born a hundred years ago, but I do not count the first forty years because during that time my body was seduced by worldly pleasures. The man who lived like that is dead. I foolishly spent forty years in this world's pursuits, and that is why I say those years are dead to me. The following sixty are years of life, my good friend, and I do not count the years of death along with the years of life. I have lived for as long as I have done good deeds, and I was dead while I sinned. I live in God, and God in me, as long as I love him in good faith.

"The life of my body is dead, and I kill my flesh to give life to my soul and to free myself from the prison of my body. Whoever loves the pleasures of the world destroys himself. He believes that he lives, but he dies without knowing it, for the sins that he commits kill him. This is why I say that he dies while he lives. Whoever sins constantly dies in life and lives in death, and sin is a death that will never end. Whoever is intoxicated with sin dies from death, for he knows not how to live. But whoever lives in good faith, without corruption and without injustice, does not die, but rather he leaves this life, and in leaving it he comes back to a life that cannot die, and he can no longer feel death."

"Master, all this seems true to me, but allow me to say this: when you say that this life is not properly called life, then I reply that neither is temporal death really death, and I want to know why."

Barlaam said, "These words are entirely true. Those who live in this world and give themselves over to its pleasures are impoverished in their wealth, and they kill themselves by the lives they lead. The present life is not really life, but those who would gain heavenly glory gather true wealth in the tithes of charity, penitence, and peace, with which they purchase the paradise that God promises to his friends. This paradise is enduring joy and eternal life, a life that does not fear death and into which death cannot enter. But those who live in sin are marked with death, and they will be judged and die an eternal death."

The king's son replied: "Good master, I believe what you say. You are fortunate to know this and to live deep in the wilderness where the pure servants of God the Creator worship him day and night. Master, what do you live on in the wilderness? Where do you get your clothes when you are so far from people?"

"Good friend, we live on the fruit of the trees and the herbs that we gather, for we find wild fruit, herbs, roots, and nuts growing near the hermitage. We do not plant in the earth. We live only on what the sun, the dew, and the earth wish to give us. We are not tempted by avarice or greed. We enjoy our lives without dispute and envy. This is how we live in the wilderness. We do not break the earth to sow or harvest, and we do not eat bread unless God sends it to us.

"Now I will tell you about our clothing, which is very harsh and coarse. Each of us has a hair shirt made from hard wool. We wear them for a long time, in both summer and winter, and we have no other clothing. These clothes cover us as long as they last. Once we put them on, they will not be removed before they rot. That is the order of our life."

"Who dressed you so well, then?" Josaphat asked.

"I borrowed these clothes when I came here to find you, for I did not want anyone here to see the clothing I wear in the wilderness hermitage.

"Now I have revealed to you why I came here and I have shown you how to win your salvation. I do not know how much you have understood. If you understand my words and hold to them well enough to become a Christian, you can free your soul from the prison of death. I have explained to you the meanings and the figures of the scriptures, and I have revealed to you what was hidden in your heart. That is what I came for, and now I must return."

"Show me the clothing that you wear when you live in the wilderness."

The saintly hermit took off the robe that he had put over his hair shirt. Josaphat saw that his flesh was blackened and ugly, and the hair shirt was torn, for he had worn it a long time and in all kinds of weather. The rough, hard garment covered his flanks from his waist to his knees. He was nothing but skin and bones. His stiff coat was not made of ermine, nor did it have sable borders. There was no luxury to the garment: it was not adorned with valuable decoration, it was not made of rich cloth, nor was it beautifully colored. It was so rough to handle that it could not be lifted or put on without pain. It was cut from coarse wool and was so rough and sharp that it pierced the holy hermit's flesh. The coat suited the holy man who wore it, and he was comforted by its roughness. He put it on more willingly than another man would don a coat of ermine. The roughness seemed soft to him, and he rejoiced in the coarse fabric that irritated and tormented his body. He disciplined his body by wearing rough clothes and kept it thin by fasting. He fought against the devil by living a harsh life. Ah, God! How could he bear such suffering?

The king's son wanted to keep his teacher's company and the comfort it brought him. He marveled to find his abstinence so strong and his repentance so strict that he suffered day and night. Josaphat cried tenderly because of it. "Good master," he said, "can we go away together? For I would feel great sorrow if you left here without me. Allow me to go with you into the wilderness. I know that anyone who remains here for long will lose his soul. Good, dear master, let us leave together, for no one who seeks to live a good life should stay here."

"That cannot be, good friend, for I believe that God has another plan. You must wait for the place and time that God in his mercy will arrange for you to be with me. For now you must remain here to serve and worship him. If you fear him and serve him with all your heart, you will earn forgiveness."

"Since it is God's will, so be it," Josaphat responded. "But baptize me now—I am ready—and teach me how to remain loyal without wavering, so I will know how to serve my Creator and my Father who is Lord and Creator of the world.

"I will give you as many of my possessions as you want, and whatever clothes and shoes you wish to take," Josaphat added. "Take however much you can to drink and eat. I will provide for you and purchase whatever you wish to carry back with you. Master, for God's sake, pray for me without ceasing. Your prayers will help me, but your departure will bring me sorrow. I must bear it if I love God and want to serve him."

"Good friend, you should indeed seek to be baptized," Barlaam replied. "But it is foolish to offer us gifts. I am amazed that you wish to give your possessions to rich people when you yourself are so poor. It is neither good nor right that the poor man give to the wealthy. This offense should be pardoned, because you believed your perception that we live in poverty in the wilderness, but you are wrong. Whoever serves God is rich. Worldly men cannot recognize this wealth, even though it should be easy to see, since whoever loves and worships God does not suffer poverty. I pray that he will save you and give you his love."

Josaphat said, "I promised my possessions to you and I would have gladly given them. But your heart is strong and pure, and you do not need anything but God's love and God's will. Now baptize me in the good faith, for I love God greatly and believe in him and wish to love, serve, and honor him with my whole heart."

Barlaam baptizes Josaphat

"Now take heed," said Barlaam, "for I will indeed baptize you." And he began to speak:

"Today is the day of your birth.

"Today you must have firm belief.

"Today you recognize your Creator.

"Today you become the servant of your Lord.

"Today you are freed from your sins.

"Today you put away the old man.

"Today you become beautiful before God.

"Today is a new day.

"Today you leave behind the false religion.

"Today you become a man of good faith.

"Today you abandon the devil.

"Today you join God at his table.

"Today you enter the right path.

"Today you leave sorrow for joy.

"Today you enter the good life.

"Today you join God's kingdom.

"Today you are wise and powerful.

"Today you become wealthy.

"Today you receive a rich crown.

"Today is the day he gives to you.

"Today you go to find God your Father.

"Today you are servant and emperor.

"Today you put down sorrow and anger.

"Today you become both king and lord.

"Today you enter paradise.

"Today you become a friend of God.

"Today you show great prowess.

"Today you become a great noble.

"Today you receive great power.

"Today you come to life from death.

"Today God wishes to revive you.

"Today his mother comes to speak to you.

"Today you see all the saints.

"Today God loves you and dwells with you.

"Today he shows you his strength.

"Today he gives you his shield.

"Today he wishes to sanctify you.

"Today he gives you your reward.

"Today God purifies your heart.

"Today he gives you great sovereignty.

"Today he raises you up out of your corruption.

"Today you are a son of the scriptures.

"Today you are the son of your Good Father.

"Today you are his man.

"Today you are his brother.

"Today you shall know your God.

"Today your dignity will increase.

"Today you must purify your thoughts.

"Today great honor comes to you.

"Today you leave poverty.

"Today is the day of plenty.

"Today is the day when the Holy Spirit will descend to you."

Barlaam chastised, admonished, and taught the king's son to turn toward the path of good faith. Josaphat agreed with everything he said. Barlaam promptly consecrated the font and baptized the king's son. He changed the old man into a new one, but he did not change his name. Barlaam asked Josaphat what he believed, and when Josaphat demonstrated that he believed as he should, Barlaam marveled at the strength he had gained. He was brave and strong in his faith. Barlaam had admonished and taught him well. Barlaam sang the mass like a priest; then he gave Josaphat communion. Josaphat received the body of God with great fear. He was

not afraid to believe, but he was afraid of taking his Lord
within him because he feared that the lodging was not well
enough built to hold such a noble presence. He feared taking
the noble and precious body of God into his unworthy body,
but he was also most happy. So he felt both joy and fear, but
joy had the greater part and he received the host with true
happiness. Sadness is appropriate, for one should feel sorry
for his sins, but he should also be happy that God abides
with him. God is so merciful that he always listens when a
man prays to him sincerely, no matter what sins he has committed.

The king's son rejoiced and believed that all his sins had
been pardoned, as the hermit had taught him. Barlaam rejoiced at Josaphat's baptism because he understood that the
young man had renounced the world. He admonished him
gently, and then took leave of him to return to his lodging.

Josaphat detained Barlaam for a little while longer. He
sent for him often to seek his teaching, and he asked difficult
questions about God. Barlaam answered him, for he knew
all the scriptures. He calmed the young man's fears, and
whenever Josaphat could not see the truth, Barlaam enlightened him.

The servants who watched over the king's son wondered
about the identity of this man who came to speak with him
so often, and they spoke about it in secret among themselves.
They were afraid of the king, who had charged them to watch
over his son, and they did not want their vigilance to be
found lacking. They agreed to betray the king's son, but in
their agreement they disagreed. A false note sounded in their
harmony, and there was discord in their concord because
they agreed to do a wrong. Zardan, the one among them
who loved Josaphat most, came to speak privately to the
king's son. "Have mercy, good lord!" he said. "I am afraid of
your father's anger. He put you under my guard, and I watch
over you. I should not have allowed a stranger to come and
speak to you without your father's permission. I do not know
what he taught you, but I fear that he is one of the Christians

and that he will convert you to their religion. If your father knew about it, he would put me to death.

"Now I pray you to ask the king's permission to speak with this man, and if you will not—please do not take this as disloyal—I can no longer allow him to come talk to you. I am afraid of the consequences. If you wish to continue to see this man, go to your father and tell him that you have taken a dislike to me. Say that my services no longer please you and you cannot tolerate me. This way you could save me and remove the blame from us both."

The king's son replied, "Friend, before I do this, I ask you to hide and listen to the wise man when he comes to speak to me. If his words and actions cannot convince you, then I will have wronged you and I will help to reconcile you with the king, but first do as I ask."

Zardan replied, "Yes, I will do as you wish."

Barlaam came to the court soon thereafter, and Zardan hid in the prince's room. The old man sat down and reasoned with the king's son. He spoke the words of his lesson from beginning to end. He taught the king's son about God and told him that he should serve God with a good heart, and that he should despise the world and all its beauty. "Notice the summer flowers," he said. "Look, for example, at the fading rose. The bush holds the rose in the light as long as the flower lasts, but no one cares about the bush once the rose fades, for without the flower it is nothing. And the flower begins to fade as soon as it is cut. The rose is a very beautiful flower when it first appears, and although it is prized for its beauty, as soon as it loses its color it is considered worthless. The rose, then, is very beautiful, but it changes quickly. So too with man when he dies. No man is so beautiful or so noble that he will not perish like the rose. As soon as he dies, he is lost if he has not done any good deeds to earn God's mercy.

"Those who believe in idols have sinned without recourse and they will die without forgiveness, for God will condemn them. Only a man whose heart has been hardened by pride would deliberately imprison himself in hell, where the wretched are condemned to dwell forever without forgiveness. It is good to believe in God, for as the true story tells us, whoever believes in him and serves him with a loyal heart will receive a noble reward. God will give him a rich crown to wear forever.

"God our Father took a virgin as his mother. He was baptized in the Jordan River and preached his holy name there. He fasted in the wilderness for forty days for our sake and let himself be tempted by the devil who assailed him. He raised Lazarus from his tomb in Bethany and pardoned Mary Magdalene for all the sins of her body. This God became our servant. He allowed one of his disciples to sell him. He was bound and beaten and hung on the cross. He suffered death for us, and on the third day he was resurrected. He ascended into heaven above, and he will come down from there to judge the world. This God asks you to live such a life so that you will reign with him." With these words Barlaam finished his sermon and left to return to his lodging.

The king's son called Zardan out of his hiding place. "Did you listen to what this man recounted here?" he asked. "He came to instruct me, and I could be destroyed if I believed what he says. He teaches me that the pleasures of this world are worthless. He wants to trick me and turn me to a religion that my father, the king, does not tolerate. He thinks my father's gods are false, that nothing compares to his God, and that no other god is his equal. This is a wondrous claim, and I marvel at the notion that God is so great that he has no equal."

Zardan understood that his lord was testing him with great subtlety. "My lord," he said, "it is wrong to ask a man a question he does not know how to answer. You test me with your words, but I know that you would not have listened to this man if you did not wish to hear him. His words have entered into your heart, and you think they are good and right. He has ignited you with the spark that fires the Christians. My good lord, I believe you have adopted this faith, and the king will be distressed to learn it. He killed many Christians for your sake. He drove them from his land and exiled them. When they still dwelled here, I often went to listen to their preaching. If your father, the king, knew that the wise man came to you and spoke about such things, I would pay dearly for it. I know that for certain."

The king's son replied, "You should remember the lesson you just heard, for it is true and could bring you great profit. If you wished to believe in God with a loyal heart and recognize him as your Lord, your soul would be blessed and you would be saved in God's court. But you are hardhearted and foolish. If you would cast the chains from your neck and loosen yourself from your bonds, he would relieve you from the sins that will burden you.

"I am disappointed," Josaphat continued, "for I hoped that belief would illuminate your heart. You have eyes but you do not see, and you are blind yet you see. You see clearly, but the clarity is false. You are, then, blind even though you see, and you lie even though you know the truth. You cannot take yourself out of this paradox, only because you do not try. You are damned by your lack of effort, and all your rewards will be lost.

"I ask you to say nothing to the king, for if you told him, you would cause him distress. You are his man and he is your lord, so you should not tell him anything that would upset him. You should also test your heart and constrain your thoughts so they do not fail before God." Zardan would not listen to this advice. Josaphat tried to admonish and teach him, but Zardan would not heed his words.

Barlaam returns to his hermitage

At sunrise the next morning, the saintly hermit came to court to tell the king's son that it was time for him to return to his wilderness hermitage. Josaphat was sorrowful about his teacher's departure, because it would separate them. Only with great pain could he bear to hear Barlaam speak of leaving. The hermit admonished the king's son and said that he could not remain. He wanted to return to his life in the hermitage, and it weighed heavily on him that he was not already back there.

The king's son agreed reluctantly and with great regret. He cried and complained, for he was consumed by sorrow; his happiness had changed to ire and he did not know what to say. Nonetheless, before he gave Barlaam leave to depart, he asked the hermit to take something from the treasury for himself and his brothers, to give to those of them in need. But poverty is not to be feared, and Barlaam refused. "Then I would ask you, good master, to leave your rough shirt here for me in exchange for a new one," Josaphat said. "Good master, I beg you, I will wear it in remembrance of you and of my repentance."

"Friend, I cannot make this exchange," the hermit replied. "Only if you find an old hair shirt for me may you have mine in exchange." The king's son sent for one, and Barlaam took off his garment and gave it to Josaphat. The prince thanked him gratefully and accepted it with more joy than he would have received a silken cloth. He held it very dear, but nonetheless he wept at Barlaam's departure. The good man had taught him that he should serve his Creator with all his heart, and that he should devote himself to worship every day of the week. He should live every day chastely, so the devil could not trick him. Barlaam had begun to show the king's son the fortress and the walls that would defend him against the devil. And when Barlaam left him, Josaphat remained sad at the separation from the master whom he loved because of his good lessons. He began to pray to God and his Holy Name and asked that he keep him from sin. Josaphat undertook the difficult work of fasting and remaining vigilant. He did good deeds and called frequently on his Creator. He served him well in his heart and loved him. Those who were with him in the palace marveled greatly at it.

Zardan, the servant to whom the king had entrusted his

son, watched over Josaphat closely and worried that the
young man's conduct might bring him harm. He feared the
king and tried to find some way to avoid his judgment, which
could be harsh and hard. Zardan's anger weighed on him but
his sadness kept him quiet. Then his angry thoughts showed
him how he might escape the king's fury, which he rightly
anticipated. He went home and pretended to be ill. He knew
he had acted against the king, and he regretted his kindness
to the king's son. He thought that he had looked after him
badly, but he was wrong because he had cared for him well.
The king's son was a Christian, and he had learned about the
good religion while under Zardan's guardianship. Zardan
thought the prince had taken the wrong path, but it was
Zardan himself who was wrong. He was brought low because he failed to be lifted up by belief. He did not believe
what the king's son believed, and he was wrong not to do so.
Zardan thought the king's son was lost because of his belief,
but he was not.

Zardan was afraid the king would kill him. He pretended
to be ill, and the king heard of it and immediately sent him
the best doctor in the land. King Avenir asked the doctor to
do all he could to heal Zardan and promised him a rich reward if he succeeded. The doctor devoted himself to discov-
ering what was wrong with Zardan. He tested his urine
many times, but found no evidence of illness. He said to the
king, "I cannot heal him, because I cannot find anything
wrong with him. If he is ill, it is because he suffers from some
concern." When the king heard the doctor's conclusion, he
thought his son must be angry with Zardan, who did not
want to reveal that Josaphat's anger caused his illness. The
king suspected something and sent word to Zardan that he
would visit him the next day, for he wanted to know what
was making him sick. Zardan was surprised by the message
and he rose early the next morning, got ready, and went to
the king. Avenir was angry: "Why do you test your strength
by coming to me this morning, when I said I would come to

you? I meant to demonstrate how much I loved you by coming to your house."

"Sire," Zardan responded, "I am not so ill that I cannot come to you. I have served you badly, for I have not cared for that which you commended to me. I think, without ceasing, about the wrong I have done you, and my sorrow and sadness about it have put me in this state. If you knew the sorrow, pain, and loss I have caused you, I believe you would kill me—if you did not take pity on me. Death would be a just judgment, and, Sire, if your mercy does not save me, I must be condemned to die."

"You? But why?" the king asked. "What have you done? Tell me! I will not judge you for it."

"I will tell you, for good or for ill. King, your son is a Christian. A man named Barlaam converted him. I do not know who he is—I saw him only once.[1] I realized then that he would cause my downfall. Sire, he reasoned with your son, and Josaphat held it against me when I admonished him for it. I told him that I would tell you about it, and he had himself baptized right away. He kept preaching to me and tried to convert me, but I refused, and he asked me not to say anything to you about it. Barlaam went back to his hermitage because he did not wish to stay any longer."

The king was silent. The sorrow and anger he felt in his heart took away his speech. He became mute and restrained his anger only with great difficulty. His heart welled with tears. His gain turned to loss, his joy to anger, and his happiness to suffering. He saw his wealth become poverty, his treasure turn to lack, and his courage to cowardice. He had lost everything, and he felt his life had become a kind of death. He saw his joy become sadness and his nobility abased. He despised his kingdom and his crown, and he felt he had lost his power because he lost the happiness his son brought him. The king abandoned himself to senseless anger, and his rage gave him the strength to speak despite his sorrow. He sent for Prince Aracin (he was his master councilor and an

astronomer). The councilor came quickly to Avenir, and the
king asked for his advice, for he needed it badly. "The thing I
most feared has happened and I am distraught. Advise me,
for my son has fallen into Christian belief. Alas!" the king
lamented, "I believed he feared and honored me enough that
he would never do anything to displease me. Barlaam betrayed him. He manipulated him and tricked me. Alas! He
killed my son and murdered me. My son used to love me, but
he has become my enemy. He is my son and he should love
me, but now he betrays me without reason—he kills himself
and murders me. He has gone against reason, his belief deceives him, and he believes a lie."

Aracin said, "King, good sire, let go of your sorrow and
anger and do not be dismayed. I believe I can give you good
advice. Let us find this man who came from so far away to
trick your son. Let him be followed and captured, my good
lord, and brought before you. By royal command, let him be
tortured until he publicly renounces his teaching. When Josaphat sees him renounce his God, then he will know without
doubt that his belief is false and that our gods are stronger."

"This is good advice, if Barlaam can be found," the king
responded immediately. "But tell me—if we cannot find him,
how will we put him to the test?"

"I will tell you," the prince replied. "I know a wise man
whom I will have brought to you. He resembles Barlaam in
appearance, dress, and age.[2] His name is Nachor. He is wise
and old, and he is clever enough to fool anyone. When Barlaam is called before your son, Nachor will come in his place,
disguised so your son will not recognize him. Send for your
rhetoricians and all the astronomers of your land and have
them gather here. Nachor will appear before them instead of
Barlaam, if you will agree to it. At the beginning of the year,
when you are at peace in your palace, with your son at your
side, you will call for your wise men to argue their beliefs
with Nachor. He will pretend to be Barlaam and defend the
Christians' faith and their religion, and he will let himself be
bested. When your son hears the debate, he will know that

he was wrong, and he will do your will." The king was relieved and encouraged by this advice, and he approved Aracin's plan.

Prince Aracin assembled a great company of men and sent
his spies out in all directions, but they could not find Barlaam. Aracin himself went into the wilderness and traveled
across it for seven days, because he knew that he would receive a rich reward if he could find Barlaam. He tracked him
as far as the Black Mountain, but he could not find him. Instead he found more than three hundred hermits there. They
lived a life that would be bitter and harsh for those kings and
counts who use their worldly gains to buy rich food and
clothing, and to pursue pleasure without charity. (What return do they expect from the miserable gifts they offer, from
their anger and resentment, their mistreatment and imprisonment of the poor, and their demands for ransom that the
poor cannot pay? They crucify the poor with the chains and
shackles of their laws. They trust in their own authority, but
their power is evil and no one should put hope in it. They
wield their power over the poor and force them to live in misery, when they should share their wealth. Our God who suffered the passion on the cross would be wrong to take pity on
high nobles—they are judged by their own unjust conduct
toward the poor.

Ah, my lords, repent! Wicked noblemen, consider the ways
of the world! My lords, why do you not remember your own
dead ancestors? The scriptures teach us that whoever does
not do as he should will receive death. They say that Herod
and Nero and Pilate and Lucius are dead, but this is a lie, for
I tell you without hesitation that I could find one hundred
Herods in this country if I looked for them. Pilate and Herod
are alive, and they live quite well in France and in Lombardy.
Herod does not lack for anything as long as the king is in
Paris, and I believe Pilate is the lord of Vermandois. Today
there is no count or king who may not rightly be called a
Herod or a Pilate, since today nobles reign over an evil world
and they delight in wrongdoing—such is their power and

their domain. They are too greedy to understand evil, and evil engenders in them the desire to do more evil. Felonious and disloyal nobles, pay attention to this story! The hermits who lived on the Black Mountain were not consumed by violence like you are.)

This Aracin, the king's councilor whom I told you about, took a great company of men with him to look for Barlaam, whom he thought he could capture. He put all his heart, knowledge, and power into the search (he tried to deceive the king's son, but Josaphat could not be deceived by the words of a pagan), and he arrived at the hermitage. The hermits living in the wilderness wondered who had come to pursue them so assiduously. Like the hound that bays after the beast it tracks, Aracin raised his voice and barked after the hermits, blaming them for what Barlaam had accomplished with the king's son, whom he had deceived. But did Barlaam deceive the prince? No, he saved him from error, for Josaphat lived a contradiction when he worshipped the creation and despised his Creator.[3] Aracin worked on his lord's behalf to try to make Josaphat renounce his faith, but the king's son did not care for false belief. He believed truly in the God that the king's councilor rejected. Aracin was foolish and deceived himself. The king's son believed in the true faith and knew how to guard against all that Aracin tried to do.

Prince Aracin fails to find Barlaam

Aracin was on the mountain with a great company of men. He followed the hermits into their wooded hermitage. They did not flee from him, and they rejoiced when Aracin and his men captured them. They were taken to the prince. One of the hermits was old, white haired, and dressed in a rough garment. He carried holy relics in a pouch around his neck. Aracin looked at him and knew that he was not Barlaam. Aracin knew Barlaam well, and he looked everywhere but did not see him. When he saw that Barlaam was not among them, Aracin cried out, "My lords! I have captured you. Tell me now, where is my enemy? Tell me, for he has deceived the king's son."[1]

The old man who carried the relics was master of them all, and he responded gently, "There is no enemy among us. He dwells with you, I believe, and leads you astray. We are not against you, for we live with God."

"Listen to me," Prince Aracin demanded. "Show me Barlaam. You know him well, I believe. He has deceived our king's son."

"He has not deceived him," the old hermit responded. "Barlaam never preached in order to deceive the prince or take him away from you. He wanted only to teach him God's law. Barlaam taught him, and he learned. Barlaam came to free him from his false beliefs, and he has surely succeeded."

"I seek Barlaam because he most certainly has done the king and all his people a great wrong," Aracin said. "Show me the way to his dwelling."

"I will not do it," said the hermit. "If he wanted to talk to you, he would have come here voluntarily. Our religion forbids us to take you to him. Our love and fear of God command obedience. Do not interfere in our affairs."

The prince grew angry when he heard himself so easily dismissed. "Understand this," he said furiously, "if you do not take me to Barlaam immediately, you will die. The pyre is ready, and you will suffer the most painful death possible. No doctor will be able to cure the wounds I will give you."

The old man responded, "We do not fear death, or threats, for we know that whoever wishes to leave this life need not fear death. This life is the true death, and whoever lives in the world does not really live. The threat of death is double in this world. Death ends life, but life itself is like death. Whoever lives in sin is dying and does not really live. Whoever does not repent unceasingly of his sins dies even as he lives. Whoever would live in this sinful world cannot expect to live, for when he begins to sin, then he dies, for sin makes him die. This man is full of death and sin, and sin is the death that will take him without recourse. Sin and death wound his heart and his understanding. No one can sin without death.

"We live in repentance and purify our thoughts. We do not fear death, for no one can escape it, and your threats mean nothing to us. We do not fear the sword you raise against us, for we have forsaken this life. We came to this path through repentance, but your journey leads you away from it. Do whatever your false heart tells you to do, for none of us is ready to do what you command. You seek Barlaam. We know where he lives, but no matter what threats you make we will not reveal it to you."

Aracin understood that his threats would not make the hermits tell him where to find Barlaam. He was livid, and in his rage he had them tortured. He had them beaten with straps until blood dripped from their wounded flesh. The Saracens tortured the holy hermits, and Aracin beat and cursed them, but he could not make them speak.[2] (What was it worth in the end, when it was all for nothing and he could not make them reveal where Barlaam dwelled?) Unhappily and against his will, Aracin decided to take them to King Avenir. He and his men continued to strike and torment the hermits, and forced their abbot, the old preacher who carried the relics, to lead them across the wilderness.

Aracin and his men cursed God and his servants as they traveled, and finally they arrived at the king's palace in the city. Aracin presented the captives to King Avenir. The uncomprehending king looked at them with fury, for he saw a people he did not love. (In fact he hated them, though this was wrong.) He decided to take vengeance on them since he could not find Barlaam, and this decision revealed his character and made his sin even worse. He commanded his men to torture the hermits: he had them beaten without pity and showed no compassion for their pain. He believed he would gain honor by beating and insulting them.

Then he stopped the torturers. "My lords," he said, "come

forward and tell me the truth about Barlaam. I have sworn
that if you do not tell me, you will die shamefully today."

"King, you should not expect us to follow such an order.
You cannot make us take you to Barlaam by beating or tor-
turing us. No pain will make us tell you where he is."

"Tell me, then," said the king, "how do you dare to carry
bones around your neck?"

"We have faith in the holy bodies we carry for remembrance," the master replied. "Those who now dwell in glory
will help us reject this world and be saved, and for that we
owe them reverence and honor. Any man who would live according to the good religion should honor the saints. Whoever would keep his house clean and free of filth can see the
standard by which he must measure himself if his false heart
does not falsify the standard. The sinner chooses a standard
and then decides what he can do to change it so he will measure up. The house that should be kept clean is a man's body.
The body takes the soul to a dangerous crossing where the
roads and tolls belong to the devil. This is why we carry the
bones of the dead, to remind us that the body must die and
rot in the putrid ground.

"Pagan king, this is the wager you have made, and you are
already losing. King, you will die, do not doubt it, and in fact
you are already dying while you live. You cannot escape
death. You do not believe, and that is the cause of your death.
You are dying and you do not know how you should die or
how you should live, because you are drunk on the pleasure
of the sins that kill you. You think you have lost your son,
but he has been led into the way of salvation. This is a straight
way, and whoever follows any other direction strays from it.
Now do what you will with us. We do not fear your threats
or your tortures."

The king was enraged and commanded that all the hermits be killed. And I will tell you exactly how. First he had
their tongues cut out, and his men did it without sparing any
pain. He treated them vilely. He had their holy eyes gouged
out, and then, to assuage his anger, he had their hands and

feet cut off. He made them suffer a grievous martyrdom. He took angry vengeance against those who had done him no wrong, but they willingly received the pain and the martyrdom. They offered the pain to their Creator, for they suffered the pain for him, and they exchanged their suffering for joy, since God gave them their reward and they would have it forever. Their souls are in paradise—whoever loses in this world gains much in the next. The saints who lived in the wilderness merited the crown that God gave them for their torture and martyrdom. There were twenty-seven of them.

Gui has told the story to this point and translated it into French, and here he finishes the story of the hermits' martyrdom.[3] The story says that our Lord received their souls well, because the pains they had endured had brought them to their Creator. The martyrdom they suffered here below made them emperors and lords in great glory above.

King Avenir sent for Aracin. "I am very disappointed that Barlaam cannot be found," he said. "Go find your master Nachor and bring him to me. I want to know if he can return what Barlaam stole from me. I will ask Nachor if he can break my son away from the false belief that causes fear in my heart. Go quickly, good councilor."

"Sire, right away." Prince Aracin went to Nachor, who dwelled in the wilderness (not to serve God, though; he served the devil and devoted his wisdom to the devil's ends). Nachor was skilled in divination and lived by art and trickery. He was knowledgeable about evil but knew little about the good. Aracin told him about his plan and asked him to use all his skill to bring the king's son back into the right path. Nachor agreed, and Aracin returned to the king. "Nachor has agreed to come and he will be here tomorrow," the prince reported, and King Avenir thanked him.

Aracin was impatient. He rose early the next day and called for the king's knights. "My lords," he said, "I have news of Barlaam. Last night one of my sergeants saw him in the wilderness. He fled there to hide because of the crime he

committed against the king. Get ready and come with me.
We will use my man's information to find him, and then we
will take revenge for the wrong he has done to us." The
knights were happy to hear the news and they assembled as
Aracin had commanded. They entered the hermitage and
combed the woods, seeking the hermit who had converted
the king's son to the good faith.

Nachor came out of his cave as though he was lost and confused, and he pretended to be sad and mournful. He listened
for the cries of those who sought Barlaam, and when he heard
them, he fled through the wilderness where the hermits lived.
First he ran to one side, then another; he showed himself, and
then he hid. He pretended to be angry, and Aracin was very
pleased to see that his men believed Nachor was the man they
had come to capture. "Stop him! Don't let him escape!" they
cried. "If he escapes, the king will be angry, and we will suffer
for it!" Aracin's men pursued Nachor as he ran from bush to
hedge. They spurred their horses in pursuit and captured Nachor, but they thought they had taken Barlaam. Nachor did
not know what to do, so he pretended to be sad and hid his
pleasure with the appearance of fear. The soldiers treated him
badly, and he pleaded Aracin for mercy.

Without revealing anything about his plot, Aracin asked
the captive his name. "My name is Barlaam," Nachor responded. "I am a Christian and I believe in God, who created
everything, including you and me." Aracin was very pleased
by this response (he knew who Nachor was, but none of the
others recognized him and that pleased him). He went
quickly back to court and had Nachor brought before the
king.

King Avenir addressed the false Barlaam. "Show me what
kind of man you are. Why have you treated me this way?
Why have you separated me from my son? Evil Barlaam, the
devil is in you and you have done me a great wrong. Why
have you taken my son from me?"

"King, you have not lost him," Nachor responded. "He is
not lost if he believes in God, and he will receive a rich re-

ward for his belief. I thought to do a good deed when I made your son a Christian."

"I wonder why you do not fear death," said Avenir. "You have spoken treason and you will die in great pain and without redemption if you do not renounce this error."

"You are foolish to threaten me," Nachor responded. "What you call an error, I consider a good deed. I do not fear your threats or judgment."

The king pretended to be very angry. He sent for his master councilor and commanded him to take Nachor away and have him closely guarded. The councilor locked him in prison.

News of the hermit's capture spread quickly throughout the country. When the king's son heard it, he cried tenderly. He spent the whole day praying to God that he would spare his master from martyrdom. Josaphat was overcome with sorrow. But God sent his angel to protect him from the deception and change his sorrow to happiness. The angel revealed the king's betrayal to Josaphat and told him about his father's efforts to deceive him. Then the angel left the prince.

The king sought to trick his son by any means, to make him renounce God. He was grateful for Aracin's advice and thanked him generously, for he did not care about the means as long as he could accomplish his end. But his elaborate plans would be undermined by divine commandment.

King Avenir attempts to win back his son

Two days after Nachor's capture, the king considered how he might make his plan work better. He went to speak with Josaphat, and the young man came out to meet him. King Avenir was so angry that he did not deign to approach his son, though he had always kissed and embraced him when they met. He sat on a royal couch and spoke angrily to Josaphat. "Son, what is this? Explain what I have heard about you. I loved you more than anything, and now the Christians have misled you. Never did a father love a son so much—you were treated more royally than I myself am. You were my sweet son, my joy and my solace. You were my legacy and you were the staff that would sustain my body weakened by old age. Son, what have you done? Consider it carefully! I was you and you were me, and my love was doubled in you. All my thoughts were for your honor and your good. You were my wealth and my love, my power and my succor. You were the best thing in my kingdom.

"Now you have blinded me, and this is how: my light has been extinguished and I am in darkness. My measure is unmeasured. My sweet water has turned bitter—it was clear but now has become cloudy. My honor has turned to shame, and my nobility has been lost. My wealth has become poverty, my gain turned to loss. My ancestral tree is dead at the roots, and my love has turned to hatred. You claim to be wise, but you know nothing. I am your friend, but you despise me. You disinherit me of my own land, for you go to war against me in my own country. You cause me to lose honor, and you make me suffer when before I was happy. Good sweet son, dear sweet friend, you have become my enemy! I have lost all my happiness! That which I most feared has come about. You have never doubted my love, yet you have given your body, your heart, and your thoughts to a stranger. Sweet son, this is most certainly a foolish bargain. The gods are very angry about it, for it has greatly pained them that you have given yourself to another.

"Josaphat, my son, how can you forsake our gods for some unknown man who was hung on a cross? Surely you can understand that if he were God, he would not have allowed himself to be hung. This is just a story that people tell. Good son, amend this shame. Listen to my advice and I will try to appease the gods. Come now and sacrifice to them. They will have mercy on you, and I will be happy. Come willingly to them so they will forgive you."

"Father," Josaphat replied, "listen to me. I am right to be-

lieve in God. I have come out of the shadows and into the
light. I have left unbelief to make an alliance with God. I
have yoked myself to my Creator and given him all my love.
He formed and made me. I am his servant, for he taught me
to serve him, and I will do so as long as I live. He made
Adam, our first father, by whose fault we live so wretchedly
in this world. Adam did not obey his law, for the devil tricked
him, and he was judged harshly. But God looked on man and
took pity on him and was born on earth to save him from
sin. He became a man to free us from our prison and was
born—do not fail to believe it—of a virgin, Saint Mary. He
was betrayed by his disciple in exchange for money, and then
he was hung on the cross, where he willingly suffered death
for our salvation.

"Our nature was ennobled when he took our form. We
should be grateful to our Father who became our Brother. He
promises us an everlasting glory, which we should remember
and contemplate in our hearts when we come to God. I worship and believe in him, I serve him, and I am baptized in his
name. I know no other god besides the Lord of righteousness
and justice, and at Judgment Day he will render to each the
reward he has earned. Whoever dwells with him will be
richly rewarded. Father, consider whether you might attain
this reward. Leave your belief, for it is despised on high, before our Lord. Believe in the Savior, for he made every creature. If your thoughts were clean and pure, you could attain
heavenly glory.

"Father, your gods are powerless. They do not know good
or evil, and they have no strength. Look at them. Do you not
see that there is no value in them except in their adornment?
And if they have no knowledge, what are they worth to me?
If they cannot hear me, what do I gain if I pray to them for
forgiveness? They are worthless gods since they have no
knowledge or power. They are the devil's creations, and no
one should believe in any god who is not Jesus Christ. The
holy hermit taught me this, and I learned it well. I believe in
God and in his power, for he is a true God and a true Lord.

No tongue can speak the strength of his divinity. He became human for our sake and came down into this lost world to free us from peril.

"Father, I feel great sorrow because you do not believe in the Creator. I have often prayed that he would take pity on you. I suffer for you because I know that you will be shamed if you do not wish to love God. I see that obedience has no place in your heart—you are hard set against conversion, and God will not accept such stubbornness. You resist the good faith and make yourself into a murderer, for you kill yourself with your sins. Your body enjoys its pleasures, but your soul is in danger as long as you refuse to believe. You do not believe in God who created you.

"King, you do not know what will happen to you, and your lack of belief will earn you the harsh pains of hell. I have sworn my allegiance to God, and I do not fear irons or nails, for imprisonment would free me, and the tortures of martyrdom would earn me a royal crown. It used to be true that I was your son, but the natural law that made me your carnal son has been superseded by spiritual laws. The Holy Spirit will not descend to a man of bad faith who does not love God and his law. Now hear me, I tell you the truth. I have left you because you have separated yourself from me. You yourself split us apart. Do you know how? Because you remain in foolish devotion to your gods while I follow the good faith. You separate yourself from God, the all-powerful Lord. You owe your rank to him, but you turn it to shame and destruction instead of thanking him for it. Father, you have gone to war against yourself—you are your own enemy. King, become a king and a friend, a friend of God, who is King of your soul! God is courtly in all things and will be pleased to help you rule this kingdom. Then I will be your son twice over. But if you do not believe, you will no longer be a father because you will lose your son."

You need not ask how the king responded. He was furious and spoke angrily to his son. "What have I done wrong? What have I ever denied you? No father ever did as much for

his son as I have done for you. And the only result is that I
suffer greater misery. Good son, the astronomers prophesied
well when they said that no good would come to me from
you, and they were right to predict that you would destroy
me and my kingdom. Never did any father love a son as much
as I loved you, but now love must turn to hatred, for you are
proud and presumptuous and accuse me of many wrongs. I
tell you truly that I will hate you more than anything in the
world, for your belief confounds me.

"I ask you, without anger, to take mercy on me because I
am your father. And if you will not, then you betray me.
Good son, think carefully about what you should do. You
are my son. I am your father. Consider what that means. I
seek no other joy but that you leave the error of your belief."

Josaphat said, "Father, you admonish me in vain. If I did
your will, I would suffer harsh consequences that you do not
understand because you refuse to believe. You suffer because
of my well-being. I am the servant of the Lord who created
me. This is not wrong—it is right. You were my father, but
truly, by God, how can I belong to a father who does not belong to God? I have gained true understanding, and you are
not my father—my father has become my enemy. I have lost
my father! And yet, no, I have a Father who is a more exalted
king and emperor than you are, for this Father is Lord over
all the world because he created it. This Father formed you,
Father. But you have betrayed him.

"Father, why do you hate the Father who made you my father? He wasted his effort when he made you so handsome
and noble, a rich ruler with power over a great land. You
offer him hatred and strife in return! It is wrong to go to war
against him when he suffered death for you. You offer him
hatred because you hate him. Father and not Father, you do
not know what his war and hatred are, for your war is the
renunciation of the joy of paradise, and your hatred is the refusal to believe. He will take cruel vengeance on you. Do not
torment me further, for it would be foolish to try to make me
think that I should seek some other kind of happiness. Do

not try to make me abandon God's commandments, for no reasonable man should serve any other god.

"Father, for God's sake, beware of this world that flees so quickly. Whoever gives his heart over to it offers his love foolishly and destroys himself. See how the flowers perish—at the beginning of the summer they are born and come out of the earth. The flowers are beautiful then, but they soon fade and disappear. So too with the pleasures of the world and all its creatures. For a short time they are beautiful, but they last only a brief moment. Father, for God and for his mother, let us now become son and father. First become the son of God, and then you will be my rightful father, and I will be your son and companion when I see that you believe in the Creator. Dear friend, how painful it is that we are separated from each other because you will not believe in the One who created us both! We are separated because you refuse reason. We cannot be companions because you are foolish and set yourself against me, against right, and against faith. Father, you will repent in the end, when you see God's vengeance (this will be at Judgment Day). Then you will remember the sweet days of pleasure and the many privileges you enjoyed in this world, but they will be worth nothing to you then. It is true—it will happen! You will be judged harshly, and repentance will come too late, for in hell there is no comfort. You make such great preparations only to put yourself in great danger of being lost! Father, your lack of judgment makes you your own murderer.

"Do not lament for me, for I am on the right path. I lament for you because you stray from it. Your own heart is against you. You think it is loyal, but it has betrayed you. Your guest has treated you badly—your guest is your foolish heart. You have hosted him and he has betrayed you. Saint Paul says in his letter that a man's fickle heart puts his body and soul in peril.[1] Do not be afraid because of your sins—you can reconcile yourself with God if you ask for forgiveness. He died for all sinners, and, Father, you would be wrong not to pray to God for forgiveness since he suffered death for you. Father, you believe that you have gods, but they have no power, they know neither good nor evil, and belief in them will bring you nothing."

The king despaired. He thought his son's disdain for his beliefs and his gods was a poor return for all he had given him. He would willingly have cursed him for it, if nature had allowed it, but he could not curse his own son. Nonetheless, he spoke harshly to Josaphat. "Son, I am sorry that you were born, since you cause me such pain. You have invented very foolish ideas. You stubbornly set yourself against your gods and your father, and you refuse my instruction and my love. I want you to understand that if you will not follow my commands, you will be put to torture, for you speak too foolishly. You are not my son or my friend. You have become my enemy, and I will treat you as one. You act against nature and ignore her laws. I am your father, and yet you do me such wrong! By all the gods, you act so strangely toward me that I could easily believe someone had used a trick to substitute you for my true son. It brings me great sorrow to see you." King Avenir could bear to stay no longer.

The angry king left his son, and Josaphat knelt in prayer to ask God for forgiveness and for the strength and intelligence not to disobey him. "God, Lord and Father, help me, for I worship you and pray to you. Consider me with mercy and forgive my sins. All my hope, strength, and power are in you. Good Lord, have mercy on me. I am your servant, you are my salvation, and I put myself entirely in your care."

King Avenir calls for a public disputation

While the king's son prayed, his father sought some trick or plan he could use to change Josaphat's mind. He sent for Aracin and asked him how he could draw his son away from his belief and his love for God. Aracin came to him in friendship and counseled him: "He is sensitive and harsh words offend him. You should coax him with soft words for he cannot bear anger. Speak sweetly to him and you will bring him back to your love—otherwise you will accomplish nothing."

The king took Aracin's advice and went to talk to his son again. He kissed and embraced him and drew him close. "Beloved son," he said, "I felt great anger and pain when I saw that you were lost to me through your belief. Dear son, leave your foolishness and come sacrifice to the gods. Listen to reason and do not argue with me, for I am your aged father. You should be a king! You should rule my lands for me and end my wars, but instead, sweet son, you abandon me. You give me more pain than the entire rest of the world, and it hurts me that you resist me and will not do anything for me. Son, what I ask will bring you honor. Submit to me here and show respect to me, for you owe me your obedience. You should try to make me happy rather than angering me.

"Dear son, do you not know that I have heard many Christians speak about their lives? But I saw little good in their foolish belief: it was nothing but a lie. I have known some wise and learned men in my time. If they had thought this faith was a good religion, they would not have remained with our own. Son, I think you are mistaken when you anger the gods who raised you up so high that all Indians and Persians recognize you as their lord. You have made your father into a sorrowful man, for it makes me sad to see you deceived by a bad religion. Listen to my advice and follow it as you should. Good son, come back to me. Accept my counsel and I will give you great honors."

The young man was wise and brave, and he saw that this was not good advice. He knew in his heart that his soul would be in danger if he obeyed his father. He responded sensibly to the king: "All that I should do, I would willingly do if I could. If I had a good father who believed in God and worshipped and served him, and devoted all his thoughts to him, then I would be eager to do his will and follow all his commandments. But, Father, your actions and your refusal to believe prevent me from obeying you, for I must not damn my soul just to do your will. And if your demands were reasonable, then I would be wrong not to grant them with my whole heart. Good father, if I did not love you, I would be disloyal. But we are separated because you would imperil my soul and set me against God and his law by asking me to do your will. I must not obey you, and it is not wise to ask me to do so. Father, I have never had such happiness as I have found as the servant of our Lord. It is right that I turn away from my family if you forbid me to serve he who is Lord over us all.

"Father, I do not care about your empire. If I wore a crown, I would soon lose it. My reign would be short and my crown ill gained. The gods worshipped in your court are deaf and mute, and there is no power in them. Your belief in them is wrong, and you are wrong to blame me for the good belief I have found. This world will not endure. You know that we all die—think about what will happen to you after your death! Father, all our ancestors are dead, but they will be raised up when they hear the holy angels' horn on Judgment Day. What will happen to you at that hour? Do not believe that your gods will help you then. You will be condemned to dwell forever in pain, without relief or succor. Good people will go to enjoy the happiness they deserve, but you will take another path, and the way you have chosen will cause your soul to be lost. If you delay too long, you will be too late. Father, for God's sake, make haste! You wait too long to go to God. I will not leave his light because of your orders or entreaties, or because of anything you say. This is what our Lord demands of me."

The king was sad and angry because he saw that his son's resolve would be hard to weaken. He tried many approaches, but could not find a way to bring his son back to his faith. Neither prayers nor promises could change Josaphat's mind. Then the king remembered the disputation Aracin had proposed. "Son," he said, "you have reasoned with me about your belief. But let it be debated before the people so they can judge by reason and right which belief is better, mine or your master's. I have captured this Barlaam who taught you the misguided belief that causes me such pain. I have him in my prison. He will be brought to my palace and heard by all my people. I will send for the Christians who abandoned my country so they too will come. I will offer them safe passage and receive them with honor. I will also send for the grammarians, the rhetoricians, and all my astronomers. Then you will hear their disputation. If your man speaks reason and shows me true faith, I will believe in your God. But if my clerics show that the Christians are wrong, then I want you to agree to come back to our faith and leave the false belief that brings you such dishonor."

The wise young man was not deceived. By divine commandment, he agreed. "I will do as you wish," he said. "May God give us victory and help us by his mercy. I give myself to him and trust in him."

King Avenir's summons went out through the country. He called for both the wise and the foolish in his letters, epistles, and messages. He invited Christians, Chaldeans, and Indians. He assured the Christians safe passage, promising not to cause them harm. The king summoned many people, and a vast multitude came. Never had there been such an assembly in his country, but the story tells us that the only Christians present were Josaphat and Barachie, a wise and respected man.[1] Only these two took the side of our Lord to defend him (Nachor was not a believer; he was a false Barlaam). The other Christians stayed in the wilderness hermitage. They did not dare to come argue the points of their religion, because they feared the king. They knew that a man who will not listen to reason will try to dominate reasonable men when he sees he cannot prove his belief to them.

The king and all his council came to the richly covered tents and pavilions erected a short way outside the city. The sides of the tents were raised so that the disputation could be heard by all, and the people assembled around King Avenir to listen. First the king imposed silence, so no one would interrupt the proceedings. He sat on a throne richer and more

precious than any ever seen. As the story tells it, King Avenir
did not have enough silver or gold in his treasury, nor was
there enough anywhere in the world, to match the value of
his throne. The rhetoricians, princes, nobles, knights, and
high clergy all had rich seats molded from gold and embel-
lished with more emeralds and precious stones than I can
name. Never in Athens or Troy was such a rich gathering
held (if the story does not mislead me), nor so many wise people ever assembled. I tell you the truth; I do not lie. John, a
bishop from Damascus, knew the story well and translated
it. Another John loaned us the book, and we borrowed it
from Arrouaise. This John was dean of Arras and was a good
Christian. He was a nobleman, from a great and noble family, and he loved the story of Barlaam. So the story came here
from one John through another.[2]

Gui de Cambrai, who translated this story into French and
put it into verse, says the king was seated at the parliament
when Josaphat arrived. The king welcomed his son and had
him seated beside him on a rich throne. Everyone admired
Josaphat's beauty, his manner, and, most of all, his wisdom.
King Avenir called for silence, and the people quieted. Nachor was brought forward. He pretended to be anxious and
sad. He called himself Barlaam, and the people thought he
really was Barlaam, but they were badly deceived. The disputation would be great, and the betrayal would be painful.
The traitors were wrong and they would suffer, for their false
belief would fail them. The nobles were apprehensive, and
King Avenir studied his son closely; he thought he could use
the disputation to deceive him, but God gave Josaphat true
understanding.

The people sat down. The king stood before them and
spoke loudly enough to be heard by all. "Now hear me, my
lord rhetoricians, grammarians, and philosophers! Today we
have assembled for an important debate and to put forward
claims and arguments that will defend our laws and faith so
a false religion is not promoted. If you win, each of you will
wear the crown of victory and receive honor, glory, and ac-

claim. If you do not win, you will all die. I will have you hanged or burned, and I will have your ashes thrown to the wind. I will seize all your possessions and sentence your heirs to eternal servitude. Now I have told you my intentions. I am emperor and king, and my words have been heard here before you all."

The king's son then declared so all could hear: "King, you have spoken with royal authority and justice. The judgment will be respected no matter who loses here. You have spoken as a good lord should, and I will do the same in addressing my master, whom I see here before me.

"Barlaam," Josaphat continued, turning to Nachor, "when you came to find me, I had many privileges and pleasures and I was happy and at peace in my palace. Then you chastised and counseled me until I left my parents' religion and became a Christian in exchange for the rewards God promises to those who love him. Barlaam, you promised me these rewards, and I left my religion because of them. Now I say to you that you must defend our religion against those assembled here. I do not want your lessons to be hidden. Let them be heard openly so your opponents will be confounded. At the close of their disputation, let them perceive without doubt that their belief is false. Let our glorious and precious light appear today. Let the holy spiritual sun appear.

"Today is like a precious stone: it should be glorious and full of great strength. This day is your shield. If God gives you the honor of victory today, I will serve him forever as best I can and with a true heart. But if you are vanquished, I will not hesitate to take immediate vengeance for my shame. I alone will act, and by the Lord I serve, no king or count or sergeant will touch you. I will tear your heart from your body with my own hands. If your words are struck down, the disputation will have mortal consequences for you. I will allow dogs to eat your body, and I will cut out your tongue to show that no one should be so presumptuous as to mislead the king's son and dishonor him."

When Nachor heard Josaphat's words, he began to feel

shame, for he was a wise and learned man. He understood that the king's son threatened him harshly, and he wanted to defend Josaphat's position, no matter how it might end. God caused his change of heart and made him defend our faith.

The Chaldeans begin the disputation with Nachor

The king sat on his throne and the crowd was silent. The son who caused him so much worry sat beside him, along with Barachie and Nachor. The king could see the treasure to be found in the truth that he wished to dispute.[1] The pagan philosophers, grammarians, and rhetoricians were lined up against Nachor, and they sharpened their wits, ready to destroy the good faith. The Indians waited to hear the disputation and see which side would win. The king commanded the arguments to begin. Each of the clerics should use his wisdom to try to best his opponent.

One of the rhetoricians rose to defend his religion in response to the king's command. He called proudly to Nachor and spoke haughtily: "Do not lie to us: are you this Barlaam who challenges us, along with the king and his son whom you corrupted and whom you taught to worship the crucified one? Are you the one who shamed our gods?"

"I truly am Barlaam," Nachor responded, "and your gods mean nothing to me. I converted the king's son and brought him into the good faith. I delivered him from death. All those who worship your mute gods are foolish and deceived. Our Lord, who dwells on high, will reward us for our faith."

The rhetorician responded, "Why then did our worthy ancestors, the wise rhetoricians, keep our faith? We are learned men, and we do not worship other gods because there are not any gods better than ours. Do not hide it from us: how do you dare to say there are other gods or another lord besides our gods, whom our religion commands us to love and worship? Our gods make counts and kings. They rule over all people, but your God was taken and bound and later crucified. Why do you believe in him? Why do you serve him? In serving him you abase yourself and become a servant. You are wrong to believe in one who could not prevent his own death."

Nachor responded in a reasoned and learned way.[2] He waved his hand to silence the people, and said to the king, "I came to you for God's sake and to save you from danger by showing you that this belief is false. Consider the earth and the sky, the sea and the sun. Look at the moon and all the elements—the air, the stars, and the winds. They must all move against their own will. A god who must move and cannot be still; this is not a true god. When he moves against his will, something makes him move, and the thing that makes him move has greater power than the god. Of what value is a god who moves, when he is not powerful enough to hold himself still? This is not a god, according to my belief. The one who makes him move, he is the god, for he has the strength to make the elements move.

"Let us consider more closely the ways in which we believe. The Christian fears God, but the pagan is blind and does not acknowledge him. Christians love the pious Jesus, but the Jews worship in error: they recognize the Creator but they are lost in their religion and do not understand the good faith. They remain in sin because of it, and they too are blind. Their religion is like a covered cup. Under the cup's cover there is good wine, but they believe it holds only dregs. They are deceived, and they do not taste the wine. They do not understand that the scriptures gloss their holy book, and that their religion is written figuratively.

"There are three kinds of people who worship false gods (the gods are false because they cannot think and they are not alive), and I will name them to you: the Egyptians, the Greeks, and the Chaldeans. They invented their religions from their own foolish ideas, and they defend them out of habit. They are masters of the false religions they themselves created.

"Now let us consider these false religions and whether there is any truth in them. The Chaldeans were the earliest, and I will first speak about how they began to worship the elements. They made statues of them, using rich and valuable materials. They used their own craft to make gods, and they held the gods they made dearer than their own Creator. They made their lords out of molten gold. It is fitting that such gods be guarded carefully, for they could be stolen! There is no intelligence in these gods if they have to fear for their theft. How can these gods save me when they cannot save themselves from others? How can they care for others when they cannot care for themselves? There is no reason in these gods. They are full of corruption and have corrupted many others. So I say to you by clear reasoning: these gods know nothing and they are worth nothing since they cannot save themselves. You should know that whoever makes a church or altar for them is foolish.

"King, now let us consider the elements, so that it can be heard before these people what sort of sanctity the elements may have and whether they have any power. I say that those who hold the sky as their creator make a foolish error. There can be no deity in the sky because it turns against its own will, and since it can be forced to turn without ceasing, I submit that anyone who makes the sky his god is foolish and misguided. (It is logical that whatever is made has a beginning and an end, and so this god begins and ends. This is a subtle distinction and important to understand, for a god cannot have a beginning, and my God never began and will never end.) The sky cannot be still since it moves with its light, and the stars that dwell there move from sign to sign. They disappear and then they rise again according to nature's laws, for time is regulated: there are winter stars and summer stars. So the sky turns. In one season it brings heat, and in the other it brings cold. It is constrained to act in this way, and I have proven that for this reason the sky cannot be a god."

One of the wise and learned masters rose and said, "Now listen to this. We all agree that the earth is a god, and I do not think you can dispute it, for we live from her fruits. She causes the grass to appear, meadows to flower, and trees to bear leaves. She gives us a great abundance of bread, wine, and meat. Without her, we could not live a single day. I submit to you that the earth most certainly is a god that we should worship."

Nachor responded, "You do not speak the truth. The earth has no power, for men shame it regularly for their own needs. They wound it where formerly it was whole. They have no pity for it and walk on it with their feet. In many foolish ways they take a great ransom from it. They plow and break it, and it seems to me that the earth is often stained with blood. It is a sepulcher for the dead, and it rots with the bodies. It can also die and never again bear fruit. The sower who would spread seed in such a place is a fool. For this reason I rightly prove that the earth cannot be a god—whether or not it wishes, the earth must suffer wounds and die."

Another cleric rose and spoke eloquently: "Since you have shown the logic by which the earth cannot be called a god or considered divine, then I say that, on the other hand, water is certainly a god, and I will prove it. All people need to wash and to bathe, and they need the fish she gives us. She devotes her power to providing what we need in many ways. For this reason, I say that water is a god, and no master can contradict me."

Nachor responded: "It is not like that—your false belief has betrayed you. The water that your tongue praises is subordinate to man, for man can easily make it bloody or give it some other color, and it can be corrupted and stained. It can be chilled and frozen or used to clean away filth. The scriptures reveal to us that water is God's creation. And so I prove that it is not a god."

One of the other rhetoricians was the brother of Plato and

strongly opposed to the Christians.[3] He was a tall, thin,
white-haired man, and he was richly dressed in silk and wore
an elegant hat. His face was ugly and his hair braided; his
beard fell to his waist, and it too was woven into many braids.
He was faithful to his pagan religion. His eyebrows brushed
his eyes, and he had a very proud look. He held a staff in one
hand and with the other he arranged his hat. He spoke impa-
tiently to Nachor. "Heed my words," he said. "Fire is a god,
as you know very well. All Christians know it, for they use
him daily. No one will dispute this. Fire serves many needs,
for he cooks food and warms people. He also makes our
courts more beautiful. Fire succors us in a thousand ways. It
is then true, do not mistake it, that fire truly is a god, for he
helps all people."

Nachor responded, "Not so quickly. Allow me to respond,
if you please. There is no doubt that God made fire so it could
serve us. A man carries a flame from one place to another to
light a fire, and he cooks meat with it. But I tell you that whoever makes a flame into a god is foolish. Fire was never a god,
nor should it be taken for one. Master, reconsider this god.
Can one not extinguish a fire? Whoever crowns it puts it out.
A god that can be constrained is a bad god, and I do not
know of anything that can constrain a real god. And for this
reason I prove, according to your logic, that fire is not a god
and has no deity in it. Our Lord created it."

Varro, a great grammarian (his brother was Caesar), rose
upon hearing these words. He was wise and learned, but he
was also rash—he trusted so much in his own intelligence
that he became impulsive. He began to sharpen his tongue
and called for silence. Then he spoke logically: "If you would
deny that the wind is a god, then I will prove it using reason.
You err when you disparage our gods. You dispute with us
before the king who stands here as our judge and lord, but
your only argument is to shame our gods. You cannot refute
my claim that the wind most certainly is a god, for when the
earth is wet and inundated with rain, the wind blows across
it to dry it and restore its former beauty. When people are hot

in the summer, the wind comes to cool them. If you admit reason, you have to judge that the wind is a god and also one of the elements. He is a true god, as I believe in good faith and so should you."

"Friend, this is not right at all," Nachor responded. "You speak against the scriptures' lessons. The wind was made and serves others, and whoever believes that the wind is a god is mistaken and lost, for it does not rule over anything. And since it does not rule, then it was made to serve, and a god cannot be a servant. A god would be shamed by serving others, and so I say that the wind cannot be a god. When the wind is forced to grow strong and weak, then it has no mastery over anything. No one can say that the wind is a lord."

Amalichon, an Indian who hated Christians, rose to his feet, angry and disdainful of Nachor. He was Aristotle's nephew and companion, and he was cruel and sharp-tongued, but also wise, brave, and wealthy. His learning and his lineage would have given him great authority if he had put his understanding in God. He was lord of a city. He was learned, generous, and noble, and he was descended from Saint Denise. He had one hundred knights with him, and the court was under his control. If anyone made trouble, he would take cruel vengeance for it, and for this reason he spoke without fear.

He began to harangue Nachor (he thought he would win the dispute this way): "We should believe without doubt that we will always be blind if the sun does not shine and give us light. Our eyes are worth nothing to us if the sun does not illuminate us with his light. He lights the day, and day does not dawn if the sun's light does not appear. Your reasoning is completely false if you argue that the sun is not a god. There is nothing to dispute here, for everyone believes it. The entire firmament is illuminated with his precious light. There is no denying it."

"You have spoken well for someone who is in error," Nachor responded. "But if you are truly wise, you will see that you are wrong. By your leave, I will show you that you have

your argument backward when you make the sun a god because of its light. This cannot be, for notice, dear master,
that the sun rises against its will and sets out of necessity.
And when its light is brightest, it has to accept that a cloud
can cover it. Its rays are hidden when it is cloudy and its
strength is compromised. Whoever makes the sun a god has
no understanding. The sun was made for man and serves
him. Moreover, it is less than the firmament. For this I say
with confidence, I have shown the proof, that there is no
power in the sun—the sun is not a god and should not be.
Whoever makes a god of the sun is mistaken."

Tanthaplamos rose quickly at these words. He was enraged that Nachor had slandered his gods. He was a Chal-
dean, born in Lesser India, and he was a good and wise
cleric. He knew many languages and all the liberal arts. He
had made the moon his god (remember that the Chaldeans
worshipped the elements as gods). "I will show you through
reason that the moon must be recognized as a god," he said.
"Her divinity is demonstrated in her ability to choose her
shape: she is horned when she wishes or round. And yet when
she appears there is not less of her, nor is there more. She
merely gives less of herself to the world when she gives less of
her light. No one can fail to serve her as a god. This is what
the Chaldeans believe and anyone who wishes to find true
belief should also believe it."

Nachor responded with reason: "Using your own argument, I will show that the truth is the opposite of what you
claim when you make the moon into a god. This cannot be
and never will be, and the scriptures do not recognize it. You
have deceived yourself. I do not know anything about a god
with horns—the moon goes into an eclipse and disappears,
when it should be most powerful. According to this logic, the
moon becomes both larger and smaller. No one can convince
me that a god can wax or wane. Your astronomy is false
when it claims that the moon is a god. The moon is a work of
God who created it."

Aradynes suffered when he heard his gods and his lord so

strongly slandered, and it is no wonder if he was troubled. He rose furiously and looked angrily at Nachor. He wanted to offer a strong and unforgiving challenge. "Master," he said, "it is not right to argue with us about such fundamental things. We are all angry about it. We Chaldeans speak now and later the Greeks will take their turn. It is a great endeavor to defend yourself against all of us, but there would be no need of defense if you understood the truth."

"You are wrong," Nachor responded, "but your words comfort me. You speak from error, but I trust in reason. Reason will give weight to your argument, if you know how to use it, for there is great weight in reason. Whoever recognizes reason understands what is right. But now say what you wish to say, and I will respond without anger."

"I want you to acknowledge your arrogance," said Aradynes. "You have attacked our beliefs and denounced water, earth, fire, wind, sun, and moon. I am surprised the king allows it. But now hear this: since they were all made to serve man, then I tell you that man himself is a god, and I will show it to you by reason. Man has dominion over everything—he holds wealth, honor, power, and nobility under his power. He is lord over many people who praise and honor him and bow before him and worship him."

Nachor responded wisely: "By faith, you lie and yet you speak the truth. It is true that God was born as a man—so I say to you that it is true that God is a man. But you mean it another way, so you are wrong when you say that god is a man. That is a great lie. A man is born and enjoys his youth. Then he grows old and feeble. He is sometimes sad and sometimes happy. He needs to dress himself and to eat and drink. He experiences regret and becomes envious, angry, and covetous. He is base and often corrupted. He can be wounded by swords and lances, and inevitably he will die. So it is foolish to claim that god is a man and man is a god, as the Chaldeans believe. But Christians understand this differently: God came down from heaven to take human form, and God became a man, not by mistake, but to redeem us from death. And so I tell you that because he was born in this world for our sakes, God is a man, but it cannot be true in any other sense."

The Chaldeans were beaten, and none responded further, for they did not dare dispute Nachor when they saw themselves so well confounded.

The Greeks join the disputation

Maximilian, a cleric who was very learned about the Greek's religion, saw that the wise Chaldeans had been silenced, so he rose and addressed the king. "My lord, I do not know what to say. The Chaldeans spoke well and Barlaam refuted them. But we do not share the same religion. As I understand it, the Chaldeans worship all the elements, and it is fitting that they do so. But this devil leads us astray. Let him now ready his tongue to meet our challenge.

"We have gods and we know that they are gods. Our gods have proven themselves worthy, for they come to the aid of all those who pray to them for mercy. I will speak the truth about Saturn, who is one of our gods.[1] He is worthy of great honor, for his deity is great. He is the lord of the elements. He is the god who first formed all the firmament, and he made all people. In his first book, Ovid tells us that Saturn commanded the world to be created, and for this reason everything exists according to his design."

"Listen, King, to how senseless this religion is," Nachor said. "The Greeks believe foolish things, and they make gods from twin images, some male, some female. Their belief is greatly impoverished and they do not know what they say. Now they make a god of Saturn! Certainly he is no god, for Jupiter, his son, killed him, as Ovid tells us. He cast his father into hell and conquered the sky, to become its lord and commander. And he threw the good members of his father into the deep sea. There Venus, the goddess of love, was conceived in a wave, and then there was no longer night or day. Woe to him who would recount this story as if it were true and have us believe it! It is nothing but an invented fable, and those who would have us believe it are servants of the devil."

At these words Mandran rose, grieved by what he heard. "What?" he asked. "What do you mean? That Jupiter is not lord of the gods with power over the heavens? What Ovid recounted is true, for we find it in holy books, and Ovid was a wise man who spoke only the truth. You will not dare to attack Jupiter! He changes into many forms, and we should serve him. He acts as he pleases and he is an exalted and powerful god. He is so wise and valiant that no one can oppose him without abasing himself. I do not think you will dare to confront him, for even if you only appeared to slander him, he would take a cruel vengeance. I warn you to say nothing against him. You would not be able to oppose him unless you used some trick or ruse."

Nachor laughed. "Friend," he asked, "have you lost your mind? You speak like a madman. You say that Jupiter is a god—he who bound his father hand and foot and put him in hell? And that is the least of it: this Jupiter of whom you speak was conceived in adultery. Ha! What a learned claim! Woe to anyone who makes a god of one engendered from adultery.

"I will tell you who he was. I have learned that he was disloyal and lascivious, and he did many evil deeds. Jupiter used magic to take many different forms, and he took after his father in that he committed adultery many times. He took the form of a bull for the daughter of King Agenor. Europa was the girl's name, and she was comely and beautiful. One day she was by herself in a meadow, a short distance from the city, when Jupiter came galloping toward her in the form of a bull. She welcomed him and made him a crown of flowers. She did not suspect any tricks, but Jupiter betrayed her. When she sat on his back, he galloped away with her beyond the sea to a place where her royal father had no power. There he took her virginity. The news spread through the country that Europa had been lost. When Agenor heard it, he sent his son Cadmus away until he could return with his daughter. Cadmus was then banished, for he would never find her. The story recounts that he left his father's country and when he did not find Europa and did not know where else to seek her, he built Thebes. Since Cadmus could not find his sister, he stayed there. His father and mother mourned their son and lamented their misfortune—King Agenor had lost his son along with his daughter, and he claimed that he was cursed, since from one harm he had made two.

"That time, your god changed into a bull," Nachor continued. "Another time he made himself into gold to trick Danaë, but she did not perceive the deception until he had betrayed her. For another lover, Leda, he changed into a swan. It is not reasonable to think he is divine, for this is not good or fitting behavior for a god. Another time he changed into a satyr for Antiope, and into lightning for Semele. Jupiter was a deranged and licentious man, and he had many children with these women. One was called Liber, a second Zethus, and other children were Hercules and Apollo, Artemis and Amphion, and Perseus and Castor and Helen and Pollux, and Sarpedon and Rhadamanthus. Minos too was one of his offspring. These are his sons—he also had nine daughters. Only a foolish devil-god would engender so many children. On the other hand—King, do you not know this?—he was a great sodomite and had with him a sweet young man called Ganymede."

(What worthy acts from these filthy and heretical gods, when they make a female from the male! I will speak of such acts briefly, for I want to condemn them here.[2]

You who denature nature by breaking her laws, listen a little to this. May God never have mercy on you as long as you practice such unnatural sin! Ah, shameful sodomites! You play a shameful game when you pervert the chessboard and allow yourselves to be mated from the corner—to mate in the right way is much better.[3] You will never share God's joy as long as you allow yourselves to be mated in this way. Whoever would admonish you should speak harshly of such acts. But for all this, you do not stop. Whoever lets himself be mated without a queen goes against nature, and it is much to be lamented when the chessboard is sullied by such a disloyal stain.

Whoever deliberately spreads his seed where it will not grow disobeys nature, and may God allow you to perish, perverse Romans and Frenchmen. The evil game came from the Greeks and now it has entered Champagne and thrives in France. The clerics were first to adopt it, and they taught the game to knights. The deed is base—anyone who would leave the clearing for the woods is like a foolish peasant. Indeed, the act is so vile and nasty that even to speak of it is evil, and so I will leave off here and return to the story and to Nachor, who responded so well to the Greeks that he confounded them. He described Jupiter truthfully when he said that he was full of trickery, and that he was an adulterer and a sodomite, an enchanter and a heretic.)

"King," said Nachor, "listen to me. These Greeks make an adulterer their god. They have a base religion and are deluded, for what they say cannot be true. They all believe in bad gods. Whoever can refute them should respond harshly. They do not know anything about God, and what they think of as divine is just trickery. They should keep quiet about Jupiter, for he was an evil character. They should abandon their gods and their beliefs, for there is no truth in them."

Archemorus rose and spoke loudly. He could not hide his anger when he heard his gods slandered. He was distressed by Nachor's characterization of Jupiter as an indolent and licentious adulterer. He did not know how to defend his gods except by making a good argument: "You would not deny that we should worship Vulcan as a god, for he is most powerful. He is the best and most valiant smith in the world and he should not be denied."

Nachor was alarmed by Archemorus's claim: he made a god from a blacksmith! "King," said Nachor, "he who makes Vulcan his god would deceive us. Vulcan was a blacksmith, and he forged to earn his livelihood. I have never heard of a god so poor that he had to use his skill to gain food and shelter. This is mistaken belief."

Ebruaceus rose, aggrieved by Nachor's words. "If Vulcan cannot be a god," he argued, "we must seek others. Master, can Mercury not be a god? He has done many wonders. I advise you to consider whether he could be a god."

"Surely I have not understood you," Nachor responded. "Mercury was an evil fortune teller and a covetous thief. Such a being cannot be a god, and it is shameful to believe that he is divine."

Sergestus rose and asked, "Is Aesculapius not a good god?"

Nachor responded, "No, good friend. He knew how to make potions and poultices and other things. But you are foolish to argue that a doctor should be a god—that is perverse and contrary to reason. In the end Jupiter killed him with a bolt of lightning because he had wrongly killed the son of Darius of Lacedaemon. If this Aesculapius were a god, he would have saved himself, but he could not. Thus I dare to judge that only a fool would make him a god."

Narradien stood. He hated Nachor and grew angry when he heard him speak: "I hear you say many false things, but you will not deny that it is right to sacrifice to Mars and honor him as a god of war. We hold him as our lord."

Nachor responded, "It would never occur to me that Mars could be considered a god. Oh Lord! What a god we would have in him! He is a sheep eater and took a licentious old goddess named Venus as his lover.[4] Vulcan, your god there in the heavens, was also her lover, and he discovered her with his friend Mars and chained them together. Only a foolish god could be caught in such shame. And if he was so talented in war, why did he not save himself from Vulcan who bound and shamed him?

"Do not continue to stand and name others, for I will say more about your gods than you can, if you will hear me. You make Bacchus divine, and you say that he is the lord of wine because he drank a lot and seduced other men's wives. He

was drunk every night, for drinking was his greatest pleasure, and in the end he was killed." (What will they do, those
who drink wine and become drunk and then lie about it
when they are accused? I put the blame on others, but I am at
greater fault than any from here to Salerno, for I do business
in taverns just like Bacchus, whom Nachor considered base
and showed to be a wanton drunkard, not a god.)[5]

Nachor also spoke of Hercules, greatly esteemed by the
Greeks, and said that by reason no one should think he was a
god. "He was as licentious as the others I have described. He
was also very cruel. He killed his wife and sons, the story
tells us, and in the end he was burned in a fire. Only a foolish
and base god would allow himself to be burned.

"I will also tell you the truth about Apollo. He was a minstrel and a good hunter. He spoke to people and told fortunes
to earn his wealth. I do not know what to say of a god who
sells his tricks. Diana—who was his sister, I will tell you the
truth about her—was considered a goddess by the Greeks because she was a great hunter, and she liked to train hunting
dogs. She loved the woods and rivers and knew them well.
King, you can judge whether such a goddess should be vener-
ated.

"These gods should be forgotten. No one can say why such
people should be made into gods, and there is a great misun-
derstanding here. The Greeks scorn God and his love because of their false beliefs, but no man should doubt him, for
he is Lord and God."

Another of the Greeks stood to challenge Nachor. "You
have insulted our gods, but you do not know what you say
when you abase them. You say that Diana is nothing but a
huntress, but what would you say about the goddess Venus?
Show me here, before the king, if you have found any fault in
her, for she is worthy of great devotion."

Nachor responded, "Friend, here, before the king and his
people, I will tell you who Venus is. I will not say more or less
than this: she was a disloyal wanton woman, and she did
many evil things in this world. And she took too many de-

bauched men as lovers: Mars, Vulcan, Adonis, and also Anchises."

This Anchises was the father of Aeneas, who was a lord of the land and lived happily in his house outside Troy.[6] Dares Phrygius tells us that Aeneas betrayed his lord, King Priam, who had given him great honors. Now I will tell you the story truly, for Virgil, who also tells it, wrongly excuses Aeneas for everything. Dares accused him of betrayal, and he was at the siege of Troy and knew the truth of the story.[7] Do not hold it against me, my lords, if I stray a little from the story, for I need to abridge it to show the truth—it would be too long if I recounted the whole siege of Troy and, by your leave, I will recount it here in a few words.

A great army was mustered because Helen had been kidnapped, and the Greeks assembled from all parts: kings, dukes, princes, and counts—all came together to avenge their shame. They camped before Troy and besieged the city from all sides. Those inside the city sent for help, and knights came from every land. Great and worthy men besieged Troy. Noble Hector, the greatest of all knights, was killed there. He was well matched—noble Achilles killed him, as the story tells us. Achilles took vengeance on Hector because he had killed his companion Patroclus. Later Achilles regretted it, when he was killed because he took Polyxena as his lover. Her brother Paris spied on Achilles at the temple, then killed him there. Polyxena did not know about it, but vengeance for Achilles's death turned against her. Dares recounts that Pyrrhus, Achilles's son, tortured her and dragged her naked through the city by her hair. Pyrrhus acted ruthlessly to avenge his father, and the wretched, innocent maiden paid the price. And Aeneas, who accused her of the betrayal and delivered her to Pyrrhus, betrayed Troy shamefully. Not a king or count was spared death. This is what Dares tells us truthfully. He says, if I am not mistaken, that Troy burned for three days, and that Aeneas betrayed the city and fled as soon as he could. The story tells us that his wife was burned and died there. When he saw the city was on fire, he went to

the boats that he had provisioned. He put to sea and good
winds took him to port in Crete. From Crete he went to Car-
thage. If the story does not lie, Dido was queen there, and she
loved Aeneas greatly. Aeneas told her everything about the
siege of Troy and its burning, but he lied about the end. He
recounted the destruction, but he hid his treason. He remained with Dido for a long time. Then he had to leave her,
and when he no longer wanted to stay with her, she killed
herself for his love. He crossed the sea with a great force and
arrived in Lombardy, in the land of King Latinus.

At first his arrival caused fear among the people, but later
he became lord of the land and led it in many wars. Before
that, the king's daughter Lavinia became queen, and Aeneas
won her in battle against Turnus. He married the beautiful
young woman and gained her rich land. Aeneas had a greatly
renowned son called Ascanius, and Romulus, founder of
Rome, and Remus, founder of Rheims, were from Aeneas's
lineage. They were brothers, but Romulus became emperor.

Their descendants included Brutus, who freed Corineus
and Locrinus from slavery in Greece. He brought them along
with a great company into the land of Aquitaine. Turnus was
killed there, along with his people, I believe. They founded a
great city and named it Tours in honor of Turnus. Then they
left and passed through Neustria. (They conquered Neustria,
which we now call Normandy.) They crossed the sea in great
numbers, and when they came to port they conquered En-
gland after a long and arduous war. At that time the land
was unclaimed and Brutus called it Britannia. He had London built to restore Troy, and they said that the city was built
to resemble Troy. Corineus chose a part of the land and gave
his name to it, and accordingly they named it Cornwall. Locrinus was on the other side of the country, and by right he
named his land Logres. The land was divided, and Brutus
was its overlord; as its emperor and king he made laws and
established customs.[8]

This is what the Trojans did, but no matter who claims
that Aeneas was a faithful man, I maintain that he was dis-

loyal and that he caused the betrayal and destruction of Troy. Everyone in the country came from his lineage—the foolish and the wise, kings, dukes, princes, and counts—and Virgil hid his shame. This is what these people did and how they ended their days. Aeneas was the son of Venus and Anchises. Now there is nothing more to say, and I will return to the story.

Nachor concludes his refutation of the pagans

Nachor spoke reasonably and did not seek to quarrel. He demonstrated his learning before the king and his people by refuting the Greeks. He showed that they should not believe in the deity of Venus: "This Adonis, her lover, do you not know how he died? I will tell you the truth, for I know it well. It is true that he was a very good hunter. (The story would be too long if I were to tell you how he came to her and then what happened to him, so I will tell you only a part.) One day Adonis went hunting with his dogs (this pagan was wise and knew the forest well). He was very tired when he came upon a great boar, and it attacked him. Adonis understood that he would die if he could not defend himself, but he had not expected danger and was unarmed. The boar charged, struck him in the groin, and killed him. Venus despaired at his death. She cries for him still and will continue to mourn as long as the world endures.

"King, consider my words, and acknowledge that the Greeks have been defeated. They have responded poorly and their claims are found false. I have proven to you that they speak falsehoods. They betray themselves, for they would have you believe things that can be disproved by logic. They make gods out of licentious men and thieves. We know that we should not believe in these gods or serve them, nor should we worship or cherish them. We should not do anything for them if they sin against God.

"Good king, my lord, you have heard what the Greeks had to say," Nachor continued. "You have heard the Chaldeans, and now you will hear the Egyptians, and you will see how well they speak and with what reasoning they will try to defend their faith. Listen well to how they will try to prove their religion before me. You will hear the disputation and you will judge whether they are able to use reason to prove that they are right. If they wish to speak before I do, I would first tell them that their belief is just as bad as those we have already heard about, and according to God, we hold it to be false. But if none dares to come forward, then I will speak to show reason through logic and without dispute. You are the king and you will judge who will have the upper hand."

Ptolemy was born in Egypt, and it grieved him to see Nachor disdain his religion, so he spoke up loudly. He marveled that the king never said a word and that he did not show anger either before or after Nachor spoke. Ptolemy himself was angry that the king did not say anything.

This Ptolemy of whom I speak was the most learned man in the world in physics and astronomy. I do not lie when I tell you that he was the son of that Ptolemy who killed his lord Pompey. Caesar had exiled Pompey and led a great war against him. Pompey fled and came to Ptolemy, who was his vassal and held his fief from him.[1] He came to Ptolemy for protection, but Ptolemy saw his lord was weak and vulnerable, and he betrayed and killed him because he wanted to serve Caesar and do his will. He cut off Pompey's head and presented it to Caesar. "My lord," he said, "I come to tell you that I have ended your war. Let peace be my reward. I have earned your love by killing my lord for you." "I am truly sad that it is so," said Caesar. "I will give you your reward according to the words of your own song: you are an enemy to us all since you have killed your lord. I could not trust you if you would kill your lord without hesitation. You have earned not love but death." He had him seized immediately and beheaded in front of his people. This is the kind of love and reward that traitors should receive.

The Ptolemy who stood before the king was the son of that Ptolemy executed by Caesar for the murder of his lord. He was a wise cleric, very learned and respected. He was a noble man from a great lineage and spoke well in his own language. (His speech would have been faultless if there had been any truth in what he said.) "I don't know who you are," said Ptolemy, "but you are too rash. The Egyptians have a better religion than any I see here. You are foolish, and I am dismayed that you would contradict us in this way. Our religion cannot be denied, and you cannot dispute it, for there is no lie in it."

Nachor responded courteously: "You speak reasonably, and I regret that you have fallen into such error, for I see you are a wise and handsome man and appear to come from a noble family. But attend to my words if you would understand my argument that the Egyptians are foolish and know little about what is good.

"They lack good sense when they make Isis their goddess. This Isis about whom I speak took her brother Osiris as her husband. They had a son named Horus, who was a handsome young man and looked like his father. Typhon killed Osiris, who was his brother, and Horus took vengeance for it—he avenged his father and uncle against his uncle.

"This is good material for gods!" Nachor exclaimed. "Everyone should believe in them! Their divinity is good and true! King Avenir, for God's sake, their foolishness is obvious. Do not believe the Egyptians, for they lie openly to you. Their belief is clearly wrong—we really should not even listen to them. They make a sheep into a god, and a bull and a heifer, a crocodile and a pig. They make gods of an eagle and a hawk. Against all reason they make a cat into a god, and a wolf, a dog, or a dragon. Since there is no logic in any of that, let them understand according to reason that they cannot defend their gods, because their powers are too weak." The

Egyptians, the Greeks, and the Chaldeans heard that he had argued well against them.

"I marvel at one thing," Nachor continued. "That devils persuade them to make gods out of murderers and traitors! The books of philosophers and poets have revealed the falsity of their belief. The books about their faith that have been translated have not revived it. King, consider reason now, since I have put the question to rest: the ancient authorities tell us that the gods are of one nature, but since one of their gods can kill another, the nature of these gods is divided. When one is condemned by the other, the gods' will is divided since they do not share a common desire, and they do not care about what is right since they act against nature. The stories that preserve their memory are fictions. Physics and astronomy show them to be wrong, and these gods' divinity is proved only by allegory. I will show you more, if you will hear it, King. You know that the Egyptians, the Greeks, and the Chaldeans do not believe in the Creator, nor do they know him as Lord. Now let us consider how the Jews believe.

"When God liberated them from Egypt, he held them dear. They had lived as wretched slaves in the service of Pharaoh. God parted the sea and they passed through. The water never touched them, but those who pursued them were drowned when the sea closed again. Moses, their master, announced their salvation to them, but they did not heed him and betrayed themselves through their lack of faith. The scriptures tell us that Moses wrote the law in Sinai. The Jews did not understand it, and their belief was wrong.

"Prophets announced the coming of our Lord, according to their religion. My lord, good king, listen to me. He was born among them, but they did not recognize their Lord. He took flesh and blood in the virgin Saint Mary, and she never had the company of a man. This is the truth: her virginity was not damaged or destroyed, corrupted or violated. She was a virgin before and a virgin afterward, she remained a virgin then and is one now. Despite her virginity, by truth, miracle, reason, and power, our Lord became human in her and was born among us through this miracle. He willingly suffered death: they put him on a cross like a thief, and he accepted it in order to redeem us. Then, by his commandment, on the third day he was resurrected. For forty days he spoke with his disciples, and each day he showed them how they should preach his Holy Name. After forty days they saw our Lord raised into heaven. The apostles went throughout the world and preached the sacraments of Christianity, and for this reason they are called Christians. One of them, I believe, came to preach in this country and announced the holy law that Christians hold in faith.[2]

"They followed the truth, and those who follow it today will be great lords in paradise forever. Christians have a true belief, for they know God truly and they believe in him. This makes them true Christians. They are bound by truth, and there is no untruth in them. Their religion does not mislead them, for they believe in the light that illuminates the whole world. If you consider it carefully, you will see that I do not deceive you with my words. Christians are in the right path, but misbelief leads the Saracens and the pagans astray and sets them against the Christians, who speak truly of God. They are of God, they come from God, and they belong to God. They dwell with him today and forever.

"I do not speak lightly. Do not believe me, believe the scriptures. They bear witness to these truths. I do not tell lies, but everything these men say to you is false. Beware of their lies. Your clerics do not draw on the testimony of an ancient book, and they are so ignorant that they speak as though they were inebriated. I believe they will keep quiet now. Their responses have failed, and you would be wrong not to have them burned or hanged. You should take vengeance on them when they abandon their Creator and promote the idea that there are other gods and other religions. Take care, my lord king, to see if they can prove it by reason according to the words of our lesson."

Nachor heeds his own words

Nachor spoke very well, and King Avenir listened to him carefully. The king was pained and angry, but Josaphat was most happy. The king's clerics all kept quiet. None of them responded to Nachor, and that was how it should be: no man should speak against reason and right, for reason confounds those who offer unreason, and whoever is guided by reason can easily overcome those who speak against it. Whatever speeches and debate, whatever great pride and unreason the king's clerics brought to the defense of a false belief, they could not have convinced anyone.

The king's son rejoiced when he saw that his side was defended so well by an enemy who did not know God. He heard a true judgment spoken by a mouth that did not know reason. Nachor's arguments confounded his companions. He shared their lack of belief, but he judged them in his arguments. He was against them even though he shared their religion, and he spoke so well for the Christian religion that everyone took him for a Christian. The king was speechless: he dared not show his anger to Nachor since he had instructed him to argue well for the Christians, and he had repeated his instructions before the entire assembly. But the king had meant something else; he did not anticipate that things would turn out as they had. He was certain that Nachor would let himself be vanquished in the dispute, but he defended himself with logic and proofs, like a good cleric, and he vanquished all the others.

The disputation was lengthy, and they heard arguments until evening. The king wanted to restart the debate in the morning, and so he ended the proceedings and they all separated for the night. Josaphat said to the king, "Sire, you have held a good trial today, and your side has been bested. It is fitting that your clerics go with you and that my master accompany me. We will go to my palace to consider how we will respond to further arguments. This is reasonable, I

believe, and if you wish it otherwise, you will have to im-
pose your force, and that would not be appropriate. Sire, I
have chosen the good side, and you should not use force
here if you do not want to undo reason. A king who gives
himself over to unreason will be judged to have forfeited
his crown."

The king understood the justice of his son's advice and marveled at his wisdom. His intelligence exceeded his age, for his
astute understanding did not reflect his youth. The king agreed
to all he asked, and he regretted that Josaphat believed in the
Creator. He truly believed that Josaphat was wrong, but he
himself erred more foolishly than his son. King Avenir was
sorry that his rhetoricians had not defended their faith. He
thought that Nachor would convert his son, and so he agreed
to accompany the clerics who despite reason refused to believe. Nachor went with Josaphat.

The prince went joyfully to his palace. He was happy because Nachor had won the day—he had confounded the pagans who could not respond to his reasoning. He called
Nachor aside. "I know that you are not the Barlaam who
preached the Christian life to me," he said. "You are the astronomer Nachor. I am very angry that you would try to trick
me into mistaking a wolf for a lamb in plain daylight. It would
have been a serious offense to deceive me, but it has gone well
for us today, since although you are foolish and ignorant, you
spoke with great learning to gain the advantage in the disputation. Do not hide it, Nachor! You are a wise councilor, but
your great intelligence does you no good. It remains in shadow,
even though it glimpses the light of day. Your intelligence is
dead and lodges in a dead man, for you die when you do not
believe. Is the religion you have defended today not a good
one?

"Your coins are worthless because they were not well
struck, and by your coins I mean your intelligence: it has not
been cast in the right mint. You see what is right, but from a
distance. Your view is troubled, and if your sight were in-
formed by your intelligence, rectitude would be restored. But

you refuse to see what you understand. Rectitude rightly teaches that clerics should be like knights. A cleric must be good at learning, just as the knight must be able to defend himself. The cleric must perceive deception and use debate to defend himself and do battle, but against whom? Against the lords of hell. No one will ever be so well covered with armor that the devil's sword cannot pierce his thoughts. A man's thoughts are his only protection, and they must be strong enough to defend him against the devil, who attacks constantly.

"Nachor, the Lord you defended today teaches you. You have vanquished yourself in your victory, and if your heart does not learn from it, you will have lost the victory you earned. You won but you have also lost if you do not repent. Consider your thoughts: you knowingly kill yourself, and yet you know very well whom you serve! You serve evil and yet you recognize the good. Your works go against your intentions. If you know good and you do evil, your works work against you. How can you refuse the truth? You know the good, you wish to lodge it in yourself, but your works make you a liar. You speak the truth but you lie in your works. Your sin is obvious when you do not act according to what you know.

"Friend, you are truly learned, but your works do not reflect your knowledge. I find your tongue sterile, for your heart goes against your words, and you continue to refuse what your heart commands. You abandon your heart and then you destroy it when you allow it to be ruled by evil. Sin is born in your heart and betrays you. Do you know what the peasant says in his book of proverbs? 'The worker is known by his works.' Your works show who you are, and I find you to be an evil man. Evil possesses you if you do not tear it out by the root that has taken hold in your heart. Friend, examine your thoughts and use your intelligence to seek the truth, for your time is short. You cannot decide the time of your death, and you are wrong to kill yourself through sin. Your repentance will be heavy, for you do not sin out of ignorance:

you know very well that you do wrong. Your intelligence betrays you, and if your heart does not repent of the folly you
have undertaken, the judgment will be harsh. Give God
thanks for your victory today and put yourself in his glory
since he taught you to speak so well. Good friend, God
formed you carefully in his image and today he spoke the
truth through your lips. Make a place for him in your heart
since he has come to you! Acknowledge him, since your Lord
has come to lead you out of error. Believe in your Lord and
you will do a good thing! Nachor, you know that the pagan
clerics have no truth in them—you have shown it today.

"Now listen to what I say to you: I brought you here for
two reasons. First, because if you had gone with the king, I
believe he would have caused trouble for you, since today you
spoke the truth against his will. And second, because I will
reward you for speaking so well for me today before the king.
But now hear what the reward is: if you will follow the counsel of your own reason and intelligence, you can enter the
path of salvation. Nachor, you have understood that it is not
right to hold to other beliefs and other faiths. We should believe only in the Creator who divided night from day. You
know that you will not remain long in this world. You are
not so strong that you will live longer than others. And if you
cling to the world, you know that you cannot live longer than
it does, and friend, the world will end. When your body dies,
the world will end for you. You sin more gravely than others,
for you understand that the world comes and goes, and you
know how we should live in it and how we should believe. I
see that you knowingly believe what is wrong. You believe in
false gods, with full awareness of your error. Your works
judge your belief."

Nachor sighed piteously when he heard the king's son describe his error with such compassion. "Sire," he said, "I
know that at Judgment Day I will hear my sentence. I know
with certainty that there is only one God who made the
world. The holy scriptures taught it to me, and this knowledge lights my heart. I know that we should cease bad prac-

tices as quickly as possible. I love God with all my heart. The
scriptures and my own reason have shown me that I should
not serve any other. I will serve him, for I believe in him."

The king's son rejoiced to see Nachor enter the right path
in response to his exhortation. He encouraged him gently:
"Friend, have good faith, for it is a sin to lose hope. As soon
as you ask for forgiveness, you will have it—I promise you.
Your crown will be prepared for you if your heart devotes itself wholly to the service of our Lord. If you win his love,
your repentance will be light. There was never a sinner so
disloyal that when he prayed sincerely to God and served him
well, God did not love him. Nachor, do not be afraid. Abandon your error and your folly. Depend on God, hold him as
your guarantor, and do all that he commands. Put yourself in
his hands."

Nachor responded, "I will do it. I will not refuse to believe
any longer, and I will serve my Creator night and day with all
my heart. You should take care for your own faith, because
the king is greatly burdened by it and seeks ways to bring you
back to his religion. Take care that betrayal does not steal
your reward. On your advice, I will go away and devote myself to caring for my soul. I will not see the king again."

Josaphat wept with happiness. He embraced Nachor and
encouraged him gently, and he commended him tearfully to
God. Nachor left; he asked for nothing more. His courage
was strong and he went to the hermitage that he desired ar-
dently to attain. He traveled until he came upon a hermit.
Nachor fell at his feet, recounted the events of his life, and
asked for forgiveness. He made a sincere confession, and
then he was baptized, for the hermit he found was a priest
and was happy to baptize him and keep him as his companion in repentance. Nachor served God well for as long as he
lived and his soul was saved.

The next day King Avenir rose early. He knew that Nachor
had left and had failed to keep their agreement. He wished to
take vengeance on those who had spoken so badly at the disputation, and he had them beaten and tortured. The king

was full of anger and did not believe he did them any wrong. He cursed them and had their eyes torn out of their heads.

The king weighed his own thoughts as he considered the disputation. He recognized that his belief was false according to Nachor's reasoning, but his heart impaired his understanding and encumbered his will. He thought of God, and then he pulled away from him. He undid what he had done. He saw clearly, then saw nothing, and then feared what he saw. He did not know what part to take, for he believed his life would be worse if he left his gods and began to serve God. He was dismayed by his thoughts and examined them carefully. When he considered both sides, he was doubly confused, but he could not forget all the pleasures he enjoyed. He lived a comfortable and privileged life, but he lost his soul because of it, for whoever serves the devil can expect a very bad reward. King Avenir began to doubt his gods, and he did not go to them or involve himself in their affairs.

The king's noble and handsome son was a good young man—sweet, brave, wise, and pious. He offered his body, his heart, and all his understanding to God. He remembered his master, Barlaam, and kept his commandments. His heart and thoughts flourished from charity and dew. The dew was his tears: they confounded the sins of the body and watered his heart. He willingly undertook everything he knew to be right. He set his body to fasting and his heart to prayer, and he served God piously. Wealthy men came willingly to hear him speak about God, as he often did, and Josaphat spoke well. Many were converted and received forgiveness from God. Josaphat was perfected in speech, works, and deeds. He lived with great restraint, for a wise man curbs his body as long as he is lord of it, I tell you truly. The king's son prayed often that God would permit him to see his master again and, if it pleased him, to dwell with him.

King Avenir neglects his gods

A high feast day approached. King Avenir usually organized a great celebration, but he was lost in his own unhappiness and did not make any preparations. The clerics who served false gods gathered together to consider how they might convince the king to celebrate the feast. They could come up with only one idea, and they decided to follow it.

A sorcerer dwelt nearby. He was a treacherous necromancer called Theonas. The king loved him and trusted him more than any other man in his kingdom because he knew Theonas was very wise. By common agreement, the clerics went to visit him. They flattered him by speaking well of his character and rank. They told him the king wanted to leave their faith, and they described the disputation he had organized as a contest between their religion and Christianity. They told him about Nachor's betrayal and that he had left the disputation and converted to Christianity. They also told Theonas about Josaphat's stubborn determination, and claimed he harassed and tormented them with his Christian faith. Then they told him that the king had made no preparations for the feast day. Whereas he usually ordered great festivities, now he did not even mention the feast. He did not plan for it at all, and, more important, he did not seem to care about sacrificing to the gods. "Ah, Theonas, good and cherished lord! Save us from this tragedy! Come with us and ask the king to honor his religion. If you do not consent to come, our religion will suffer."

Theonas was greatly distressed to hear the clerics' complaints; he agreed to go back to court with them. When he entered the palace, he went directly to the king. King Avenir rose when he saw his friend and received him with great respect and pleasure. His worries were calmed by Theonas's arrival, and he had his friend seated beside him. The king told him about the battle with his son and explained that he had lost the victory he anticipated.

"Good sire," said Theonas, "whatever the Christians say is entirely false. They don't know anything, and their words are like a dog's bark. Sire, let your courage be as exalted as your station! If you turn against reason and persecute your gods, your kingdom will suffer great harm and misfortune.

"There is none so bold that he would dare to speak about Christianity within my hearing," Theonas continued. "I beg you, sire, do not be sad or angry. Celebrate this great occasion with happiness and joy, and I will tell you how you can honor your son and love him again. Go to the festival with this understanding, and trust that I will not disappoint you."

"I will gladly do so," said the king. He became joyful and changed his mind about neglecting the feast day. He called for his messengers and sent them throughout his kingdom. King Avenir dispatched letters, charters, and seals throughout his realm, to call his noble barons and friends to the celebration. He promised that in place of incense they would imbibe the smoke of sacrificial animals. (People who cover their gods in silver deserve such base rewards.) The summons spread throughout the country, and all the people came, each bringing a sacrifice to offer. The king made a great effort to please his gods. His people made sacrifices, as he demanded, and Theonas too made an offering. The king was ashamed because Theonas had reproached him, and he rejoiced at the feast. (Was it really a feast day? No, truly, for it was a celebration based on ignorance and did not acknowledge our Lord. The joy the pagans take in their festivities has no flavor, for those who rejoice without God cannot taste true pleasure.)

When the celebration had come to an end, the king turned to Theonas. "I have done your will concerning this feast day and now you must give me my reward," he said. "If you know a good sermon that can draw my son to our side, then go preach it to him, for it is time. If you are successful, I will make a golden statue in your likeness and will worship it as long as I live."

"Good king, do not worry. I know how to advise you. If

you wish to recover your son and deliver him from the error of his belief, have all the servants removed from his palace. Find beautiful, noble young women to serve him, and have them dwell with him night and day. Carnal flesh demands its rights, unless it is unnatural. (And the practice of unnatural carnal desire is condemned.) Once desire is freed, it will tolerate no limits, it will know no moderation, and it will follow its course, whether for shame or honor. Your son's carnal nature will counsel him to do things that will cause him to fall from his high convictions.

"If you would convert your son, send for the young women. Choose one hundred of the most attractive and most noble, and install them in his palace. He will not be able to resist them, and when they join together, the pleasure of their union will change his thoughts. Tell the beautiful young women about your son and say that whoever can seduce him will wear a rich crown—she will be queen. In this world, a woman is the thing that most draws and confounds a man and that most binds and enflames him.

"I will prove it to you with a parable," Theonas continued. "There was once a king who possessed many cities and castles. He was very wealthy, but he had no son. He sorrowed in his heart, for he had no one to whom he could leave his wealth when he died. (He was right to be sad, for whoever has a poor and miserable heir loses his power.) While the king was still lost in his sorrow, a son of great beauty was born to him. The king rejoiced greatly and sent for all the clerics and doctors in his kingdom. When they were assembled, he asked them what they foresaw for his newborn child.

"They replied, 'Let us see him before we speak.' They came to the child's cradle and studied him. Then they revealed their thoughts. 'Sire, hear our counsel: if your son sees fire or sunlight before his tenth year, it is certain he will lose his sight in both eyes.'

"The king was distressed and immediately asked for counsel. Following his clerics' advice, he built a deep, wide pit that no light could enter, and then, with great sadness, the king enclosed his son and his nurses inside. I tell you, King Avenir, the son lived there for ten years and did not see a single ray of light.

"After ten years had passed, the king's son was released from the pit. My lord, the truth is that he had never seen anything and so he did not recognize anything he saw. His father commanded that he be shown everything in his kingdom: men, women, clothes, and horses; youthful men and young women; silver, gold, wood, and stone; flowers of all kinds; bulls, cows, and sheep; furs and silks. They led the boy from place to place, showing him all these things. The child cleverly asked the name of everything he saw, and they named each thing for him. When he saw women, he asked, 'What things do I see here?' One of the men replied jokingly, 'By your leave, I will tell you: those things you see are the devils that deceive counts and kings. When they embrace and kiss men, they harm and torment them.'

"When they had taken the child everywhere and shown him all things and taught him their names, the child returned to the king. His father asked, 'Son, what pleased you most in all that you saw?'

"The child replied, 'I will tell you truthfully: nothing pleased me as much as those devils that deceive men.' And when the king heard him, he marveled that his son loved women more than any other thing he saw; but nature cannot lie.

"This parable proves that the love of women is a serious thing," Theonas said, "and it is easy to manipulate a man who is with a woman night and day. There is no stronger love in the world than the love of women, nor is there anything by which men can be so easily bound."

When King Avenir heard this advice, he was eager to put it to use. He sent for one hundred of the most noble and beautiful young women in his lands. He had them dressed in rich silks and furs. He thought he could use them to win over the son who had converted to God, and he expected to mount a strong attack. Who would lead the attack? The beautiful

women and the devil, who sows evil.[1] The devil knows very
well how to plant evil in women when he trains them. How
does he train them? And in what? In debauchery! Malice,
pride, and presumption abide comfortably in women, and so
does the devil. When the devil joins forces with a woman's
beauty, there is no man who cannot be turned to evil. When
pride enters a woman's heart, the devil will reign over her
and she will not care about a friend's admonitions or gentle
words of warning. (I do not speak of all women—that would
be an exaggeration—and I believe there are many good ones
who would not wish to do wrong.)

King Avenir spoke to the women he had assembled. "Hear
me, noble ladies: you are the most beautiful and highborn
women of my country. I will tell you why I have brought you
here and dressed you so richly, and if you will agree to my
plan, you will receive good recompense for your beauty. Do
you know what I offer you? You will serve my son's pleasure
in everything. He was made a Christian against my will. I
wish to crown him king, and whoever has possession of his
body will become queen. I say to you openly that whoever
can make him sin will be first lady of the empire. Be attentive
to him and try to excite and attract him until you can draw
him away from his foolish faith. This is my heart's greatest
desire. I am angry and sorrowful that he is so vanquished by
foolishness."

The king commanded his son's courtiers to leave his palace, and he sent the young women to join Josaphat. The
women went eagerly. They vied with each other to serve the
prince, for they all hoped to win the crown. The king's son
would have to be more wary than usual, for the devil had bet
against him and he deceives many men. The women in Josaphat's palace were eager to seduce him. If the young man did
not guard against the prick of desire's needle, he would be
taken in by their attractions and fall into sin. May God save
him, for he was being attacked by great forces! But I do not
fear his fall, because he had a true heart.

The young man was in great torment, and he fought

against nature. He needed wisdom and restraint to prevail in such a difficult contest. Each of the women came to speak sweetly to him, and if nature were not defeated, he would eventually have to sin. He fought back with fasting, vigils, and prayers. He took God as a shield and a lance to use in his defense. The women who came to besiege him did not care about his prayers. They showered him with sweet words and courtly greetings, as was appropriate to their task. They teased him and laughed.

"Young sire, what are you thinking?" they asked frequently. "You are not at all jealous and you do not care about pleasure! Should a king's son act like this? You are handsome and highborn, a prince from a distinguished lineage, but your heart is not noble. Since you will become a lord and king, you should become more courtly, and you will know nothing of courtliness if you do not learn to love.[2]

"It is good to take a lover as long as she is worthy," the women encouraged the prince. "Love, good sire! Love! Love! Do not worry so much! Thoughts are only good when they serve love. You know well that valor and worth can be earned through love, and a young lord should always think about acquiring worth."

"Yes, I do want love," said Josaphat, "and I already have a love that I will cherish as long as I live. My love is complete, for it possesses my whole heart. I think night and day of my true love. The thought of my love is sweet and good, for now it is fresh and new to me. I would never have any pleasure if I did not think about this love more than any other. This love holds me and binds me, and no other love can take my heart. The more I think of it, the sweeter it becomes. If others knew what I know, they would envy me for having such a rich love."

One of the women responded, "Reveal her to us, by your leave! There is no shame in revealing her identity. Is she a king's daughter or the daughter of a count?"

"She truly is a king's daughter. Her nobility is beyond compare, and it is far higher than your lineage. No one could describe it without naming wonders. My friend is brave and wise, and my love for her is well repaid. She esteems me and takes me for her friend. I give myself entirely to her in everything. I devote myself to her. I surrender myself to her."

"Tell us her name!"

"Her name? By God, I cannot tell you her name because I do not see in you any understanding of the kind of love I describe." At these words he rose and went to pray to God. He addressed his plea to the one who had claimed his love. But he prayed to him about a different love, one that it is not right to claim. Josaphat did not wish for this other love, and he asked God for mercy and forgiveness, and weeping, he thanked God for protecting him from such great adversity. Still weeping, he asked that he protect him even more strongly in the future.

A beautiful princess tempts Josaphat

The young women were filled with wonder. They told each other that the young man had lost his mind. One of them was more knowledgeable than the others. She was from an old and noble lineage, the daughter of a king who had lost his throne. She had been exiled from Sidon, where her father, as I understand, had been lord and king. She was a relative of King Apollonius, who fled his lands (I believe you have heard much about this King Apollonius's life, and about his victories and his defeats).[1] This lady was beautiful and noble, and, aided by the devil, she devoted herself to seducing the king's son. The young woman had a dark and evil heart, and she wanted Josaphat to give into pleasure. She was not afraid to seduce him, and she went to his bedside, entering his room boldly (for women have a brash courage when they set their minds to something).

The devil came to confound Josaphat. He observed the young man and inspired the lady's words. "Sire," she said, "I was the daughter of a rich king who ruled a great country, but now I have been disinherited. If you do not take pity on me, you will commit a great sin. I am a wretched orphan, I have neither father nor mother, and I am willing to become a Christian for your sake. If you will help me, I will leave my foolish belief."

"Beautiful lady," the young man responded, "if you wish to do as you say, that would be a good thing. No one who is not a good Christian will ever see God, who died on the cross. It is right and good that everyone should seek the Christian faith, for in this world there is no pleasure, joy, or happiness that does not eventually turn to sadness. Beautiful lady, think carefully on this! Because you speak so well and because you are from such a distinguished lineage, you would be very wrong to allow yourself to be lost. If you follow your good intention, you will enter the right path."

Good Lord God! No one can appreciate the value of an honest man! An honest man does not devise tricks. Others may contemplate evil, but he thinks only of good. Eve came forward here, with deception in her heart. But she did not find Adam, for this young man's heart was strengthened by sanctity and knowledge. Josaphat believed the lady spoke the truth, but she lied from a false heart. Adam met Eve again here, but Adam acted more wisely than he did before. Eve wronged Adam, but this Adam protected himself better against the Eve who tried to trick him. This Eve was a bad wife to Adam, but this Adam did not return her enmity. If she had wished it, Adam would have been good to her, had she intended good for him. But the lady did not want to understand his intentions, she wanted to deceive him, and if the young man did not beware, he would fall into the trap set by this beautiful trickster.

"Good sweet lord and friend," said the lady with the beautiful face, "if you want to save my soul, you should consider an exchange. If you will grant me one wish, I will not hesitate to do whatever you ask."

"Sweet friend, tell me what you want."

"With pleasure, my lord." Lust transformed her heart, and then her eyes, her mouth, and her entire appearance. She spoke to Josaphat with ardor and passion, and she was never more joyful: "Upon my honor, if you will marry me and take my virginity, then I will do as you wish, and I will follow your instructions without fail."

"Beautiful lady, this distresses me. Your offer is hard to accept. I would like to save your soul, but I must tend to my own, and it would not be good for me if I were to lose God by joining my body with yours. If I were lost for your sake, then my reward would be of little value. I will not defile my life for such a base union."

"What do you mean?" she exclaimed. "Are Christians defiled when they take women as wives? I believe I am wiser than you in this matter. Whoever combines marriage and religion certainly will be saved as long as he holds to both in a holy way. I am not so confused that I have forgotten the book that describes your religion. I know that marriage is a good thing when the spouses are loyal.

"Marriage is a good and reasonable law," the young woman continued. "God himself commanded it, and he joined together the very first man and woman. (But according to Christian belief, first he made them, then he joined them together.) From two he made one, and the scriptures forbid that any man should separate those whom God has joined together. Man and wife are united as companions and should not be parted. Marriage is a form of faithfulness, and any nobleman who is not married should seek to wed. A noble household is better kept when a good woman abides in it. A good wife is to be prized, and she should be exalted and loved more than any treasure. Just as a precious stone is set in gold, so a lady dwells in her household as long as she is of good repute. Saint Paul himself confirms that I do not lie when I say that it is much better for a man to marry than for his body to burn forever."

"By God, this is true," said Josaphat. "According to the scriptures, it is much wiser to marry than to burn in lust, but whoever wishes to remain chaste should avoid marriage. Whatever does not hinder me will help me.

"Dear sister and friend, are you so rash as to wish that for your well-being my virginity should be lost? I would have to find your idea presumptuous if I believed you so impertinent. You speak with malicious intent, not loyalty. I must refuse the marriage you propose because it is full of dishonor, and if it is dishonorable, there is no faithfulness in it."

"Your argument is confused," the lady answered. "You know that no man would find dishonor in this marriage. I am a pagan and the daughter of a king, and I will become a Christian for you if you will take me. You would be doubly charitable if you would make me, a pagan, into a true Christian. If you do not do it, then I am most unfortunate, for you will damn my soul. Sire, you are my damnation, but you could be my salvation if you wished to save me. You should consider this more carefully. My offer is good, and you cannot find any motivation for it that is not reasoned and right. For God's sake, I beg you, become my husband! You will redeem the inheritance I have lost if you will marry me.

"I have shown you many reasons why you should do as I ask," she continued. "The scriptures say that Saint Peter took a wife, and he was not damned for it. The holy prophets took wives and taught us to marry. I have never heard of any prohibition against marriage. What kind of man are you? You are not a true Christian if you renounce the laws of our fathers and God's religion. I will receive baptism and be saved if you wish it. By faith! You could do nothing better than to save a soul that is damned. Let me be saved by you today!"

"Sweet lady, I wonder where you have received such advice. Can you not be baptized without lusting after me? Your heart is not moved by belief if you seek to bargain for what will please you. Receive Christianity, keep your virginity, and your pardon will be all the greater for it.

"Your beauty moves me, and I swear to you that if I ever took a wife, I would take only you. But your request is disloyal. You would receive baptism by corrupting your body and my own."

"By faith, you delay too long and the new day is coming," the lady replied. "I believe your thoughts are elsewhere—you play a different kind of game. Cursed be your body and your beauty! You are a liar and you choose your pleasure where you will. Good Lord, what chastity! What a splendid young man! What joy for his friends when such a fortunate man was born! I do not lie when I say that his birth brought honor to his father, but he chooses chastity because he is taken by another kind of love that shames his family. A good couple is formed only by male and female, and when the masculine companion in a couple becomes feminine, he goes against nature and denies the woman her rights. A male who becomes female is not a man."[2]

"By God! Dear young lady, your words are not becoming. You wrongly accuse me of a great shame, and I know why. If I did your will, you would show your pleasure, but women always try to shame those who do not wish to do what they ask. Their slandering tongues are sharper than a razor and more pointed than a needle. There is no need for accusations or disputes. I will not take a wife and I will not spread seed to grow in any earth.

"Beautiful lady, I do not care for fighting with women. They grumble and complain, and they heap blame on the goodness of others. You have failed at this joust, and I would have made a bad showing if I had been defeated by you. Dear sister and friend, there is nothing more to say. Leave this battle and go seek what you want somewhere else. You want to challenge me with your debates and insults, but I have no desire for it—my heart looks elsewhere."

"Noble lord, for God's sake, have mercy on me!" the young woman begged. "Do not take revenge on me in this way. Since you will not have me as wife, grant me another favor. Let my soul be saved in this way: take my body a single time—I do not ask for more. Through this one time I will gain all I want to win. The king will give me back my land,

and I will become a Christian. If you sleep with me just once
I will be saved."

Josaphat responded, "Ah, dear friend, your body is unfortunate to have such a flighty heart. Your heart should save
your body, but it corrupts it. You mortgage your honor to
cultivate your shame! You are willing to seek your own hu-
miliation. If I granted your desire, no crown, land, or wealth,
no dominion, power, or promise of inheritance would com-
pensate for the virginity that would be so shamefully lost. If
you believed, you would become a Christian, but for as long
as you are a pagan, you will not be loved by God. Since you
have God in your thoughts and you promise to believe in him
if I do your will, why do you put your body at risk? You
should purchase your baptism, but you would sell it for pleasure!

"I have vowed my chastity to God, and I will not break my
vow. Your family standard is still clean and true, and you
should not stain it. If you protect it, anyone who tries to taint
it with shame will waste his time. If you understand the
scriptures, your standard will be dyed with the good. For
God's sake, listen to what I tell you, for I chastise you for
your own good! If you keep your chastity, much good could
come to you from it."

"For God's sake, good sire, listen to this," the lady replied.
"King Avenir sent me here to honor and serve you, and to
give my body to you. I wagered more than he asked. He told
me that if I shared my body with you, he would give me back
my land, and I offered to do even more for you: I offered to
become a Christian. My Christianity would be your salvation, for if I were saved by you, you would have done a good
deed and the reward would belong to you alone. But you are
a harsh Christian." With these words she sighed and wept.

Josaphat looked at her and felt pity, and he also feared that
he might sin. The sight of the lady was very moving, and he
was torn between two choices. If he did not do as she asked,
he thought he would wrong God, and if he did what she
wanted, he feared angering him. The devil excited him and

made him want to take the lady. He wanted to do it but he resisted. The weeping lady begged him with all her might to take her side. Pity drew him, but he did not understand that sin entwined with pity.

He rose abruptly and went into another room. He knelt in prayer to God and his Holy Name. He asked for counsel, for he had great need of it. He fell asleep while praying, and Saint Michael took his soul and carried it into paradise. The young man was comforted to see its great pleasures, but his delight was cut short when Saint Michael showed him hell and the enduring sorrow and great torments inflicted there on those disloyal to God. Saint Michael also showed him the treacherous betrayal that his father had plotted, following the advice of Theonas, and Josaphat marveled at it. Then he woke and shuddered from the fear that assailed him. He was greatly dismayed, but God calmed him. The king's son rose quickly and began to pray immediately. He begged God for forgiveness and asked that he free him from temptation. His head began to ache and hurt badly. He lay back down.

Theonas confronts Josaphat

Josaphat was ill, and when the king learned of it, he came quickly to his palace. "Good son," he said to him gently, "I regret that you are ill, and I have never been more concerned."

"Father, you caused this illness when you tried to betray me," Josaphat replied. "I would never wrong you in this way. You sent temptations to seduce me, but God showed me your treason and protected me from it so that I was not deceived. Father, you were disloyal and when you sought to harm me, you did wrong to yourself. Why do you have no pity for me, your son and friend? You are my father, but I have lost faith in you. I am most unfortunate.

"Father, let me go away with my master, for I do not wish

to stay with you any longer. I care nothing for your empire, and I will never want to rule it. I do not care about your cities, nor do I desire your crown. I want to go to a hermitage and lead a more difficult life, for I have too many pleasures here. Let me go, by your mercy! If you keep me here in such distress, I will die of sadness. Let me go, I beg you. Let me go or I will die! Death is close and holds me by the heart. Nothing holds me here any longer."

King Avenir was afraid and sorrowed for his son. He went back to his palace and sent for Theonas to come right away. The king cried tenderly for his son and complained to his advisor. "I did everything you asked, but to no avail. Your plan failed, and my son has fallen seriously ill. Now I do not know what advice to believe. I thought the plan was a good one, but we have failed."

Theonas said, "Listen to me. Send for your son to come here before me, or rather let us go to him there since he is so sick with sorrow that he will be unable to come to your palace."

"Master," said the king, "let us go." King Avenir rose and led Theonas to his son.

Now I know that Josaphat expected an argument, even if he did not yet know its subject. The king sent Theonas before him, hiding his anxiety. Theonas admonished Josaphat loudly and berated him repeatedly. "Friend," he said, "what are you thinking? Explain to us what you want! You have angered our gods, and if you would be king and reign over this country, you should follow your father's advice and embrace them. Now you have lost all your friends."

"No, friend, I have not lost them—I have regained them," Josaphat answered. "If keeping these friends would cause me to be damned, then I would do a great wrong. I speak the truth openly: God is my King, God is my Lord, and I do not wish for any other empire."

Theonas said, "But listen to me, friend. You speak very foolishly. Do you know who gave you life and who gave you to your father so that you would be his heir? I will tell you, for it is true: the gods gave you life. But you have challenged their authority. Your foolish thoughts and your mistaken belief have cost you the love of the gods and your father's love as well."

"Oh, you shepherd of lies!" the king's son responded. "What an evil diversion you create, and it will lead only to wrong. Your aged face and your white hair reveal that you have lived a corrupt life. I believe you must be descended from the giants who built the Tower of Babel. (It did not please God, and he showed them his displeasure, for they all died in the end.) Why do you mock Jesus Christ? Be assured that he would not permit it if he wanted to punish you for it. This clemency should give you hope, but you do not understand. It will all become clear to you on Judgment Day.

"Wretched man, what do you believe in? Acknowledge God and his strength, and understand that he made you. Do not worship the creation—worship the Creator and make him your Lord! You have to purchase your gods, and you cannot hide that they were made and shaped by a man who gave them whatever form he wished to look upon. If you know how to listen to reason, admit that when a man makes his god, the man was made before the idol was created. A man who makes gods is an important man indeed! I find you very ignorant if you believe in a carved thing that was forged by man's art. It is only a thing, a carving in wood or stone. Even if the carving were noble and beautiful, it would still have no tongue or spirit, no mouth for speaking, and no heart for feeling. It is a phantom and a vain thing. No matter how much you serve your gods, there is nothing in them but what they are made of. The one who carved them is their father, and the god is less than the man since the man engendered his lord.

"Ah, Theonas! You are foolish if you believe this. There is no reason in this religion, and I do not accept your advice. You are a wise and learned man, and I marvel that your heart is so confused. I will never serve your gods, and I will never believe in them. I will believe in my Creator and serve him night and day, for he healed all my wounds with the blood he shed on the cross. Instead of sacrificing some beast, I will sacrifice myself to him. I will not fail to make an offering, for I will sacrifice my entire body to him.

"God became a serf, for to take human form is to become enslaved. Human life will always be servitude because it will never be without pain. Our Lord took the form of a serf and he suffered martyrdom. He was resurrected on the third day, and now we wait for the Creator to come and judge the world.

"God is everywhere, just as he is in heaven above. This is what we believe. He is in every place and he is one. We believe that he cannot be divided and no place can enclose him. I will give you an example so that you may understand. (These demonstrations are necessary.) Do you see the sun? Its rays spread across the country into many places. It shines on a dunghill just as it shines on a church. The church does not lose its light because the sun shines on the dunghill—the sun reaches everywhere and illuminates everything. The sun is not any weaker or stronger because it shines everywhere, nor is there less light in it. So I say truly that God is in all things and in all places without any lessening of his sovereignty, as the scriptures tell us.

"God has two natures: one is divine and the other human, for on the cross he suffered the pain of death as a man. This is not a lie, and you should believe it. He did not die as God but as a man, and he was resurrected as God. He broke open the gates of hell, as the scriptures tell us, and through his commandment he freed those who waited for him there. He redeemed our sinful nature when he took our form and ascended to heaven, where the angels welcomed him. Whoever does not believe this is wrong. You should believe in such a good God who has done so much for us. He commands obedience and requires continence. He teaches forgiveness, peace, and faith and asks us to follow his commandments. People should keep his laws, but they stray from the right path.

"Look at yourself: what gave you life when you were made out of base matter?" asked Josaphat, turning to his father. "Oh cruel king, listen to reason! You set your heart to follow your desires. If you will not reconsider your false beliefs, remember what you are made of and how you were given shape in the womb of your mother. If you knew who made you and what he needed to form you, you would come join yourself to God, who joined himself to you when he took your form.

"You live in sorrow, and it will not end. You will die in sorrow and your flesh will be a pasture for worms. Your heart is perverse when you will not exchange the devil for everlasting life! Your heart and body will be damned to unending pain. Acknowledge the legacy the devil leaves you: a prison full of pain, darkness, shadow, and innumerable sorrows! Oh, fool, leave this misguided path and come to the Creator who will give you the stole of immortality and the joy of paradise, and you will rejoice in them all your days!"

"None of this is true," Theonas said. "The life you describe is not as good as you would have us believe. Your people are poor priests. They are rude peasants from lowborn families. They have no learning, whereas wise and noble clerics study and teach our faith. Kings and counts follow our religion, and it has been taught for many years. If it was wrong, it would not have lasted so long. Many people follow it now because it holds so much reason and learning. Our religion is not false, and yours is full of lies. How could your people speak the truth when they have no power?"

"By God," Josaphat responded, "now Theonas speaks like a fool and does not follow reason. If our religion had been translated into philosophy, the arts of astronomy, grammar, physics, or rhetoric by clerics, and if it had been promoted by kings, then it would have been shaped by human ability. Our faith has a different form, for it was spread by humble people who exchanged their low station for courtly service to God. Our religion is good and beautiful, and it reigns over all other religions. The strength of God is demonstrated when modest people prove it.

"Now our religion grows and rises, as yours loses its value. It is a great honor to rise high, but the one who rises should anticipate a descent so he is not harmed when he falls. If the ascent is pleasant and easy, take care in descending, for while rising one should take care to ensure that the descent will not be harmful.[1] Fools climb stairs without anticipating the descent, for in the descent one sees how high one has climbed. The ascent of a false religion is not remarkable. It does not really rise. In fact, it falls because of the wrongdoing of those who promote it. This ascent should not be trusted, for as a false religion rises, it goes further backward than forward.

"Our religion merits belief because the scriptures that bear witness to it are entirely true and report God's words. God made our religion for us. Why did he make it for us? To save us. No craftsman could make it better, and a richer work was never made from such base material. But the creation that does not acknowledge its creator is foolish, and Theonas does not remember the Creator who made him! He goes against reason when he makes a god of his own creation.

"Theonas, look and see the dangers of your belief. You choose your own death and perdition. You are drawn by the devil who made Adam and his companion Eve commit the first sin. Your heart is wretched and vain when you do not recognize that you are wrong. Wretched man, renounce the sin of your disbelief! You can know with confidence that Holy God is Lord and Father of all the world. He is its emperor, and only a fool does not recognize him. Your foolish thoughts deceive you and blind you to reason. I pray to God, and his Holy Name, that he will encourage you to follow the good, for I see that you err in all things."

Theonas was moved—the Holy Spirit illuminated him and opened the eyes of his heart. He was distressed and did not know where this desire for God had come from. But God's strength can make a heart blossom and put forth flowers and fruit. Theonas struggled to express the thoughts that animated him. He spoke bravely to the king. "King Avenir, we have been vanquished by your son, who knows the path to salvation. Believe in God and good will come to you. The God of the Christians is great. His holiness and faith are great. Our religion has been disproved by the words of Jesus Christ, for what your son says is entirely true.

"Tell me, my lord Josaphat," Theonas continued. "Will God have mercy on me if I pray and ask him for it with a true heart?"

"Yes, by God," Josaphat responded, "there is no sinner in all the world, however disloyal his sins, who will not be saved through repentance. I rejoice in your salvation when I see you turn to the right path. Do not doubt God—your prayer will be heard since it comes from a true heart. Do not be troubled any longer. God is happy for all sinners who come to his love, and he opens their eyes to his great mercy. God is so merciful that if you offer him your heart and your body, he will ask for nothing more as long as you keep the offering clean and pure."

Theonas rejoiced greatly at Josaphat's words. He bid farewell to the king and then departed. He repented truly. First he went back to the cell where he lived and built a great fire and burned the books of magic he had used to work against God. Then he went to the wise man whom Nachor had joined after he converted. Theonas fell at his feet, weeping, and confessed his sins. The wise man gave thanks to God for his repentance. He taught Theonas about God and then baptized him. Theonas became a new man and a new knight because of his teaching. It happened to Theonas as I have recounted it to you. He prayed and wept until he was reconciled with God.

King Avenir gives half his
kingdom to Josaphat

When the debate was over, the king felt he had been badly
served by his advisors because his son had not been turned
away from the God he loved and served. He had tried to
change his son's belief and he had failed. King Avenir was sorrowful because he did not know how to draw Josaphat away
from Christianity. He sent for his courtiers and his councilors,
and Prince Aracin was the first to arrive. When they were all
assembled, the king asked for their advice, but no one spoke.
The king marveled that none of his men knew how to advise
him. He could not enjoy his honors and privileges as long as
he was separated from his son. (The king hated his son because he had converted, but he was wrong to do so.)

Aracin thought about how to counsel the king, and then he
addressed him: "My lord, I do not know what advice to offer.
He is your son and you are his father. You would act against
nature and lose the name of father if you harmed your son or
had him tortured. Nature forbids it and would not allow it.
But by your leave, I will give you this counsel. If you want to
convert him, divide your kingdom in two and give him a
crown. If he has to devote himself to the world and to solving
disputes, it may draw him back to you."

All those present praised the idea, and the king himself approved it. When he rose the next day, King Avenir went to
Josaphat's palace. "Son," he said, "agree to my wishes, and if
you do not, I will no longer love you. I will have you crowned
and give you half my kingdom. If you do not earn my love by
accepting, you will never leave the prison of your palace. You
know that you have disobeyed me. Now take care to understand and do not resist my will in this. I want you to be lord
and king. In this way you can live as you wish and rule your
own land. You must obey my wishes."

Josaphat looked into his heart and understood that he

should agree so he could escape his father and follow his own beliefs. "Father," he said, "I want to send for the holy man Barlaam, but you do not allow it. You are worldly and understand things only in terms of the world. No matter what I say, you are reluctant to believe in God and pray to him. I will agree to what you ask. I do not see any danger for myself in it. In fact, I see more reasons to accept than you do. Since I must elect the better of two bad choices, I will not deny your will, if this is what you ask of me."

King Avenir rejoiced when Josaphat agreed. He had his kingdom divided, and he kept the smaller part and gave the larger to his son. He had him crowned that very day. Great joy broke out when the crown was carried forward. Counts and kings were present, and the coronation celebration lasted two months. When the festivities came to an end on the sixtieth day, the king had all his people gathered to witness the gift of his realm's capital and its surrounding castles to his son. He sent Josaphat into his new empire with many people, accompanied by great rejoicing. All the people of his country came to meet their lord with happiness and honored him. He thanked them, but he cared little for the inheritance, the land, or sovereignty.

Josaphat entered the city and found many idols there. It was well furnished with plenty of wood and water, and the young man went immediately to inspect its resources. He saw the city was well situated in the midst of abundant vineyards, fertile prairies, and well-worked fields. He loved it and held it dear. He did not see evil or crime in the city, except in the people's belief. The city was tainted because its inhabitants did not believe in the Creator.

There were many towers in the city, and its new king put crosses on top of each. Then he had all the temples destroyed. He ordered the people to tear down their walls. The king encouraged his people, and they did not leave even the foundations standing. He had every idol in the country burned, and not a single one escaped the fire. In the middle of the city he built the Church of the Holy Cross to serve God and his laws, and he converted his people, not through force, but by teaching them and showing them the right path. He worked joyfully to change their false belief, and they never made any complaint about it. King Josaphat converted his councilors, and all the city's inhabitants believed in God because of the many miracles God showed them in response to Josaphat's prayers. He acted with great humility and did not take pride in his kingdom or in his office, for Josaphat wished only to serve God. King Josaphat was happy with his people and grateful for his crown. He had become a king of Christians when before he had ruled over pagans.

John, a bishop from Damascus, came to India when he lost his bishopric because Saracens destroyed his city.[1] He went into Josaphat's realm and befriended him. The king was very happy to receive a bishop. That very day he made him an archbishop, and there was great rejoicing in the city. Many were baptized that day, including princes and counts. The archbishop preached to the people and taught them the scriptures, explaining their meaning and showing the people how to believe. He demonstrated his teaching in his own deeds, and he converted the city through his teaching and his own actions so that it became a model of learning and good works. Noble and great is the king whose city and country devote themselves to the service of God. (I forgot to say something about the archbishop. I speak truthfully when I say that it was he who recorded this story, for he knew it well and told it exactly as it happened.)

Josaphat kept the archbishop with him for more than twenty years, as I understand it, and he converted all the people of the land. King Josaphat glorified God and his laws, and he brought the people of India out of their foolish belief and reconciled them with the Creator. He converted all his own empire and part of his father's. Christianity spread and multiplied because the pagans wanted to receive the good faith. King Josaphat was very pleased. He praised God and served him even more devotedly when he saw that his service was effective. He rejoiced in his heart to know that his inheritance was so widely shared. His archbishop converted all the land, and those who were blind saw clearly when they believed in God.

King Avenir was dismayed to learn that churches and chapels had been established in his lands, and the loss of his castles and cities to the Christian religion saddened and troubled him. Those who served God abandoned him, and he experienced more conflicts than peace. He remained alone in his palace, burdened by the loss of his country and sorrowful because he had lost it to his son. He complained about it frequently and thought his son betrayed the laws of nature when he disinherited his father.

He sent for his lords. He thought that if he could not win his son by persuasion, he might find victory in war. The king's councilors assembled on the designated day. Few came, for Christianity had robbed King Avenir of many of his vassals, and those who had become Christians did not respond to the king's summons. The king saw that he had lost power and his court was diminished; it had once been full of great lords and knights, but now it was deserted and empty. "My lords," he complained to the few who were present, "I will disclose to you something that torments me. My son wants to take my land and my reign from me. I have honored him too well, and he offers enmity in return for all the love I have shown him. Now I am greatly sorrowed and must fight back. Counsel me on this and come to my aid, for I have decided that I will not leave things as they are. My son is now my enemy, since he offers hate in exchange for the love I have shown him."

When Aracin heard the king, he said, "By the gods, my lord, I believe that you have delayed this decision for too long. Josaphat has acted against us for a long time. He is presumptuous to limit your right to rule, and my heart is saddened to see him rise above you. Sire, consider how you will avenge your shame. Your son shows his arrogance when he takes all your cities from you, and his sovereignty costs you dearly. I am sorry to see your nobility abased, and it was un-

fortunate that you gave him his own kingdom. He is more of
an enemy than a son."

"My lord Aracin, I did it on your advice," the king responded. "You advised me to give him his part of the land.
Your counsel has led me to war!"

"My lord, I advised you with good intention, but I now see
that I was wrong, and I beg your pardon for it. Your son was
crowned by my counsel, and it turned out badly. I am sorry
and I offer you all my help. I will follow your orders to my
utmost."

The king responded, "I have confidence in you. My lords,
you hold your fiefs from me, tell me whether you will support
me."

They all responded with a single voice, "Good king, we
offer our help to you and we are eager to avenge you and the
insult to our gods. Revenge is required, and your decision has
been too long deferred."

The king saw that they were loyal, and their desire for vengeance made him happy. He sent messengers to summon his
vassals. Following the advice of Aracin, he sent word to Josaphat and demanded that he renounce his crown and his
lands. If he did not, the king warned, he should prepare to
defend himself. If he did not return his father's lands, then
the king would call for his vassals. From India to Damascus
and from Athens to Byzantium, they would assemble to join
the battle against Josaphat and his people. King Avenir
vowed that he would take all his lords from him: their houses
would remain empty and there would be none to serve him.
King Josaphat would lose his land because he had given it a
base religion. King Avenir's message was delivered faithfully
by one of his counts.

"What?" Josaphat asked when he had heard the message.
"He will make war on me? He forced me to take the land,
and now he will force me to give it back? Since he will try to
take it by force, I will use force to keep it. I do not fear death
for any wrong I have done. I will not submit to his debased
rule unless I am taken in battle. My laws are followed in the

land that he would take from me, and since I am its lord and king, it is reasonable and right that my laws be followed. It is mine in all justice, and I rule it well. I have taken it from his gods, and I will hold it for God. Tell the king and his lords that even if harm should come to me, war will not make me abandon the city. Go now! May God give my father understanding so he will act justly toward my people."

The count left Josaphat and brought his response to King Avenir. The king said, "I have lost my country if I do not win it back through battle." He did not delay and was tireless in his preparations. He assembled his army and sent for his friends, wherever he could find them. His messengers went out to call for support in the name of love and sovereign right. He sent a messenger to the lord of Byzantium, who was his friend and his relative, lord over many people and count and sire of the city. (At that time it was not the empire it is today. Now it is called Constantinople, but it used to be called Byzantium. The coins called bezants—we still have them today—come from Byzantium, and they take their name from that city.)

The lord of Byzantium came with many people, to bring aid to his beloved kinsman. Polidonus of Athens also came with many men, to help the king of India whom he loved.[2] King Avenir assembled many men of his own. India was filled with knights, and the king was a good companion to them. He took it as an insult that his son thought he could resist him. The king planned to attack his son with such force that the walls of his city would not protect him.

When the knights were all assembled, they set out with great pleasure. There were sixty thousand men, and they formed a noble company: fifteen of them were highborn kings and a good three hundred were dukes and counts. They rode for short days because of the great army they led. (A well-armed host should not endure long days of travel.) For more than ten days they journeyed from the king's city to his destination. Now I will return to Josaphat.

The king's son was in his city. He asked the archbishop

and his high lords for counsel. "My lords," he said, "you must advise me. The king, my father, wrongly intends to take my land from me."

The archbishop replied, "My lord, I have heard that your father hates you. But he is mistaken, for his enmity is caused by the divine law that you spread in his land. He would destroy your country, but, Sire, if you trust my advice, you will not give it to him without a battle.[3] You have enough people to defend this land, and it should not be given up to the Saracens. They will install their idols here and bring down the holy church. My lord, you have labored to convert this land, but you will see it revert to evil if you give it to your father. The country will be lost to God, who made you its ruler.

"I do not advise you to undertake a battle with your father merely to save a fortress or a tower, a city or a castle," the archbishop continued. "God is the sole reason to keep the land. It is right to undertake this war, for a good Christian should always rule over pagans. Christianity is newly established here, but this city is mistress over India and the entire region. The pagans are our enemies and seek to harm us. They come to fight against us only because of Christianity, and they think they will conquer us and destroy our religion. You should not give the land back to your father—you should defend it against him. This is not your war. It belongs to God and the holy church. You are God's knight, and you must be willing to defend him. I tell you that you should not fear anything in your duty to God. And you, lords who listen to me, take care to defend yourselves well, for the city is good and strong and you know that our strength is greater than theirs. My lords, why are you frightened? We have people to send against theirs, and we have the Creator on our side. Since they do not have him, we have the greater strength. Become his knights, for he asks you to defend him."

The archbishop's words lightened Josaphat's heart. He saw that his men were encouraged by the reasoning they heard. The people in the city were frightened, but the fortress was well stocked with arms and horses, and there was plenty of

food. King Josaphat prostrated himself in prayer, to ask God
to help him and to pardon him if he had sinned. Josaphat and
his people needed God's help, for they anticipated a cruel
battle.

King Avenir goes to war against his son

The angry King Avenir rode with his great host toward Josaphat's land and did not stop until he reached the city. Inside,
they told King Josaphat that his father had laid siege to his
city, and Josaphat wept with pity. Avenir's men pitched their
tents outside the city walls. They camped beside a lake they
intended to use to defend their position. Before Avenir arrived and put up his tents, Josaphat had burned the fields and
all the houses outside the city walls. (The poor people always
pay for the actions of the rich!) Secure inside their city, Josaphat's men climbed to the top of the walls to look upon the
enemy camped beside the water. Avenir's men were sorry
they had camped so close when Josaphat's men began to
shoot arrows, and forced them to retreat.

Josaphat was in his castle with his people and was not
afraid. His father, the king, was lodged with a great army
outside the city, at the base of an ancient wall. I tell you truly
that the apostle Saint Thomas was in this place for at least
two years. He built the first church in India there, and it was
later dedicated to the saint because he baptized many people
inside. The king's tent was on that site, and he put the gods
he brought with him on its ancient altar. This was a foolish
thing to do and later it cost him dearly.

Polidonus of Athens (he was the king and duke of that
land) was camped at a spring where the water was sweet and
clear. This was the source of the Méandre, whose waters are
good for navigation and go by André, a city in Africa. Dëin-
fans of Byzantium, the most powerful of all the noblemen,
was lodged beside a wood where there were many wild

bears. Protesilaus, from Britain, of Menelaus's lineage, camped by an estuary above the water of the Tabari. Why should I tell you all the names? The list would be too long if I recounted the name of every one of King Avenir's men. They were all lodged together, as they should be, for they did not stop in any other place. They played musical instruments, the horses whinnied, and the standards they had set up waved in the wind. Gold glistened in the sun, and the indigo and vermillion colors of the tents glimmered. When evening came, the most valiant men of the company took the watch, and the night was long for those who stayed awake to watch the city.

The night passed, day returned. From all sides, they rose and armed themselves. Their armor shone, their shields showed many colors, and the gleam from their helms and hauberks rivaled the sun's rays. When the companions were all armed, they were divided into ranks. King Avenir joined them eagerly, for he wanted to be in the first attack. But the king of Britain took the honor from him when he asked permission to lead the advance.

Both sides prepared carefully. The archbishop and Josaphat considered the assault seriously. They met to take counsel with each other, but first the archbishop sang the mass and Josaphat received God's absolution. Then they debated what they should do. King Josaphat was confident and trusted God, and he vowed that nothing would prevent them from confronting their attackers. The archbishop agreed, and by the king's commandment, they all armed themselves. The king was first to put on his armor. He had never before taken up arms, but he intended to demonstrate his power and strength to his enemies. A valet brought him a prized Greek horse (no count or king had a better one). He mounted skillfully, for he knew how to ride. With a loyal heart, he asked God his Creator to have mercy on him that day, and on his people who prepared for battle. He marveled to see them so joyful and happy to go to war. Everyone in the city was armed; they had all mounted their horses and taken ranks. They were ready for battle.

King Avenir's men rode toward the city and began the assault. King Josaphat's men let sharp arrows fly from the parapets and defended themselves bravely. There was a fierce battle, and the knights from Britain attacked as hard as they could. They were very good archers, but Josaphat's men came against them in strength and many were wounded. Any man who could pull a bow attacked or defended.

King Josaphat cried to his people: "Open the gate so we can go outside. Let us see which of us will fall first in the battle." They opened the gates, and the well-armed battalions went out in tight ranks. They immediately began to fight without pity or fear, and the battle was engaged from all sides. They broke hauberks and chain mail, and they cut horses' reins. When their lances were broken, they immediately drew strong, sharp swords and trenchant axes. Vermillion blood bathed the steel, and the weapons looked as though they were bleeding. They fought hard and paid for their blows with their flesh—the field was strewn with bodies whose souls had departed, and with hands, feet, entrails, and heads without brains. Riderless horses roamed the field— many were wounded, many had escaped their reins, and many were killed. Wounded men cried out in dolorous laments. Some drowned in blood and many were trampled to death by horses.

The battle was heavy and hard, and the engagement was long. The king of Britain fought well. He was a good knight and a pagan. He rode hard against the Christians, and he and his men attacked with force. This king thought hard about how to take the Christians, but they defended themselves well. They had many men, and they had God and his strength to help them. The two sides came against each other again and again, with great charges and blows. The battle was equal on both sides, it seems to me, and each side harmed the other.

A castellan from Josaphat's city had armed himself well. He was nobly attired with lance and shield, and he charged forward to do great damage. He encountered a well-armed duke who was weakened from the loss of blood and went to joust against him. The knights broke their lances, then drew their swords and struck each other relentlessly. The duke was brave and attacked with great strength, and the strong blows they exchanged damaged their shields.

The battle was hard, and it was almost over when another echelon came at the defenders and revived the battle. The pagans ambushed the Christians, who would never have lasted if God had not helped them, for the battalion came upon them all at once. The battle was almost lost, I believe, when the archbishop and King Josaphat arrived to help the Christians. They returned to the battle with renewed courage and earned great honor. Each fought as well as he could, and the archbishop struck many strong blows. He knew if the battle were not won, Christianity would be lost. He fought well and broke many mail shirts; he split many helms and killed many pagans in the battle. His blood-drenched sword was twisted and dented, and his damaged shield had taken at least a hundred blows. He fought with courage, as did the entire army.

The Christians defeated the king of Britain and Miradeus of Babylon, who was the son of Semiramis. (History records that she was the founder of Babylon, but she was not the first to build in that place, for in earlier times giants had foolishly built a great tower there to rival God. He punished them by giving them a language that troubled their thoughts so that they could not understand each other. This tower was called Babel, and the name Babylon came from Babel.) Miradeus and the king of Britain left the battle, but they had paid their dues. They left many of their men dead on the field, and there were many dead from our side too.

Miradeus sat fully armed on his warhorse. He had done well that day and was reluctant to leave the field. He turned back repeatedly to charge against his enemy and rejoined the

battle many times. He guided his men out of the battle with
difficulty, trying to prevent the Christians from striking them
down. He was very sorry that they had been pushed back so
far. Then Arcelaus, a Christian knight, rode out of the ranks
to confront him. Arcelaus was well armed and his horse was
eager. When Miradeus saw him, he turned his horse toward
him. Both men spurred forward and each tried to harm the
other. They struck strong blows and pierced each other's
shields. Despite their armor, their bodies were also pierced.
Miradeus was gravely wounded, and Arcelaus died. He was
greatly to be lamented (he was a good Christian and a good
lord), but he received martyrdom for our Lord. When the
archbishop saw it, he was exceedingly sorrowful. He spurred
his horse quickly toward Miradeus, who waited for him, im-
mobile, on his horse. The wound on his thigh pained him
greatly. Miradeus bandaged his wound with a sleeve his lady
had given him as a love token.[1]

The archbishop struck him on the side of his shield. The
lance was strong, and he struck heavily and almost knocked
Miradeus from his horse. The knight held firm despite the
pain. He did not complain but was almost dead from his
wound. Miradeus said, "You are wrong to attack me in this
way when you see me so near death. It is not good chivalry if
you take what little life I have in my body. Your valor will
not increase if you kill me, for I am fatally wounded."

"You are wounded, friend? Where?"

"In my body."

"Then lay down your arms, for your soul is more seriously
wounded than your body, and your thoughts prevent its heal-
ing. You do not believe that you feel any pain there, but you
will. Your soul will feel pain when your body dies."

"Master, tell me—why? I have kept my religion and remained faithful to my gods."

"Then you will die disloyally because you refuse to recognize your Creator. Friend, leave this day behind you and
abandon those who attack us from outside the city! I will
heal your body and your soul."

"How will you heal my body, Master? I am wounded so seriously that I can expect only death. I do not see any other outcome."

"Friend, I promise that if you become a Christian, I will heal your wound."

Miradeus said, "I put myself in your care, for I see that you are a wise man." The archbishop led away into the city with great honor. Everyone who heard about it rejoiced.

The Christians fought well and struck many good blows. The king of Britain was defeated—four counts captured him and sent him into the city, where the Christians disarmed him. Polidonus from Athens then joined the battle eagerly. He had more than ten thousand Greeks in his company. They forced the Christians back to the city, but they lost many men. When Josaphat saw the retreat, he armed himself and mounted a great warhorse. There were many knights with him, and they went out from the city in a great force, carrying one thousand shields. "God's help!" was their battle cry.

Josaphat went straight to the heart of the battle and struck down all he encountered. When his lance broke, he unsheathed his sword and struck more blows as he moved forward, using both sides of the blade. His companions fought well too. Their banners and standards were deployed, and their warhorses whinnied from the middle of the field. The pagans would have been foolish to wait for the battle, for two thousand men spurred toward them in a resounding charge.

The Saracens saw Josaphat's men coming, but they did not fear them. The good knights greeted them with steel blades. A hard and heavy battle began again, and neither hauberk nor chain mail was worth a penny. Josaphat's strength and anger took him into the center of the fighting. No one could endure the battle without courage. The knights did not stop to discuss land or inheritance; they used all their strength to destroy their opponents. This was no rhetorical disputation, nor was any judge present to hear arguments. They defended themselves with steel blades. Banners and standards were torn, and every knight struck blows as strongly as he could. Josaphat himself struck great blows to encourage the people he had called out to fight.

Polidonus fought well. He rode toward the Christians with ardor and strength. What a shame that he was a pagan, for he was a handsome knight and sat his horse well. He went through the ranks, encouraging his men, then he went quickly to seek King Josaphat. If he could find him, he would joust with him to demonstrate his prowess. His heart was happy to see so many noblemen striking blows with strength and vigor, and he thought that he could prove his prowess and thereby bring honor to his lady.[2] He fought well and defeated many Christians, killing most and wounding others. He shouted out his battle cry.

Josaphat's shield was pierced in many places, his casque was damaged, his mail shirt broken, and his blade covered in blood. He met Polidonus and they began to fight. The shields would pay dearly for the battle, for both fought hard. Josaphat landed a blow between Polidonus's shield and casque, wounding him gravely, and the Greek was dismayed to find himself so badly harmed. Blood spurted from his wound and drenched him down to his heels. He wanted badly to avenge the blow, and if he could use his blade, he would exact a severe vengeance. He raised his arm, aimed well, and brought it down on Josaphat's helm, knocking off the circle of gold. The blow glanced off the helmet and the sword broke. Josaphat would have been deeply wounded if the sword had not broken, and his blow would have been well avenged. The archbishop saw the king fighting with fervor, and he went into the middle of the field to watch the battle and see how the king fared as he pursued and tormented Polidonus, who continued to defend himself with what strength he had left. Josaphat showed his rival that he had been foolish to attack him.

The Christians were defeating the Turks, who would not last through the battle.[3] At noon the Turks' army had turned back. The Christians had put them to flight, but Josaphat kept the defeated Polidonus in his prison. Then he turned back to his enemies. The destruction was great. The Christians chased the pagans back to the Byzantine tents; they killed a hundred and fifty men and took more than twenty prisoners. The young ruler of Byzantium entered the battle against the Christians and their king. The archbishop encouraged his men: "My lords, do not lose your strength, for Argeus is coming against you with his men. They have rested here all day while you exhausted yourselves in battle for God. For his sake, forget your fatigue! Your pursuers are close, and they descend on you with fury. Defend yourselves, for God's sake, if you love your Lord and your life!" The archbishop blessed them, and the king exhorted them and offered them his help in the battle, his wealth, and anything they could want. When the Christians heard the exhortation, they were happy for the blessing that the archbishop gave them. Their courage returned, and they rushed toward the Saracens. Their hearts were noble, and loyalty was on their side and against their enemies. They advanced in well-ordered ranks and attacked all at once.

The contest was harsh. They gave each other great blows on their shields, many hauberks were broken, and many good knights were killed. Ten Christians were taken prisoner, and five Turkish dukes who held great domains. The Christians struck so many blows that the Saracens left the field first, defeated, a little before vespers. Many were killed and their bodies lay on the field. Armed knights lay gravely wounded, and riderless horses moved across the battlefield. The ruler of Byzantium lay dead under his steed. No tongue could describe the great suffering experienced in that day's battle. Feet, heads, and entrails were strewn across the field, and many wounded lay in the meadow alongside dead bodies with gaping mouths.

Nightfall separated the armies. The exhausted Christians returned to their city and went to their lodgings to remove their armor. King Avenir called for a truce, and the battle was suspended for three days. At dawn each side went to look for the dead on the field and bring back the wounded.

Prince Aracin plots to betray Josaphat

King Avenir looked on the destruction. He had lost so many of his nobles that he did not know where to address his sorrow. Josaphat, the king's son, also had good reason for lament. He had lost many of his friends and was most sorrowful, but he was comforted to know that the dead were saved. He had all the dead buried, and the wounded cared for.

The archbishop did not forget about Miradeus. He sent for the prisoner, and the guards brought him quickly. The archbishop admonished Miradeus and invited him to become a Christian. "Sire," Miradeus said, "I need no further instruction. Baptize me, by your mercy." The archbishop rejoiced when he heard him recognize the true belief, and Miradeus received baptism that day. But before he was baptized, Josaphat, the archbishop, and all the Christians, young and old, knelt to pray to God that Miradeus might be healed of the wound that threatened him. Immediately the bells of the Church of the Holy Cross began to ring, and the archbishop and the king crossed themselves. Miradeus was healed: his flesh sealed over the wound. No wise man should have been surprised by it, for Miradeus believed in the Creator! He no longer felt any pain because a good doctor had healed him. They praised and thanked God, and all the city rejoiced because God had cured Miradeus and he had been baptized. When the ruler of Britain heard of it, he too converted immediately. Polidonus of Athens did the same, and all the other prisoners repented of their sins and were baptized. The city was full of rejoicing, and the Christians said that it was a great fortune to recover the loss of those killed in the battle through the conversion of their enemies. They thought it was a good day.

King Avenir heard the news, and his heart was very heavy at the loss of his men. He cursed the gods he served because every day he lost more of his people. He had proposed the truce in anger and sent for more of his men.

Aracin came to him. "Sire, I will go into the city and demand that they give you this land."

"Friend, you should think of another plan," the king replied. "They have no reason to give back the land. They have defended their position and continue to win more people to their side. Go quickly and arm yourself, for we must attack and vanquish them or we will all be dead or taken prisoner." King Avenir's entire army prepared for battle, as did the defenders, and when they were all armed they went out in tight ranks. Josaphat's men waited outside the city's walls as the enemy came toward them. There was great noise from both sides. They were all armed, and they attacked each other as enemies. The battle was harsh and strong, and each side fought hard. Miradeus was armed and mounted on a war horse to fight as a soldier of our Lord. Aracin fought well and led a great host into the battle. Many Christians were killed or wounded, and the field was strewn with dead pagans, including some of the highest born. If you had been present, you would have claimed never to have seen such a hard battle, or so many great blows given and so many received, so many men crying out from wounds, or so many dying in pain. Miradeus jousted against Aracin and struck him on his shield. His lance was straight and his arm was strong, and Miradeus knocked Aracin to the ground. He dropped his lance to draw his sword; he harried Aracin from all sides and cut the laces of his helm. Aracin cried to him, "Miradeus, my lord, have mercy! I yield in good faith. Make me your prisoner."

"I grant it," said Miradeus. He let him rise and had him taken to prison.

The scrimmage was fierce and the knights were exhausted. The battle had grown more intense but the Christians had almost won it. The new Christians fought well; they could no longer tolerate the pagans. King Avenir was very sorrowful when he saw that he had lost both the battle and the land. He left the field with great regret. "Alas," he said, "my great love for my son has led me to misfortune. My love was misplaced and our religion has been shamed." The Christians pursued the pagans and attacked them. While the king lamented, the Saracens were almost overcome. The battle lasted until the two sides separated at dusk. The Christians returned joyfully to their city. King Avenir was very angry and took shelter in his lodging.

Aracin plotted a betrayal from inside Josaphat's prison. He sent for the archbishop and the king, and asked them what they planned to do with him. The good archbishop began to preach to him and Aracin began to sigh. He pretended to be repentant, in order to betray them. "My heart is sincere," he said. "I am a wealthy man, the master counselor of the king and his lords. You should baptize me. If the men on the other side know that I am a Christian and a believer, I believe they too will be baptized. King Avenir's people will come to God, and his religion will grow and prosper." The archbishop rejoiced to see Aracin turn into the right path. He thought the war would be ended by his conversion and peace would return.

Prince Aracin was baptized immediately, but the felon deceived them all. He did not love God or believe in him. He deceived the Christians with his baptism, and he hoped to deceive them further by persuading them to heed his advice. Aracin called quickly for a messenger and sent him to King Avenir. He told the king that he knew how to make him happy again. Aracin would tell him how he could take the city.

King Avenir rejoiced. "Ah, Aracin," he said, "you have always loved me and known how to advise me." The king spoke to the messenger: "Good friend, tell Aracin that I will do what he asks so that he can deliver the city to me. Let him send me instructions and I will follow them."

"By God," said the messenger, "first I will tell you what he has already done because of his love for you. He has been baptized in the name of their Lord. He tells them that he believes, but he lies. It is part of his plot. He deceives them by using their religion, for he saw that there was no other way."

"How cleverly he uses his situation!" replied the king. "He

is surely my ally. Go back to him and tell him that I will do as he asks." The messenger went quickly to tell Aracin how eagerly the king had received his plan.

Aracin devised a way to betray the Christians in the city. He took pains to serve Josaphat. He showed deference before him and appeared to have a strong faith. He often asked the priests of the Holy Cross about doctrine, and he devoted himself to the religion.

The negotiations between the armies led to a truce of eight days. The Christians marveled that Aracin had been so thoroughly converted. He seemed gentle and pious, and he never ceased his adoration of the crucifix. The traitor deceived the Christians, for they truly believed that his conversion was real, and they rejoiced for it—they were never happier. Out of sovereign love, the king gave him charge of the highest tower in the city. The traitor had what he wanted then, because he thought that from the tower he could betray the Christians and their good city without any resistance. Aracin hated King Josaphat and his reign. He called for one of the messengers he had told about his plan. He sent him secretly to tell King Avenir to prepare the army, for he would give him the city shortly.

Aracin was assigned the guard of one of the city's strongest towers, and no one watched over him. If King Avenir could enter the tower, he would take the city. The messenger went to tell Avenir what Aracin planned. The king heard Aracin's instructions and loved him greatly for sending them. He summoned all his people and told them what Aracin had devised. "My lords," he said, "I wonder how Aracin thought of such a good plan. He is new to my service and devoted to me. Before the end of this week, he will give us this beautiful, strong castle." The Turks rejoiced at the news because they thought they saw an end to the war. They longed for their lands and wished to return home. The council came to an end, and the messenger went back into the city.

There was a good man in King Avenir's army who believed

secretly in God. When he heard the king's words, they seemed vain and foolish to him. He would be most sorrowful if any harm came to the Christians. "I am King Avenir's vassal," he thought. "I must not betray him if I wish to keep faith with him. I do not know if it would be dishonest to send word to King Josaphat about his father's betrayal. All good men should be offended by King Avenir's plan, but I do not dare show my displeasure. Should I not act? I believe I would betray the king if I sent word to his son, and yet I have great pity for Josaphat. If I do not warn him, it is not because I am afraid but because I would fail in my obligation to his father. However wrong he may be, King Avenir is my lord. He does not wish to become a good man for my sake, nor do I wish to do wrong by betraying him. But is it a betrayal? By faith, I believe I misspeak, for I do not see any betrayal in it. In fact, I am a traitor if I knowingly tolerate betrayal. Should I go to King Avenir and tell him so? I would be a fool if I did that, for he would not abandon his plan for my sake, and I would be foolish to reveal to him something that would cost me my life. If I did that, I would deliberately seek my own death.

"Alas!" he said, "I do not know what to do, for there is no good course. If harm comes to the Christians, then all the good I have done in this world will be lost. But if I send word to them, I will be disloyal. Yet if any harm comes to them by my fault, I will do a great injustice. This is not what I desire nor have I sought it.

"I will commit a great sin if I tell my lord's secret—these are his enemies and he is right to seek ways to deceive them. They would do the same to him. I should suffer if by my actions I prevent my lord from taking the tower. By faith, I will not take his victory from him. But if I do not, I will do wrong, for I should have more faith in God than in our laws. I will act disloyally if I lie to God, and if I reject pagan beliefs, then I should not lie. I do not believe that I will do wrong if I send news of the betrayal to the Christians. I will hold to this decision, for I will not let them be betrayed."

He sent a messenger secretly into the city, to tell King Josaphat about the plot. The king was angry and told everything he had learned to the archbishop, who was dismayed. "According to what I understand, this Aracin has betrayed us. He should die a painful death, for he has acted villainously if what we hear is true."

"Listen to me," said King Josaphat. "It would not be right to condemn him unless he is taken in the act. He is supposed to betray us tonight, but he will be watched so closely that if he begins to put the betrayal in action, we will know it." The day passed and night came. Josaphat sent his men to watch the tower.

The truce ended during the night. The army outside the gates believed the city would be lost before daybreak, because they had confidence in the traitor who had been betrayed. Aracin waited for King Avenir's men. They had armed themselves quietly before approaching the city. King Josaphat's watchman saw that they were coming, urging their horses forward silently. He saw that Aracin waited for them at the tower, wearing his arms. The watchman's warning cry echoed through the city and woke the king. The men on the walls had secretly armed themselves and went to confront Aracin. The traitor had not expected them, and he retreated into the tower. He knew he had been discovered and his plan thwarted. King Avenir's men heard the watchman's cry and knew they had failed. They saw that the city had been alerted and the banner of the king raised in the tower. They fled in disarray and went back to their camp.

Great cries were heard throughout the city and many cursed the traitor. Aracin was in the tower and he was afraid. He did not trust those who watched him from below. The tower was attacked from all sides, and Aracin did not know how to defend himself. He was ashamed and fearful, and he did not dare to leave the tower, because he feared death. King Josaphat's men sought justice. They attacked the tower angrily, and when they took it, Aracin was captured and brought before the king.

"You have committed a great sin by lying about your faith in God," said Josaphat, "and it brings me deep sorrow. Ah, felonious traitor, what were you thinking when you sent word to my father and offered him this tower? You will die, for your betrayal has been proven. You will admit your bad faith when your body is delivered over to cruel torture and a dishonorable death. You are condemned by your own judgment, since you pledged yourself to God, and you will die in great shame." King Josaphat had a fire built (this was the law then), and when it was hot, Aracin was thrown in and burned.

King Avenir converts and Christianity spreads

King Avenir heard that Aracin had been taken from the tower by force and condemned to death, and he recognized that he had been wrong to go to war against his son. He knew that those who had become Christians were in the right. Avenir acted according to his true nature. He sent a messenger into the city to ask for the archbishop. The archbishop came to King Avenir and explained the path of truth and told him how he could be saved, and the king listened well. He made peace with Josaphat and then went back into his own kingdom.

It truly happened in this way. Holy Christianity grew and God was served and honored in many countries. The newly baptized Christians went back to their lands and cast down their idols. They crushed and destroyed the statues they used to worship and instead taught the good faith. Many people were baptized, from Byzantium to Britain, and Miradeus preached holy Christianity in Babylonia. We know all this is true.

Back in his own country, King Avenir regretted that he had

dwelt so long in darkness. He recognized that his gods were evil and his belief in them was foolish. He repented for his false belief and feared he would never receive forgiveness, despite his promises and his wealth. He sent for his lords and told them about his conversion. He asked them what they wished to do. As God who saves all sinners wished it, they responded with a single voice: "Sire, for God's sake and for the sake of the cross, let us leave behind the false faith that has blinded us and let us know the Creator, for we should not believe in any other god. This belief is completely true."

Their response made King Avenir very happy. His heart was ready to serve God. He called for a messenger and sent word to his son that he and his men were ready to become Christians and leave the religion of their ancestors. When Josaphat heard the news, he praised God and gave thanks for his father's decision. The city rejoiced and its people offered their gratitude to God. Josaphat gave the greatest thanks and asked God to confirm his father's heart, so it would remain submissive and he would be saved. Josaphat would never have been happy unless Avenir had converted, and he was content to know with certainty that his father had repented. He hastened to his father's city, accompanied by the wise archbishop. When Avenir heard that his son was coming, he went out to meet him and received him joyfully. The father rejoiced to bow before his son.

Josaphat and the archbishop went to the palace, where they were greeted with honor. The father sat beside his son, who told him about this world and how it would end. Then he explained divine law from the very beginning. He showed him that God had made every creature and designed all nature. He told him that God made the first man, Adam, who bit the apple and was thrown out of paradise when his act was discovered. He explained that God came to earth to redeem all sinners, was wrongly hanged on a cross, suffered death, and then was resurrected. Josaphat taught his father well, and King Avenir listened willingly, for he believed in

God with a good heart. Avenir was baptized and all the people rejoiced. He repented for his sins.

The archbishop baptized all Avenir's people. The city was converted, and the king was happy and rejoiced because of it. The idols were thrown down and the houses of pagan worship destroyed. King Avenir had churches built and endowed with rich altars and cloisters. He loved Christianity—he repented sincerely and his conscience was happy because it was turned to God. He did not care to govern his realm and gave all his land to his son so he could devote himself to God. He prostrated himself in prayer every day and asked God to forgive the sins that condemned him to die.

King Avenir lived this life for four years after his conversion. He led a hard life and humbled himself before God. He was certain and firm in his faith. After four years, his body became weakened, but not his belief. He continued to repent in his illness. He gave himself completely to God, recounting all his sins and asking for mercy. Josaphat comforted him and taught him about God. He told his father of the forgiveness God promised him if he would confess. "Father, you must offer all your love and do all the good you can imagine in order to save yourself. Think always about God and be sure that you have confessed, for through confession you will gain forgiveness. Confession is a medicine for sinners and the root of repentance and good deeds. For God's sake, examine your heart and repent truly according to your belief. Then you may expect forgiveness on the Day of Judgment. You were dead and now you live, for the unbeliever must die even while he believes that he lives. You are delivered from the death that awaits any sinner who does not repent. Whoever expects forgiveness and believes he will receive it is healed, and without forgiveness you could never see God. But his mercy is greater than his judgment, and you can know with faith that God will have mercy on you—do not doubt it. Put yourself entirely in his hands: there is no more secure place in the world. In your struggle with this false world, be attentive to the good and guard against the evil. Do good deeds and repent of the great evil you have done."

King Avenir sighed and wept. He regretted his sins and repented with a true heart. "Good son," he said, "sweet friend, you have counseled me every day, and through you I am healed and delivered from all ills. Because of you, God rules my heart. I believe in God and give myself to him in good faith. I commend my body and my soul to him." With that, the king died. His soul left his body and joined the company of angels, and his penance was lightened because he died in true repentance.

Josaphat saw that his father had died, he who had been emperor, king, and lord of Greater India. He thanked the Creator that his father died a believer, for he knew without doubt that God would have mercy on him. Josaphat wept for his father and there was great mourning throughout the land. He wept from pity and from joy, for he was joyful that his father would receive forgiveness. King Avenir's vassals assembled when they learned about the death of their lord, and after seven days of mourning, they buried him with great honor. The body was not wrapped in royal silken fabric; it was placed in the tomb covered only by an old, worn hair shirt made of coarse wool. King Avenir was interred before the altar of Saint Mary in an abbey Josaphat had built for him. One hundred monks wearing black were installed there, and they prayed every day for all the dead and for the king who had left the false religion to worship the Creator.[1] Josaphat spent the whole day before the tomb, praying to God that he would have mercy on his father's soul. This was King Avenir's end, and this is how we should all come to God.

Those of you who wish to repent of your sins should take this as an example. This king was cruel and false and he did much evil in this world, but then when he repented he received God's mercy. Sinners, turn to your Creator, repent truly and do your penance while you still have time. Did your ancestors not die? My lords, they did, and so will you. Why, then, are you so attached to this evil world? After you die, there will be no turning back, and if you repent after your death, it will be too late. Do good while you live, as did the man this story describes—he cleansed his body of sin through the good he did in the world. Purify yourselves as he did, for he left this world in a pure state because of his penance and good deeds.

Josaphat wishes to leave his kingdom

Josaphat returned to his palace. He had brought peace to his land, and he spent his father's wealth wisely by giving it to the poor. He gave his possessions to the needy and shared all he had. He did not wish to own more than the poor people he helped, and they were in great need. When he had given away all he owned, he sent for his lords. When they were all assembled, the king spoke his thoughts: "My lords, I have sent for you so that you can hear my will. My father is dead. He could not be saved by his high position, his sovereignty, his kingdom, his great power, his fortress, his city, his wealth, or his lineage. Even I myself, his son, could not save him, and I did not wish for him to die. Now he is dead and must go to justify his works and be judged. Nothing will be hidden, and the works he has done in this world will be apparent. He will be judged for all he has done, and the same will come to all who live in this world and to all who will ever be born in it. My lords, as you know, I am a Christian like yourselves. You are my brothers and my friends, and you have reconciled yourselves to God through holy Christianity. I am in fear for my soul. For a long time I have wished to live as a hermit, and I still long for it. I stayed in this world for my father's sake, until he was willing to convert to God. Now his soul is in God's hands, and I will leave this world. I will not stay with you any longer, for I wish to change my life and dwell with my master, if I can find him. This world is like a deep well full of sweet poisoned water, and I will not dwell here—I have stayed too long and it has weighed on me for some time. Now I will take my leave of you and give you my crown. I will not be your lord any longer. You must choose another."

The noblemen of Josaphat's kingdom responded with one voice: "Sire, for God's sake, take it back, take it back! Is it true that you would leave us? This is your land and your inheritance. We would suffer great harm if you were to leave us, and only with great sorrow would we be separated from you. Sire, for God's sake, consider this: it would be a cruel sin to abandon this kingdom, for no one can rule it better. Sire, for God's sake and for the sake of the cross, do not permit a foreign king to claim the land."

The noise of the people's unhappiness grew. Everyone in the city was in tears, and everyone lamented and regretted Josaphat's decision. They showed great sorrow and cried out loudly. There was much weeping and lamentation, and the people's mourning was to be pitied because their pain would not be relieved and they would find no comfort.

Josaphat said, "My lords, cease your lamenting and leave your sorrow. Do not weep, for your king goes away for a good reason. To fight against the devil is a good battle, for the body is full of filth and a weak vessel for the soul. A man who rules a kingdom makes mistakes, and I know with certainty that no one can reign justly. Disloyalty and immoderation make war against what is right, and a ruler must do many wrongs: send men to death, say false things, go against the truth, hear false judgments, disinherit good men, and undertake wars to defend the land. Orphans must be lost, widows wrongly destroyed, poor knights ruined, and slanderers heeded. This is what earthly kings do. They do not think of the good. To save my soul, I must leave these things behind."

Then the cries were renewed along with a great clamor of grief, and the noise from the weeping grew louder. Throughout the city, they cried out in laments for the brave and wise Josaphat who wanted to leave his inheritance and renounce his crown. He did not want to hold them all his life. "Sire," they said, "for God's sake, have mercy! If you leave us like this, we will be delivered into shame. Evil kings and wicked counts will destroy your kingdom. For God's sake, good sire, listen to us. You have sixteen cities and one hundred castles. Not a single pagan remains—they have all become Christians. You brought them salvation and they have been baptized. Now you will leave them? You are their lord, their brother, and their ancestral king. You are an unfaithful friend if you would leave them like this! Listen to our supplications, stay with us out of mercy and because we beg you not to leave!"

"My lords," he said, "this cannot be. I must seek my master, for I promised to do so a long time ago. Now I will go to find him. I wish to spend whatever remains of my life in the hermitage. My lords, I am a faithful friend to you if I go to heal my soul, for I should not value a kingdom more than my soul. In fact, I am surprised that I have stayed for so long. You should not regret my departure—you should desire it since I go to save my soul. I am king and I give the kingdom back to you. God will not abandon you! I am sorry to leave you and it pains me to depart, but I must leave you to go and pay for my sins. For God's sake, my lords, do not weep, but listen to me and make peace with my decision, for you can choose a lord who will be a good king and worthy of the reign."

He called Barachie forward. This Barachie was a wise nobleman of good reputation. He had been a Christian for a long time, and he was one of the learned men who attended Nachor's disputation. I described him before, and I remind you that he was the third Christian present when Nachor won the field in the joust with the astronomers.[1] Josaphat called him forward and asked him to take the crown. He chose Barachie and freely gave him the land, for he loved him and trusted that the kingdom would be safe with him.

Barachie resisted. "It is not fair to burden me with what you yourself wish to abandon," he said. "It is not a privilege to receive what you do not want. The land and the inheritance are yours. Be wise and keep them. My lord, listen to reason: your people need your guidance. It would be wrong to leave them, and disloyal, and disloyalty is not wisdom. It is not right that you should leave your kingdom."

"My lord, for God's sake, cease this complaint," said Josaphat. "There is no point to it, for I will make you king, Barachie. I swore to my master a long time ago that I would be with him. There is nothing more to say. I am going, and I am leaving you the crown."

Barachie said, "You know that it would not be right to leave this place without your people's consent. Can pity not move you? If the kingdom falls, it will be your fault. You must teach your people. If you wish to honor your bond with them, you must govern, correct, keep, and protect them. How do you know what I will do when I am king of the land? If I do harm, as many other kings do, it will be your fault. Ah, Josaphat, do you not see that it would be wrong to betray us? The land is yours and you can very well save your soul here while you are king. If you stay, the laws that you introduced will grow stronger, but if you abandon us, they will no longer be feared and respected."

Josaphat said, "Good, dear friend, although the laws first came from me, those who have become Christians will keep them well. All India is Christian now. There is no castle or town where God is not served. The entire kingdom has been converted and all the people have turned to God. If I leave my office, it is because I am not worthy to hold it, and I wish to leave it with dignity. You will rule the people well.

"You are worthy of the crown, and worthy is the king who gives you the kingdom you merit," Josaphat continued. "If you receive it with humility, then your worth will be doubled. Consider your lineage—your family is noble enough for you to become king. Put aside your hesitation since the kingdom falls to you and the crown claims you. Be on guard against the evil in the world. Life goes quickly, and everyone is the same when the time to die arrives. You must take the kingdom, and I must go to other things."

"No, I will not do it," Barachie said. "I will not take it. You must seek another king, because I am not worthy."

Josaphat left him. The day ended and night arrived. All the people went back to their houses. Josaphat thought about how he could best acquit his obligations toward God. He spent the whole night writing a letter. He recorded his reasons for leaving his home and his kingdom. He named Barachie king and sent word of his choice to his nobles. He did not know a better man in all the kingdom or one more worthy of the honor. He humbly asked that they recognize Barachie as their king. Then he left the palace, intending never to reenter it. He left his letter on the dais and departed.

But the people came out into the streets, sobbing and crying out loudly, "Josaphat has betrayed us and he is leaving. Go after him and bring him back to the palace. If he is not willing to be king, he must be king against his will. We will keep him by force since he would force us to let him leave." All the lords went after him. They crowned him in his palace, in front of all the people of the city, and cared little for what he wanted. The noise was loud and the cries great. Never was a king crowned so unwillingly. He swore to his barons that they crowned him for nothing and for nothing would he hold court. From that day forward they would never see him on the throne, if it were up to him.

The lords proposed a compromise: they would do his will and would not force him to remain, but they asked Josaphat to crown a king who knew how to keep his law: "Good sire, choose a lord who knows how to rule us!" they pleaded.

"My lords," he said, "I will do so." He stood and took hold of Barachie and put the royal ring on his finger. Josaphat crowned Barachie against his will in front of all his people. Josaphat did not want to be king anymore. He gave the office to Barachie, for whom it was a burden, but he was forced to take it by the great cries, the loud noise, and the complaints of the assembled lords.

Josaphat counseled him gently, "King Barachie, now you

rule this land. Now you must take pains to exalt God and his law, as is fitting for a loyal king. If you wish to rule your people well, you must remain loyal to your lords. Reason and rectitude will give your heart intelligence and restraint. Carry rectitude as your standard so that unreason does not harm it. Worship the Lord God and the holy church as I have always done. Counsel the poor, and do not accept gold or silver for doing wrong. Sire, be attentive, fearful, and watchful. Be humble, eschew pride, and stop at the threshold before entering a room. Keep good counsel. Keep your land in peace. You will have a palace, houses, towers, and castles, but do not disdain the poor people of your empire because of all the honors you enjoy."

With these words, Josaphat kissed the king and the barons around him. He took his leave humbly and they all cried with pity. They were sorrowful and regretted their loss. As Josaphat departed, the weeping people surrounded him. They were most sad and sorrowful, and they were dismayed to see their lord leave. There were so many people assembled that Josaphat could hardly leave the city. All day they accompanied him and were reluctant to let him go. They did not want to leave him before nightfall, but then the darkness separated them.

How extraordinary that such a wise and noble man would leave his inheritance, his lands, and his honors for the sake of his Creator! Josaphat fled to the hermitage, leaving his land and his reign. He went joyfully and happily since he exiled himself for God. He left all the delights of the world, and he constrained his body to bring his soul to salvation.

When Josaphat's lords turned back, he fled, and never did a happier man escape. Those left behind were sad and went home confused and sorrowful, but Josaphat went joyfully to seek God, leaving behind his honors and his lands. He had on rich silken clothing, but beneath his royal vestments he wore the hair shirt that Barlaam had left him. He came to the home of a poor man, who offered him lodging and received a rich reward for his hospitality, since Josaphat gave him his clothes. Then he traveled on with joy and great haste. He carried neither water nor bread. His heart was satisfied because it was filled and illuminated with virtue. All his thoughts were with God; he did not think of anything else. He reprimanded himself and chastised his body. He lived in the hermits' wilderness and thought only of serving God. He sought never to be separated from him.

My lords, do not doubt me, I would not lie to you. Josaphat entered the place where the hermits dwelled and was enlightened by God. But the place was large and the way was hard. This was the hermitage of Sanar, a deserted wilderness and a thick wood with no paths through it. A severe drought was in the land and had lasted more than three hundred days. There were no houses, castles, or fortresses, and only caves offered the covering of a roof. No one lived there except hermits who had left the world behind. There was little joy and much suffering, exile, desolation, and a great many snakes.

The wilderness was vast and its trials were many. Josaphat entered it gladly, praising our Lord that he had reached the harsh, wild hermitage. He lived on roots and herbs; these were sweet medicines that would bring his soul to glory when its victory was perfected. The devil assailed him and took many forms to try to deceive him, but God directed Josaphat's way. He was with him and remained with him. When the devil tried to make him sin, Josaphat remembered the scriptures and made the sign of the cross against the devil, who found him so full of firm resolve that he could not discourage him or make him sin.

The noble and gentle Josaphat moved alone through the hermits' wilderness. He wandered without direction and chastised his body by fasting and going without sleep. He suffered as he walked, naked and in prayer. When he remembered the devil, he burned for God. His limbs became blackened and he was nothing but skin and bones. He had a hard and cruel bed at night, whereas before he had reposed with great comfort and pleasure in his royal chambers, but the

harsh bed seemed delightful to him and he lay there in safety.
The young man was happy and joyful because he turned his
thoughts to God. Each day he prayed for Barlaam. He did
not know what had become of him or where he dwelled, and
he prayed that God would allow him to find his master. Josaphat sought Barlaam for two years, and he suffered many trials and much pain, but God led him and would save him. As
Josaphat wandered through the hermitage, he trained his
heart as he praised and served God. Never did a count or
king love his Creator so much that he would abandon such
great honors to travel through the wilderness, living on herbs
in the woods.

A debate between Josaphat's body and soul

Josaphat's soul and his body were engaged in a fierce battle.
The body's attachment to the pleasures of the world threatened to destroy the soul. The body remembered the noble
and beautiful crown it had lost, but the soul claimed that the
earthly crown was worthless compared to the one that comes
from on high. The body replied that the second could be
gained while wearing the first. "The crown was your birth-
right and you abandoned it," the body reproached the soul.
"Now you know that you were wrong, for this life is too
cruel.

"It is a sin to mistreat me," the body continued. "You deprive and deceive me. You have become my enemy and you
try to kill me. What wrong have I done you that you would
wish to murder me so violently? I am your host and I lodge
you, but only the wood and pegs remain of my house. The
rafters are bare, and you have abandoned me. I was once
very beautiful, but you have destroyed me. You hate me and
love yourself. You were once married to me, but you destroy

our union. You harm me when you rob me of my nobility, my power, and my wealth. You have taken away my pleasures and my delights, my comforts, my privileges, my soft bed, my rich table and my good food, and the servants and valets who served me. All these belong to a king, but where are the food, the wine, and my cups of fine gold now? Where are the silver and the gold that used to fill my treasury? Where are the rich silken fabrics I used to wear? Where are the servants who served me day and night? Everything is lost and I am naked and sorrowful. Alas, I do not know where to turn. I have to stay awake all night and fast all day, and I cannot do anything about it. Alas! I have nothing to cover myself with and nothing to eat."

"Stop it, sad creature," the soul responded. "What were you, what are you, and what will you be? You were nothing, you are nothing, and you will become nothing! What is a great household worth to you, what can wealth, power, or a kingdom bring you, when you have to die in the end? As for your house, the posts and the rafters have fallen because of a little suffering, and yet there is no weight on them! See how miserable your limbs are, but I know you do not think about them and you do not care what I become! Miserable thing, remember that the joy of this world lasts only a short time— think on the enduring happiness that the scriptures describe. I believe there is more sorrow than pleasure in the joy of this world. It begins in sorrow and ends in sorrow. But the joy of heaven is so precious and fine that no one can describe it, however well he speaks. What is the joy of this world worth? What good is silken cloth? Everything grows old and every-thing fades away. There is no delight in the world equal to the pleasure of serving God."

The body did not accept this reasoning. "You are wrong, dear companion. My father, Avenir, was a king and emperor, and he lived happily in the world, enjoying honors, rich cloth-ing, and noble surroundings. He had everything he desired, and he did as he wished with his wealth and knowledge, and for a long time he did not believe. Then at the end of his life,

he believed in God and did many good deeds, just as the
Christians do. He was not lost, I believe, and he enjoyed
many pleasures in the world!

"Do you believe that God would destroy us with his teaching?" the body continued. "Why did he make this world so
beautiful if all those who live in it will be damned? Do you
say that those who serve and worship God while well shod
and well dressed will be lost? You are foolish to torment me.
God made beautiful things to delight men, for no one can
spend every minute in worship. You have betrayed me by
taking me away from the world. I was in the world, and now
I am parted from it. I had a part of the world, you parted me
from it, and now my part is very poor. I am naked, barefoot,
and impoverished. You allow me to suffer."

"By God," said the soul, "you are wrong. You are earning
life through death. Because of your poverty and nudity, and
through your hunger, thirst, and discomfort, you will become a lord in heaven. You know well that here below we decline and perish without any certainty of when we will die.
Do you know when your life will end? When I leave you, you
will be a vile cadaver to be shunned and avoided.

"What are you saying about King Avenir? It is true that he
was a powerful ruler. He had honor and esteem as long as he
lived, but in the end he repented and undertook a harsh penance to reconcile himself to God and make peace with him.
In the end he proved himself worthy to be saved, but you do
not want to carry the burden King Avenir took up. You want
to sin with hope, and whoever sins without fear should be
judged to die. This is why I keep you poor and naked and
give you so little to eat—if your house were covered with a
roof you would find comfort, but you would risk being lost. I
admonish you with hunger, and I am distressed that you reproach me, for I do it in good faith."

"By faith," said the body, "there is no good faith here,
since you are killing me. You are a traitor when you kill your
companion, and you will never come to God while you make
me live in such shame. I was most unfortunate to be joined to

you. You sin and betray yourself when you kill me, and you know it well. You do not care about me any more than you would a dog. Why do you want to kill me? You do not act nobly, and I do not see how you can profit from this, for sin cancels out charity. My companion attacks me. I am dying of thirst and hunger. I see fruit hanging on the tree and I want it, but I cannot taste it. You let me die of hunger. This is why I accuse you of disloyalty: you are wrong to wrong me, when you could treat me well. Do other Christians act this way?"

"Yes, by faith, they do. They sacrifice the body to save the soul."

"By faith, there is no reason in this. I pay too dearly for your salvation when I am tortured like this."

"What logic you use!" replied the soul. "If I were to be saved without you and you did not share in my rejoicing, then it would be unjust that you should suffer for me. But I believe that you cannot be saved without me, nor I without you. You know this too. I suffer pain and sorrow for your salvation, but you would seek only shame for me if I made you my lord. I leave you in need so that you will not be sullied by the filth of sin.

"I am your lady and you are my servant," the soul continued.[1] "You can be sure that I will never make you my lord, and I will tell you why. If I made you my lord, I would lose our Lord, and so I will not give you power over me. I know you and your pride well enough to know that you would turn my pure thoughts to great shame. It is not worth it to me. I speak to correct you, for you are excessively proud of your lineage. You think about your earthly legacy and that is why you hate this hermitage. You accuse me of treason, but you do wrong, for I am not a traitor and it is right that I chastise you."

"You admonish me too harshly," the body complained. "Give me at least a little relief, for I cannot bear this. My suffering increases every day. You know I speak the truth, for you can see how weak I have become. If I do not find water and salt, I will no longer be able to speak. I will never be able to move from here if you do not have a little mercy on me."

"Mercy for what?"

"I am starving!"

"If you were full and satisfied, you would think of even more foolish things than you do now. Your hunger makes you think of nothing other than pleasing yourself. You remember your pleasures, but I do not care, for I know that they will not do you any good and you cannot have them. Make peace with it, for they will never return. You should be happy to lose them, for a fattened body cannot live in this world without sin, and I save you from fattening yourself. You will never have another rich meal, and you must bear it. You gain nothing from feeding your body if you do not feed your thoughts with the memory of sin. You cannot put your trust anywhere else, for I have taken you away from your old life out of pity and compassion."

"As I see it, you don't have any pity for me at all since you allow me to suffer," said the body. "I would prefer that you leave me rather than stay with me like this. My flesh is pale and weak. My face is discolored. If you are my lady, you are a bad one when you neglect me like this!"

"I neglect you? By God, I do not, my friend. On the contrary, I care for you constantly. I suffer a harsh penance to save you from judgment, but rather than help, you hinder me. You seek your own death and you would destroy me too. You give me bad advice while I suffer pain and misery to pay for your pleasures. I make a distressful pilgrimage through the hermitage to win you a crown, and you should rejoice in it! Friend, what would happen to you without me? I feed and look after you, and you lust after sin. I do not know what I can say to you since you try to kill me. You cannot last long here, and you will have to die. Think about this, I do not jest! This life is but a brief passage, and you will die forever if God does not redeem you. Remember the coming judgment, the joy of heaven, and the torments of hell!"

"What?" the body exclaimed. "Are those who enjoy pleasure in this world tormented when they die?"

"Yes, truly, it is so. They are justly tormented, for the world deceives them and they do not repent."

"When a man repents before he dies, will he be saved?"

"Yes, truly, of all his sins. But such a repentance is a fearful salvation."

"How so? I will repent and then afterward I will fear?"

"To fear and repent is fitting for one who wishes to pay for his sins. If he has sinned against his Lord, should he not then fear?"

"If he would pay for his sins, then it follows that he repents and regrets his wrongdoing."

"What you say is true, but there are some who are so taken by the world that they sin unreasonably."

"So if I sin using reason, will I be condemned for it?"

"Sin using reason? By God, it is a great sin when you link reason with wrongdoing, for no one can sin by reason."

"Yes they can."

"How?"

"One can sin reasonably."

"By God, this is not true and cannot be. Our ancestors tell us that reason is always against sin. You know that reason can only include the good. Sin is evil, not good, and anyone who would think it possible to sin reasonably is not a Christian."

"Reason is essential, then, for it is true that if reason did not oppose sin, no man would ever stop sinning," said the body.

"Friend, that is true. God and reason always forbid sin. When a man sins, he lacks reason, moderation, and knowledge, but these come to the sinner through the sweet pity and mercy of the Creator."

"Now I believe that I am a sinner," said the body. "Many sins dwell in me as long as I am called a sinner. But tell me: how can anyone find reason in me without sin? I was a sinner and sin will remain with me as long as I do wrong, it seems to me. Reason, knowledge, rectitude, and moderation should rightly raise me out of my sin. But you said that in your opinion, reason would never be found with sin? But reason could be found with sin in a sinner."

"This is true—you have said it well, for when a man is sinning, reason is nowhere to be found, but then it comes quickly to chastise and blame the sinner for his foolishness. So reason comes to the sinner and chastises him for what he has done, but reason is not present while he is sinning."

"Now I understand," said the body. "But tell me truly why you keep me in such shame. You could make my life easier if you had more consideration for me."

"Yes, I could let you sin, but that would be your damnation. You will be judged for your sins. You want to damn us both, but I want to save you."

"I don't want to damn us."

"Oh yes, you do."

"Is one damned if one commits a wrong?"

"Yes, certainly, if he does not repent."

"Is it wrong to dress well or eat one's fill?"

"Yes, for there is pride in dressing well—and now I regret that I used to dress you so well—and banquets lead to gluttony, excessive boasting, and debauchery."

"True, that can happen to those who eat too well. But if one eats reasonably, is that a sin? Teach me."

"By God, no, or so I believe. I see no wrong in anything done with reason. But you are so unbridled that if you saw the opportunity to eat and drink well, you would not be able to resist."

"You have restrained me well, for I have had no such opportunity. I am nothing but bones and skin."

"Yes, and, by God, I am pleased about that. And you still have more than you deserve."

"By God, I do not. I have been brought too low—I wish you had some other body."

"Yes, you would like that. Wretched thing, you are deceived by the devil who dwells in you!"

"There is nothing in me but unhappiness and anger."

"That is exactly what I mean. What I said is true. There would be no anger without the devil."

"Yes, there is anger in me, but you know very well that I can be angry without the devil's help."

"You know that anger is a sin, and as my master taught me, sin cannot exist without the devil."

"And how can I not be angry? You took away my great empire, my privileges, and my wealth. I am thin and my flesh is stained—you have enslaved me. I am wasting away in this hermitage. You have imprisoned me, and you reward me badly."

"On the contrary, I reward you well. You put your crown and your wealth in my control, and I spent them well."

"Tell me where you spent them."

"I will gladly tell you. I gave them to God, I do not deny it, for he is my companion and lord."

"You gave them to your companion? How can that be? Does God need to take from me? Is he not rich enough? He has enough—he doesn't need my wealth."

"You are wrong. He needs it. Do you know how? When one gives to the poor, that is giving to God, as he commands. All the world is under his law. I took your wealth to save you and so God would have mercy on you."

"Mercy? He does not work by mercy, but by force, since he forced me to be miserable and poor."

"No, he did not. Tell me truly if you suffer against your will."

"I don't know why I would lie about it. I would gladly renounce this suffering, for I cannot bear the pain and sorrow you force me to endure."

"This pain is a pleasure compared to the pain in the deep pit of hell where those who sin are condemned."

"What? Are bodies that live in the world damned even when they do not lead such a bad life?"

"I do not say they are damned—that would not make sense. Perhaps they sin sometimes because the pleasures of the world draw them in. It is easier to understand for those who see God than for those who will never see him."

"See him? One can easily see him and remain in the world to serve him. One can do both of these things: love the world and see God."

"No, that is not true. No one who loves the world will ever see God on the cross, and Christians reject the deceptions of this world."

"Why? Can one not love it?"

"Not if he would save his soul. The world is poison, and whoever dwells fully in it will be damned."

"But one could live here in moderation."

"Friend, God says in the scriptures that those who dwell in the world are confounded by their love for it. If they do not leave it in good faith, they will never be with God or see his face."

"That is a harsh judgment," said the body, "and a reason to leave the world."

"Now I hear you speak with reason," replied the soul. "Whoever loves God and his Holy Name should leave the world without delay."

"Love him? I cannot love him, for he is too harsh and bitter."

"He certainly is not. He is sweet and merciful."

"But he has brought me to such a harsh place and makes me suffer, and I have lost everything I desire."

"That is not true, if what you desire is to be in heaven with celestial glory. You will go there without fear if you willingly undertake your penance."

"My penance? Have you lost your senses? Do you think I will willingly accept nakedness and hunger? This place is too harsh! I am dying of hunger and thirst! Will you not have pity on me?"

"What pity, you wretched one? I have taken you out of sin and will win you a crown that no one will ever steal from you."

"The day is long. Nothing you describe will ever happen. Where would such a crown come from? You already took one from me, and I am sorry to have lost it. It pains me to have lost my crown and my inheritance."

"Your inheritance? By God, your thoughts are disloyal. Do you not see that all those who wish for an earthly crown will die? The crown does not save them, nor does prestige or sovereignty. Don't all kings die? Friend, recognize that if you were a king, you would die. You would not escape it, for man's life is short and inconstant. If you do not leave these thoughts behind, you will gain nothing from your sojourn in this wilderness. If your heart serves envy, your good works will be for nothing, for your envious heart reveals that you are ruled by sin. You have said too much, and if you believe what you say, then you are taken in by your own sin."

"Taken in? No, I am not, for I will follow the Christian religion. But you oppress me too harshly. I cannot bear it much longer."

"You will have to bear it, for it will bring you rewards and great joy. Do not complain about it, but act without delay for your end is very near."

"What end?"

"The end of your life. You are wrong to reproach me, for you will die soon."

"You did this to me, do not deny it! You have deprived me and I am dying. You will not help me, and I am sorry that you are willing to kill me."

"Now you have misunderstood. If you were well fed and dressed in rich clothes, you would still have to die. A full belly, silken clothes, and all the pleasure in the world could not save you."

"I know all that and believe it, but I say that for me, my life would be longer if I had the company of the world and its pleasures."

"No, it would not, according to my belief. This life is not really life; it glorifies itself. Whoever is truly repentant, a true Christian and true believer, and suffers pain for God, he will live forever in happiness. If you will renounce your desires and look to God, you can live a long life."

"My reward is to live?"

"Yes, by God! Life, forgiveness, and never-ending joy.

Your reward will endure forever. Why do you care about
what you do in this world as long as God has mercy on you?
You should not care about anything except gaining forgiveness. Your flesh will rot and become a pasture for worms. At
the Day of Judgment I will come to you and we will be re-
united. We will be crowned in heaven above if you will repent with a good heart in true belief. Leave your foolish pride
behind! The span of your life is short, and you do not have
long to live. You will soon die, and on Judgment Day you
will rise again. Endure the pains and the ills: through them
you will be saved."

The body said, "I will sorrow no longer. I care for neither
honor nor pride, and I will do your will since it leads to my
salvation. The pain no longer hurts me and it passes quickly.
I no longer regret my suffering. I am eager to serve God, and
I give myself to him. Let him do with me as he will!"

Josaphat struggled and suffered greatly in the wilderness.
He loved and served God with a good heart. For two years
he sought his master without finding him. I believe it sorrowed him greatly, for he lamented often. His skin was blackened by the heat and cold, but he regretted nothing and gave
his love, his heart, and all he had to God. The devil tempted
him often and shook his resolve, but Josaphat took everything to God, who helped and comforted him. He put his
heart on high, with God, and surrendered it to him. The
devil assaulted him often and marveled that he could not
sway him, for Josaphat's heart was pure.

Josaphat finds Barlaam

Josaphat lived in the hermitage. His beard and his hair grew
long. One day he came upon a wise man living deep in the
wilderness, and he rejoiced to see him. The hermit watched
the naked Josaphat approach him. Josaphat bowed before
the hermit and asked if he knew Barlaam and where he lived

and if he had seen him recently. "I know him well and spoke to him not long ago," the hermit responded. Josaphat rejoiced to hear news of Barlaam and eagerly asked how to find him. The holy hermit led him to the path he should take, and Josaphat continued until he came to a cave in a high, steep rock. He entered it joyfully and saw his master. He greeted him and Barlaam returned his greeting, but the hermit did not recognize Josaphat. He saw a thin, pale, disfigured man, naked, with a long beard and hair and a narrow chest.

Josaphat's white body had blackened and his beauty was ruined. The young man Josaphat had been as beautiful and as freshly colored as the rose alongside the lily. He was like an enameled portrait where the red combines with the white, but now it was as though the enameling had become worn and the contrast between the rosy red and lily white was lost. The rose and lily lamented, for they could no longer combine to give him color. The red and the white had faded, his fresh coloring was lost, and his face was completely black. Only the shape remained of his face's former beauty, and his form was all that identified him as a man. He wore, around his waist, the garment his master had given him, and it was black and stained. Over it he wore a coat made from reeds. He was thin and emaciated. This is how he looked when he came to Barlaam, who received him piously.

"Master," he said, "do you know me? I am Josaphat, the king's son, whom you came to convert. My father was King Avenir. Do you recognize me? We have not met for many years. I have sought you, Master, and now I have found you. I praise God and thank him for bringing me here."

When Barlaam recognized Josaphat, he rose to his feet. He looked at him carefully and then kissed and embraced him. Barlaam could not find words to speak his happiness. He studied Josaphat and felt compassion for the beautiful, pale young man who had become so black and discolored. Barlaam could not contain his joy, and he embraced Josaphat repeatedly. He marveled at the suffering the young man had experienced on the harsh wilderness path he followed with bare feet. What painful trials he had suffered for his Creator! Barlaam and Josaphat sat in front of the rock, and Barlaam asked him about his father. Josaphat told him that Avenir had converted in the end and believed in God. He told Barlaam that he had left his lands to seek him, and that he had searched for two years and found him only after a hermit indicated the way.

Barlaam embraced Josaphat sweetly and gave him a holy kiss. They spoke of many things, and then they rose and went to pray before the crucifix on the altar. When they had worshipped for some time and talked of many things, they sat to eat. There was no rich food, no fish, meat, or wine; there were no silver plates, and not one crumb of bread. The young man did not forget to thank his Creator (it was already the hour of noon prayers). They ate apples they had found in the wild and herbs, roots, and plants. They drank bitter water. "Good son, I offer you the food your Father provides to us," said Barlaam.

"Master, there is great comfort here. It has been two years since I left my dwelling to come to this hermitage. I have found it very harsh, and never did I find as much to eat as I have had at this dinner. I must thank God for it, since he sent me to you."

"Good son, you are most welcome. How did you sustain your body in such misery in the wilderness?"

"It had more than it deserved. I must not be concerned with my body if I would save my soul."

Barlaam and Josaphat became companions in the struggle to live a saintly life. Each took the other as a model: Josaphat wanted to match his master, and Barlaam did not hide his wonder at the young man's effort and dedication. He marveled that such understanding could be found in one so young. The day had barely dawned when Josaphat began to pray. He dedicated himself to God's service, sleeping little and remaining awake to pray. Barlaam advised him to do less, but Josaphat thought that was wrong, for he felt he did not do enough. He went to pray secretly in a hidden place, because his master chastised and reproved him, but he did not cease his vigil.

They lived together like this for a long time. Josaphat did not weaken, but Barlaam came to the end of his life, and the holy angels showed him that he would die soon. He told the young man what the angels had revealed to him, and Josaphat wept. He was sad, but Barlaam rejoiced because he knew God called for him—to him, there was no better news in the world. Josaphat said, "Father, Master, tell me how you can leave me when I love you with such good faith? How can you leave me alone in this wild hermitage? I am sorrowful that you would leave our sweet companionship while I still live. My friend, master, and father, what will I do when you leave here without me? Take me with you, by your mercy! You converted me and then you had me baptized a Christian. My lord, you have done so many good things for me—you took me as your friend and you are my companion. Take pity on me and do not leave. My lord, put off your departure, for I cannot bear to remain behind. Master, for God's sake, relent and have mercy on me, for I cannot remain here alone."

"Friend, I cannot stay. I am not lord of my own life, God is its Lord and Guardian. I do not dare to question his will. I must obey his command," Barlaam gently reproved Josaphat.

Barlaam returned to his prayers. His body remained but his soul departed, and Josaphat heard the voices of joyful angels carrying it away.

Josaphat was in great pain when he saw that his master and his lord had died, but he rejoiced to know that the soul of the good man had gone to a great reward. He wept many tears and mourned their separation.

Barlaam's body remained, and Josaphat went to find it a shroud. He buried it with great sadness and with many sorrowing sighs, and then he lay to sleep on the tomb. But Josaphat's soul did not sleep—it was taken to the heavens. There he saw eternal pleasures, abundant rewards, domains, honors, and fiefs. He saw the seats of virginity and the rich thrones and crowns. Three of them caused Josaphat to marvel, and he asked who would receive them. Those who were in heaven responded, "One will be for your master, one has already been claimed by your father, and the third will be yours if you finish your penance." Josaphat was confused to learn that his father had one of the crowns. "What?" he asked, "my father who converted so recently will have a crown just as beautiful and new as mine? This is not right, for I have suffered many trials full of pain and sorrow for the love of our Lord. My father suffered very little, and he will be crowned just as richly as I am? I marvel that this can be true."

It seemed to him that Barlaam responded. "I told you many times not to envy the possessions or honors of others," he said. "Do you fault our Lord if he would crown your father with a crown as good as yours? Are you not happy that he has received forgiveness and mercy through your prayers? You should rejoice in it!"

Josaphat was contrite when he heard his master speak. Then Barlaam took him and showed him the paradise God had prepared for those who love him, and Josaphat marveled to see such great pleasure and beauty. Then Barlaam showed him the pains and tortures that await sinners in the devil's domain of hell.

Josaphat was very afraid and his fear woke him. He remained still and quiet, remembering what he'd seen. He was sorrowful to recall the misery of hell, where he had seen many naked souls lamenting the pain that tormented them. But the sight of the joy that God promises to his friends comforted him. He sat on the tomb of his master—he had no desire to leave it—and he lamented the loss of his companion. My lords, remember Josaphat's great sorrow and the misery and the pain he suffered for his Creator. He did not sleep or eat, and yet he was satisfied. He was so intent on serving God that he did not care for food. He read the scriptures often.

This is how he lived. He refused all the pleasures of the world, and his only comforts were the cave where he lived and the prayers he made—and yet he had sinned very little!

Ah, God, what was he repenting and why did he put his body in such torment when it had done no wrong? He was a very good Christian and he suffered great pain and sorrow in the service of our Lord.

The narrator laments the sins of the present world

My lords, you who hear this story, for the love of God, repent as this man repented![1] If you are enemies of our Lord, you will not understand the works and life of Josaphat. Great barons and noble lords, you hold many castles, towers, and cities, but you have not thought on this. You wear rich silken clothes, but you do not consider how little joy and how few good things there are in this world! However high- or low-born a man may be, he is unfortunate to enter the world. Why are evildoers even born? Why are there Christians who violate their baptism? Ha! It is unfortunate that the wretched have ever been born, for they will be grievously damned at the Day of Judgment, when they go before God to receive what they have earned. My lords, what excuse will they give? None at all, I believe, for they have produced neither flower nor fruit. What offering do they think they will bring?

The world is corrupt and full of evil. No one keeps his faith. But what faith would that be? By God, it is true: faith is lost, for betrayal and felony have cast her out from the world. Today the priests of the holy church are priests of evil. They treasure their possessions and are full of simony. They are infidels and sodomites, and they abandon nature's reason and laws to violate the holy scriptures. Popes, legates, archbishops, and prelates have left rectitude so far behind that faith no longer dares to chastise them. Kingdoms decline and everything in the world comes to an end. The world does not simply become worse, it is made worse by clerics—not a single monk can be found who speaks the truth without lies, even in the order of Clairvaux. Ah, clergy, how base you have become! You never tire of evil, but you are too tired to do good—no worth can be found in you. Rome, how little you are feared! What has become of your great power, feared throughout the world? You should sorrow to see yourself vanquished by money and abandoned by rectitude. You are like a prostitute who offers pleasure in exchange for a belt or a ring. You have become the capital site of betrayal, when you were once the capital of Christianity, and the Christians have left you. Your first sin was that you began to sell the sacrament and the body of God. We have to guard against you, for you would make us into new Judases. God our Lord laments that you sell him as Judas did, and you hang him on the cross again.

Remember the proverb: when the head is in pain, all the limbs must suffer. You can see this clearly: the head is hurt, for you are the head. You were once the head of the holy church, but you have brought her so low that now you rule over evil. You are the dame of the simoniacs. The holy church has been corrupted and your words and deeds make the Church into a synagogue.[2] Blame falls on you, for money rules the church.

You make your sorrowing wife a concubine when you put her body up for sale.[3] You have stolen her chastity, and she is sold a thousand times every day. You make your wife into a whore, since you let anyone handle her for money. You have a hard and base heart, and you will pay dearly for your betrayal, for your sins are known by the One from whom they cannot be hidden. You wish to blind him, for you fear he will see your acts. Ah, my lord cleric, you should be ashamed when you hear this account! Your sin is base and ugly, and our Lord knows that you make your good and beautiful spouse into an adulteress. You make the lady into a servant, and you turn away from what is right when you understand the holy scriptures but do not follow them. Your evil deceptions cause Christians to perish. Holy church has become a merchant, and priests will sing two sequences in a single mass out of greed for the offering they will receive. They sell the sacrament and think they hide their sin, but God sees it all and will take vengeance.

Oh Kings and Counts, I come back to you! The failing world is your responsibility, and you should share the blame I have just put on the clerics, for much of the evil and destruction that confounds the world comes from you. You should carry the sword to defend the holy church and her lands, but you have brought her low and have no care to raise her up. You place your interest in other things, and you tolerate the sale of the church, for you have a share in it. You take fraudulent payments to deprive another of his rights. You covet wealth and you follow your own unreasonable desires. Wealth is your lord, and you do not dare to deny him anything he asks (this brings you down), be it right or wrong. You bring undeserved suffering to those you should help and counsel. We see how happy it makes you to use your power to steal from the poor. Your palaces and your rooms remain empty and dim because you shun the company of honor and chivalry. Traitors and gossips are your ministers, and you gather with them in front of the fire. You are impoverished when you choose their hearth and chamber, since the vaulted ceilings and paneling, like the footmen who guard the door and keep it closed, are all turned to evil uses.

Evil and perverse lords, look at your works and see how impoverished they are, for you live in sin! God gave you many opportunities and you have refused them all! Evil barons, see how you are deceived. Our Lord has given you many signs of salvation. When he allowed himself to be sold again, he showed you a sign that you should have heeded. He let his city be taken along with the holy cross on which he was hung in order to lead us to salvation.[4] In the beginning, some of you took up the cross to save God's city, but you did not succeed. You fought badly and lost God and his love. The command that you should go to Damascus and conquer the pagans has been issued.[5] What will you do with your cross?

You should have taken it to the Holy Sepulchre a long time ago, but you loved your own country too much. The pleasures and delights of the world overwhelm you, and you reject the path that promises you the highest joy! You are consumed by the sin that holds you hostage. You cannot separate yourselves from your wrongdoing. You are full of evil and there is no courtliness in you. You are greedy for gain and have no desire to give. You lead a cruel battle when you destroy the poor with unjust taxes.

How did you lose his love, since you vowed to serve him by taking the cross? You became his enemy by doing the very thing that should have made you his friend. The devil seduced you and gave you the desire to take the cross so he could make you sin more than before. You have neglected your arms because of it, and your sin increases. My lords, you disregard your promise and seek a shameful delay. Your way is in peril. Wise men sorrow because of it, but the worst will fall on princes who are devoted to evil, sin, and disloyalty. They have shamed the poor. They amass gold and silver for I know not what purpose. This is a sin that destroys them. They say that they will depart, but these are only words, for they would rather stay than leave. They delight in wealth, and their evil deeds earn more every day, but they do not remember the cross. Nor do they remember their voyage, and they forget their pilgrimage because of their sins. In the end they will be shamed if they do not go. But what does it matter to them? They do not care, I believe, for they wish only to return. They do not go for the sake of their Lord but only so that people will not speak badly of them.

The world is full of dishonor: there is no prince or lord who does not do evil. All the most noble men are disloyal. Betrayal is now the custom, and all men follow it. There is only evil in the world and all who live there dwell in evil. They are greedy and envious, full of evil and foolishness. Disloyalty has entered into the belly of the holy church. Goodness has been corrupted, and no matter what they claim, there is not a single one who can or will do what God asks. Belief has turned to unbelief, and the Christians are less faithful than the pagans.

This world is lost. The nobles are deaf and mute, and they condemn themselves. There are so many evils in the world that I do not know what to say about them. You cannot find a single worthy man in a thousand.

This world is dying. It is full of evil and poison, since people are poisoned when they live in it so foolishly. Sin is now common to all, and no one hides it. They follow folly in word and deed, and they cling to the world. No sin is criminal anymore, no one recognizes his crime, and all refuse to repent—they are all evil traitors. Nature has lost her rights, for sons betray fathers, daughters do not honor their mothers, brothers lie to sisters. You will not find a loyal husband or wife in all the land. Now they are all adulterers, women as well as men. Now it is a marvel to find a wise man—I believe that you will not find a single one from here to Rome. It is the same for women. A faithful wife is slandered with gossip and her virtue destroyed through envious lies. If any honor remains in the world today, it is held by the vavasors, who act more nobly than the lords.[6] They are faithful companions and speak well to people. They govern themselves well and nobly, and hold their bodies dearer than their clothes or shoes. Each one of them lives according to his means and more nobly than the kings or counts who shame this world. The vavasors would be even more worthy if they were a little less like wolves devouring poor people. But they cannot help it, since they must take what they spend honorably wherever they find it.

I have described the vavasors because I was with one of them, and he was good company and lived a pure life. He never indulged his body with food or drink, and he gave many alms while he was in this world. No knight was considered more worthy: he was praised for his dignity and intelligence, and his company was greatly prized. I do not want to dwell on him so long that I seem to gossip, but I do not know any knight who knew so well how to distribute honors, to

whom he should give and from whom he should take, nor do
I know any knight who was more loyal.[7] Every day I heard
him say, "My lord is brave." He defended his lord often, for
people speak badly of counts and barons (but if they have
done wrong, then there is good reason for it). He was raised
up more often than he was brought low. He was not perfectly
endowed with goodness, but compared to others, in truth, he
should be praised. He was from a high lineage, and his lady
is brave and wise, without pride or excess. Her noble up-
bringing is manifest in her conduct. I have undertaken this
work for him, and I am close to the end. My lord, Gilles de
Marquais, will be named in it after his death and for as long
as Christianity will endure, along with his wife, Marie, who
by her good works took vows to God our Lord. Those who
hear this story will pray to the Creator, he who was hung on
the cross for us, that he will have mercy on their souls and on
the soul of the one who labored to compose this story, that he
give us all a good life and take us into his company!

Barlaam and Josaphat are reunited
in death

Now I have told you about my labor, about the lady and the
lord for whom I write, and about the evil and cruel world
where men do not acknowledge God: they leave him to keep
company with the devil. The world has turned to great
shame. My lords, hear the story I tell about Avenir and Josaphat.

Josaphat was in the wilderness, praising and serving God,
and he was often at prayer because he sought forgiveness. He
rejected the world and its pleasures; he fled and left it behind.
He did not care for the world. In fact, he hated it, for he
knew that whoever would serve God with love should reject
it with all his heart.

He mourned for Barlaam and lay often on his tomb. He missed his master, and he lamented and wept for him. He ate and drank very little, and lived in great discomfort. He prayed without ceasing, near Barlaam's tomb. He was both joyful and angry. He should have been happy, but he was both angry because he had lost his master and happy because he knew that Barlaam had gone to experience the joy his heart longed for. Josaphat was happy that Barlaam would wear a crown. A crown? Yes, in paradise where God crowns his friends. This crown is beautiful and good, and there is no such crown in this world here below, where riches are nothing compared to those in heaven.

Josaphat lived happily in the wilderness, waiting for his reward. He was content to do penance, for he feared the judgment and the pains of hell. He was sorry that his life continued because he longed to reach the great joy that God saves for his friends. The wise men who dwelled nearby came often to comfort and encourage him. They told him not to mourn Barlaam's death, because it had been time for him to die. Josaphat never stopped serving God and praying to him.

I could not tell you all the ways he martyred his body, but I can tell you his age: he was twenty-four years old when he left his kingdom to conquer heaven. He spent thirty-five years as a good hermit, far from the world and its pleasures. Then he left this life and was taken to heaven.

Josaphat did not spend his days in vain. He held to his strong purpose until he died. He refrained from sin and desired the good so strongly that he never slowed or tired. He did many praiseworthy things, saved many souls from the devil, and set an example for us all. Then he entered the path from which none returns and was taken to the kingdom of God, whom he loved greatly. Let Holy God be praised, when such a noble and highborn man lives so wisely that sin cannot move him. Privileged men and women should be attentive to their souls and not use their power to do wrong. They should do nothing that would cause them shame or harm.

God sent a hermit to come and provide the death rituals.

He prepared Josaphat's body and put him in the earth with Barlaam, for they had been companions in the search for God. They were laid side by side. Then God sent the hermit into India to bring the news of Josaphat's death to King Barachie. The king hastened to the grave with a great company of people. Barachie wept from sorrow and pity; he loved Josaphat, who had crowned him and given him his kingdom.

The sepulcher was opened, and they looked inside and recognized Barlaam and Josaphat. The two lords had become healthy and whole; their bodies had a sweet odor and were not at all corrupted.[1] They looked as though they had been put in the tomb that very day. The king had the bodies carried back to his country, accompanied by lighted candles and the smoke of incense, as was proper. Many people came to meet them. Many remembered Josaphat as the amiable and familiar man he was, and they received him with more joy than can be recounted. They put the bodies in the church Josaphat himself had built for the honor of God the Creator. Sick people came to the tomb from far and near, and they went away healed. Many of the pagans who were still in the land came because of the miracles they heard about. By the grace of God, many were converted and baptized in the name of the One whose honor, name, and empire will never fail. He will endure longer than my story, and he will judge both the living and the dead on Judgment Day.

AMEN. Here ends the story of Barlaam and Josaphat.

Notes

TRANSLATOR'S PREFACE

1. Edward C. Armstrong, *The French Metrical Versions of* Barlaam and Josaphat, Elliott Monographs 10 (Princeton, NJ: Princeton University Press, 1922). There is also a fourteenth-century translation into Occitan, the language of southern France.
2. Daniel Gimaret, trans., *Le livre de Bilawhar et Būdāsf: Selon la version arabe ismaélienne* (Geneva: Droz, 1971).
3. D. M. Lang, trans., *The Balavariani: A Tale from the Christian East Translated from the Old Georgian* (Berkeley and Los Angeles: University of California Press, 1966) and *The Wisdom of Balahvar: A Christian Legend of the Buddha* (London: Allen and Unwin, 1957).
4. Gui de Cambrai, *Le vengement Alixandre*, ed. Bateman Edwards, Elliott Monographs 23 (Princeton, NJ: Princeton University Press, 1928).
5. Bernard Gicquel, "Chronologie et composition du *Balaham et Josaphas* de Gui de Cambrai," *Romania* 107 (1986): 113–23.
6. Robert Ackerman, "*The Debate of the Body and the Soul* and Parochial Christianity," *Speculum* 37 (1962): 541–65.
7. Carl Appel, ed., *Gui von Cambrai, Balaham und Josaphas nach den Handschriften von Paris und Monte Cassino* (Halle: Niemeyer, 1907). The manuscript published by Hermann Zotenberg and Paul Meyer, *Barlaam und Josaphat: Französisches Gedicht des dreizehnten Jahrhunderts* (Stuttgart: Litterarischer Vereins, 1864), is based only on the Paris manuscript.

THE NARRATOR'S INTRODUCTION

1. This is a first example of the narrator's frequent interventions into the text to comment on the story.

2. The narrator frequently addresses a listening audience, rather than readers, and it is likely that the story was read aloud and perhaps even read performatively. The reader, perhaps a minstrel, may have created voices or mannerisms for the characters and performed them as he read.

JOSAPHAT LEAVES HIS PALACE

1. This is Zardan, who will appear later, and he seems to recognize Christian belief but does not embrace it. Josaphat will test him later, and he will refuse to convert (see pp. 65–66). The courtiers who accompany Josaphat on his first ride into the city also seem to recognize the Christian God (see p. 15).

BARLAAM TEACHES JOSAPHAT ABOUT JUDGMENT DAY

1. The narrator here equates Jews and pagans; in his view only Christians have a true religion and only Christians can truly do good deeds, because they do them for God.

BARLAAM RETURNS TO HIS HERMITAGE

1. It is not clear why Zardan says he has seen Barlaam only once, since Barlaam's frequent visits to the king's son caused his concern in the first place. He may mean that he was present only once when Barlaam spoke with Josaphat.
2. Later, Aracin says he has seen Barlaam many times.
3. The narrator refers to Josaphat's earlier adherence to his father's idolatry and to his veneration of idols created by men, rather than God, the Creator of all things.

PRINCE ARACIN FAILS TO FIND BARLAAM

1. Aracin addresses the hermits with apparent respect. He may speak ironically, or he may simply use a conventional form of address.

2. This is the first time the author describes Indians as Saracens. He may be conflating the Indians with Muslims, who are usually called Saracens in Old French texts. However, there is no explicit mention of Islam, whereas the purported beliefs of Greeks, Chaldeans, and Egyptians are described in some detail. It is more likely that the narrator uses the name Saracen to mean "pagan," as is also the case in some other Old French narratives.

3. This paragraph is addressed to the audience, and the author refers to himself in the third person (Gui). The passage could have been added by a later copyist who recorded the story, or Gui de Cambrai may wish to reassert his claim to be its author and translator by naming himself in the story.

KING AVENIR ATTEMPTS TO WIN BACK HIS SON

1. The reference to Paul is imprecise and represents a general appeal to authority rather than a specific citation.

KING AVENIR CALLS FOR A PUBLIC DISPUTATION

1. Barachie will return at the end of the story as the successor to whom Josaphat entrusts his Christian empire.

2. Gui de Cambrai uses the traditional identification of John of Damascus as the author of the story and identifies the origin of the Latin book from which he translates his story.

THE CHALDEANS BEGIN THE DISPUTATION WITH NACHOR

1. This is the first of many indications that King Avenir recognizes Christian truth but refuses to believe because he does not want to give up his earthly pleasures and privileges.

2. Nachor's defense of Christianity is a version of the *Apology of Aristides*, a famous defense of Christianity given by the Athenian philosopher Aristides in the second century CE. It was

mentioned by many authors in late antiquity, but no extant copies were known until the nineteenth century, when two copies of the *Apology* were found, published, and translated, and the resemblance to Nachor's speech could be discovered.

3. *Barlaam and Josaphat* is set in a distant past, and the narrator does not distinguish between historical periods. For this reason, Plato's brother, Aristotle's nephew, the eighth-century John of Damascus, and figures from other periods can all co-exist during Josaphat's lifetime.

THE GREEKS JOIN THE DISPUTATION

1. The narrator uses Latin names for the Greek gods because knowledge about Greek mythology was transmitted through Latin texts in the Middle Ages.

2. The narrator begins an impassioned condemnation of what he sees as corrupt sexual practices.

3. The narrator references a checkmate move that uses a knight, bishop, and king, but not the queen. He thus describes "mating" relationships among men, and specifically among men who belong to the social classes whose corruption he laments here and elsewhere in his narrative.

4. The identification of Mars as a "sheep eater" is probably a reference to the ritual sacrifice of sheep to Mars.

5. These sentences seem to come from the narrator, but they may represent the voice of a professional minstrel who also performed in taverns.

6. Once again the narrator interrupts Nachor.

7. Medieval authors took Dares Phrygius as an eyewitness to the fall of Troy.

8. In medieval traditions, Brutus was known as the founder and first ruler of Britain.

NACHOR CONCLUDES HIS REFUTATION
OF THE PAGANS

1. The narrator uses a feudal vocabulary to describe relationships in antiquity.
2. According to tradition, the apostle Thomas was sent to India to proselytize. He is later described as the first to build a church in India (see p. 143).

KING AVENIR NEGLECTS HIS GODS

1. The narrator begins a misogynist rant.
2. The women reference the values of courtly love, familiar to the audience from courtly romances and poetry.

A BEAUTIFUL PRINCESS TEMPTS JOSAPHAT

1. The narrator refers to Apollonius of Tyre, a romance hero whose story circulated widely in medieval Europe.
2. This lady suggests that if Josaphat does not love women, he must love men. Her accusation echoes the narrator's earlier condemnation of homosexuality.

THEONAS CONFRONTS JOSAPHAT

1. A reference to the wheel of fortune, a figure for the cyclical rise and fall of fortune, here modified to suggest that a false religion does not even really rise at all: it only appears to prosper.

KING AVENIR GIVES HALF HIS KINGDOM
TO JOSAPHAT

1. John of Damascus, long considered the author of *Barlaam and Josaphat*, becomes a character in Gui de Cambrai's version of the story.

2. The narrator identifies the king's allies using invented names meant to recall pagan lands and peoples.
3. The archbishop sanctions a holy war against the pagans. His exhortation to fight echoes calls to Crusade warfare and recalls the figure of the fighting archbishop Turpin in the Old French *Song of Roland*.

KING AVENIR GOES TO WAR AGAINST HIS SON

1. A lady's sleeves were sewn onto her garments after she was dressed in them, and they are often described as love tokens in medieval literature. A lady gives her knight a sleeve as a token of her favor, and the knight carries it as a standard in a battle or a joust. Miradeus's possession of his lady's sleeve locates the pagan knight in a courtly love context.
2. The knight brings honor to his lady by fighting well, and his prowess is enhanced because he loves his lady. This is the circular logic of courtly love.
3. Gui de Cambrai begins to call the pagans Turks, in what is surely a conflation of Josaphat's battle with Crusade warfare.

KING AVENIR CONVERTS AND CHRISTIANITY SPREADS

1. Monks are sometimes described by the color of the habits they wear; Benedictine monks wear black.

JOSAPHAT WISHES TO LEAVE HIS KINGDOM

1. The narrator counts Nachor, along with Barachie and Josaphat, as one of the Christians present at the disputation (see p. 87).

A DEBATE BETWEEN JOSAPHAT'S BODY
AND SOUL

1. The soul uses the rhetoric of courtly love to describe its sovereignty over the body in terms of a lady's sovereignty over her lover.

THE NARRATOR LAMENTS THE SINS OF
THE PRESENT WORLD

1. The narrator begins a long condemnation of worldly corruption among the clergy and the nobility.
2. The narrator uses supersessionist rhetoric to condemn corrupt clerics: they destroy Christian belief and the church becomes the pre-Christian synagogue. There is also an obvious anti-Semitic association of the synagogue with corruption.
3. The narrator describes the church as the spouse of the clergy.
4. A reference to the Muslim possession of Jerusalem and to the Crusading movements that attempted to take the city.
5. The siege of Damascus during the Second Crusade (1148) led to a defeat for the crusaders. The narrator may reference calls to the Fifth Crusade (1213–21), an attempt to retake Jerusalem and the rest of the Holy Land.
6. A vavasor is a minor noble in the feudal hierarchy.
7. Gui describes feudal loyalty.

BARLAAM AND JOSAPHAT ARE
REUNITED IN DEATH

1. The incorrupt body is a sign of sanctity, which is further demonstrated in the miracles associated with the relics.